THE EEL THAT SLEPT

*"The obstacles of the weak,
are the stepping-stones of the brave."*

Copyright © 2019 Martin Sansom

The right of Martin Sansom to be identified as the Author of the Work has been asserted by him in accordance with the Copyright, Designs and Patents Act 1988.

All characters in this publication are fictitious and any resemblance to real persons, living or dead, is entirely coincidental.

ISBN: 9781689659918

First Published in the United Kingdom 2019

10 9 8 7 6 5 4 3 2 1

Published by Martin Sansom

THE EEL THAT SLEPT

M A Sansom

Prologue

November 6th, 1835...

Robert Daintree lifted the oilskin bag to his lips and stood up to drink. He'd stopped at the creek to fill up, before heading east towards the bridge that he'd built only a year earlier. It was frustrating to be leaving now when there was still so much to do, but Charles would be arriving soon, and he needed to deliver his message in person. Charlie Darwin may have been a dreamer, but he was a sceptical man and Robert knew that the only way to convince him would be with hard, physical proof.

He looked north to the house that he'd once called home and thought back to the moment when he'd first discovered that place, marking its location with a row of Totara saplings so he could return the following year. It was a simple building, made out of tin and planks, and it gave away nothing of the wealth that he'd amassed during his time spent there. It was smouldering now though, demolished by the fire that he'd set before leaving, and now as the sun rose over the mountains Robert saw the smoke limping upwards like a final death cry.

He removed the bag from across his back and peered down at the treasure within. Most mornings, its glow alone would have been enough to warm him, but today it seemed tainted and he shut the bag to muffle its whispers.

He raised the oilskin once more to his lips and took another sip, before spitting it out. The water had tasted bad for days now—ever since the red coloured rain that had passed through a few days earlier. He would have to live with it for now though, at least until he'd made it to Otakau and the transport ship that would take him north.

He pulled another oilskin from his belt and bent down to fill it up. The icy water stung as he held it under the surface, and he gritted his teeth as he waited for the bag to fill. But the biting sensation grew too intense and he flinched away from the pain; what he would give now for one of Charlie's chemical concoctions that warmed the skin.

He rubbed his hands to ward off the cold and then plunged the bag once more, aiming to fill it to the brim. But as he did so the bag suddenly pulled him down and he fell forwards into the creek, tumbling head over heels into the fast-moving water.

When Robert surfaced, his face burning with cold, he watched, as his bag of treasures disappeared from sight. Swimming against the flow he tried desperately to chase after it, but even at full stroke he struggled to maintain his position, and he soon found himself going backwards.

The cold was crippling now and as his limbs grew heavy and numb, the world to change. Even the air inside his lungs seemed to freeze and every breath he took seemed to cut like razors in his throat. This was it, he suddenly realised—his time had come—and his heart seemed to stutter inside his chest.

And then the whispers came, warm and enticing. He still had his other bag—the one with the larger nuggets—and he reached down to grab it, desperate not to lose its precious cargo. But just like the oilskin, it pulled him downwards and he let go to keep his head above water.

"Join us…" whispered the voices. "Let go of the light, Robert, and welcome the dark."

They'd said that before, in his dreams and his stupor. But now they were here again, and their promise seemed real, not just a figment of his anger.

"Come join your wife Robert, she's waiting with us, here in the darkness."

It was a promise of redemption—a prize that he no longer deserved—and he knew he that should take it, before the offer was cruelly snatched away.

"Take me," he whispered. "Take me before I change my mind."

He regretted saying it of course—almost as soon as the words had left his lips—but by then it was too late, and as the water pulled him down once more, it wasn't the warm embrace of Eleanor that found him. Instead, he saw death and a pair of glowing green eyes.

Chapter 1

From the top of the gorge it had just looked like a plate of spaghetti. But now, as DS Rachael Blunt neared closer, a writhing liquefaction of body parts took shape and she fought back the urge to vomit.

Stopping just short of the stomach-churning scene, a raucous screeching suddenly filled the air and she turned her attention skyward. Her eyes struggled to focus against the cold, white glare of the autumn sun, and she lifted her hand instinctively to act as a visor.

When her eyes finally adjusted to the light, the horror at her feet was instantly outdone, and she gasped at the spectacle of a disembodied head, tangled precariously in the cords of a lime green bungy rope. Worse still, some of the victim's vertebrae and spinal cord were still attached, and they trailed wickedly like a cadaverous rat's tail.

Another screech drew Rachael's attention to the Black Kites that hovered overhead, and she watched as the winged raptors darted back and forth, ripping chunks of flesh with their talons.

"And erm... when did you discover the body?" she asked with a gulp.

She lowered her hand and looked to her companion as he

answered. She wanted to read his body language as he replied, as it often said much more than the words themselves.

Scotty James was noticeably on edge—a little green at the gills even—perhaps his hard man image only extended to the world of extreme sports that he'd made his career.

"I dunno really. It was probably about 7:00 when I found him, I suppose. Or maybe it was 7:30, I'm not really sure."

'...*when I found him,*' Rachael repeated in her head.

The dangling head and spine was barely discernible as a human being, yet Scotty was clearly convinced that it was a man.

"So, you're positive it's a man and not a woman—how can you be sure?"

"Well it's Jonno Hart, isn't it? He was one of dad's friends"

"And how do you know that?" Rachael asked.

The victim's face had been obliterated by the birds and what little flesh remained, now hung from the cheekbones in ragged strips.

"I could tell it was Jonno, as soon as I saw him," said Scotty. "But the birds have been pretty busy since then, so yeah, I guess it's hard to tell now—you do know who Jonno Hart is don't ya?"

Rachael knew exactly who he was, he was a TV fishing celebrity, and her boyfriend was obsessed with the man.

"And what about the body?" she asked. "In what sort of condition was that, when you first arrived this morning?"

"Yeah, that looked pretty much the same as it does now. Those eels are vicious bastards, and once they get a scent for blood, they rip everything to shreds.

Rachael studied the pool of body parts in front of her, and once again she had to fight down her urge to vomit. The longfin eels had thrashed and churned their way through the victim's body, leaving the torso an empty cage of death. The eels were of varying size, with some almost four feet in length. And the others, although smaller, were more snake-like and appeared to be just as ferocious. Their smaller bodies had allowed them to burrow their way through the cartilage that connected the victim's rib bones, and now they were gouging their way through the tendons that held his kneecaps in place.

"So how long do you think it'll be before I can re-open the bridge?" asked Scotty. "I've got swingers booked in all next week and I've already had to cancel a thousand bucks' worth of business."

Rachael was appalled at his lack of compassion, but she'd never heard of bungy jumpers referred to as 'swingers' before.

"Swingers?" she asked. "Surely, they're jumpers, aren't they?"

"Nah, we don't bungy very often these days. It's just the odd one or two per week since the new dam made it too shallow for submersion jumps. Nah, I'm talking about our latest attraction—a bridge swing—it's called 'Swing to Riches'."

"Swing to Riches?" said the policewoman. "How can a bridge swing make you rich?"

"Ah, well… now that's the cool part, isn't it—it's the gold!"

"Gold?" said Rachael, her interest piqued.

"Yeah, that's right. Every swing gives you the chance to strike gold…

…cool idea eh?"

Scotty stood there looking smug, like a cat who'd got the cream. He was a tall, athletic-looking man, with a mahogany tan and sun-bleached hair that made him look like a California surf bum—he certainly didn't look like a business genius.

"And how exactly do your swingers strike gold?" Rachael asked.

"Oh, it's pretty straight forward," said Scotty. "We give 'em a gold pan ya see, and every time they reach the bottom of the swing arc, they lean back, and they scoop up some of the riverbed.

Those old-timers from the gold rush didn't have the mining equipment we've got these days, so there's still plenty of nuggets left to find—well that's what I tell the tourists anyway."

Rachael raised an eyebrow. Scotty clearly didn't realise that he'd just admitted to fraud. But before she could say anything, he seemed to sense her unease and decided to caveat is words.

"And even if there are none of the big nuggets left, there's still plenty of smaller flakes to find of course."

"I'll have to take your word for that I'm afraid," said Rachael. "I don't know very much about gold swinging, or swing panning, or whatever it is you're calling this thing."

The mention of gold had secured Rachael's attention, not because she was interested in Scotty's stupid idea, but because wherever there was gold, there was probably a motive for murder.

She pulled out a pen and made a note in her pad...

'Contact Queenstown District Council in relation to possible health and safety breach at Moke Creek Activities Company. Potential risk of broken limbs due to extreme nature of bridge swing attraction.'

Although she didn't know much about gold panning, Rachael doubted that there was much left to find these days anyway. Nearby Arrowtown, had been the centre of New Zealand's gold mining industry for well over a hundred years, and tens of thousands of prospectors had stripped the land bare in search of the precious metal.

"Well Mr James, I'm sorry, but you're going to be closed for at least a couple of days I'm afraid—at least until we've gathered all the body parts and searched the area for evidence. I'm sure you wouldn't want your guests to find any stray fingers or toes in their gold pans, now would you?"

"Well no, I suppose not."

Rachael looked up again at the birds scavenging above. There wasn't going to be much evidence left to collect if the recovery team didn't arrive soon.

She studied the victim's eviscerated remains, and as her eyes drifted up towards the bridge that suspended them, a small movement suddenly caught her attention. A hundred feet away on the northern side of the river, a figure, stood watching from the cover of a large granite boulder. The voyeur's presence angered the policewoman and she turned squarely to face them, keen to show that they had not gone unnoticed. But when the person saw her returning their gaze, they shrunk back into the shadows, like a shade, sucked down to the underworld.

Rachael wasn't easily spooked, but it was creepy being watched like that, and a shiver ran down her spine. For a moment, she thought about shouting out to the unwanted visitor, but she had a hunch that this person wasn't going to respond willingly, and so she turned to Scotty instead.

"Do you know who that was just now, watching us from the rocks?"

"Sorry, I didn't see anyone I'm afraid. It could have been a tourist I suppose, or perhaps a local, out for a run?"

Whoever it was, they certainly didn't want to be seen, and Rachael wanted to know why. But for now, she had more important things on her mind, like how she was going to recover her victim, before the birds and the eels left nothing for her to save.

Chapter 2

Five days earlier…

As he flicked the tip of his fishing rod forwards, Jonno Hart, heard the familiar sound of his cameraman, cry out behind him.

"For fuck sake, Jonno, watch what you're doing with that thing will ya. You nearly took a chunk out of my ear, ya bastard."

Jonno ignored him. The cameraman been a miserable bastard all week, and he waited for what came next with the certainty of a wife who knows that at some point her husband is going to ask if she's seen his keys.

"…Prick."

And there it was, the culmination of a 25-year relationship. A working partnership that had seen Jonno Hart become an international TV celebrity, while his cameraman, Dave Norman, had remained in the shadows, filming his adventures around the globe.

"You want it to be perfect, don't ya?" laughed Jonno. "Stop ya whining Davey Boy and keep filming. This next one's gonna be huge—I can feel it in my bones!"

Their Māori guide, Kaihautu, looked on with steely eyes and he wrinkled his nose at the men who were fouling his river.

"Hey Kai," shouted Jonno, "I gave your number to my friend Bob, he likes his fishing on the er, 'exotic' side, shall we say. I said you'd help him find him a good spot to dip his rod. Bob likes to 'dip his rod', doesn't he Davey Boy?"

The cameraman ignored Jonno's crass innuendo. After 25 years he was used to the celebrity's macho banter, and now he didn't even bother to get irritated by it. Jonno was just a dickhead, and one day he'd get what was coming to him—hopefully, sooner, rather than later. To be honest, Dave was surprised that Jonno hadn't found himself in hot water years earlier. He was the most racist, homophobic, misogynistic bastard that the cameraman had ever met, and he seemed to make enemies wherever they'd travelled. But then again, that's probably why he got on so well with Bob—he was a dirty old pervert as well—and Dave knew exactly what Jonno had meant when he'd mentioned Bob's 'exotic' tastes.

"Hey, Davey Boy, did you see that hot little thing Bob's got working for him down at the hospital? The lucky bastard told me that she sometimes gets changed in their storage room. I said you might have a spy camera that he could borrow, ya know, just in case she's stealing pens or somethin' while she's in there."

This time Dave's patience faltered, and he was about to say something when the Māori beat him to it.

"You know… you really shouldn't talk about women that way, don't ya?"

Kai's words had formed a question, and although Jonno couldn't see it because of his blind ignorance, the cameraman sensed that it was more of an order to shut up or face the consequences. He was desperate to see Jonno knocked out cold, but as he was also in the big man's firing line, he decided that a distraction was called for instead.

"Did you see that Jonno? Look over there to your left, it's an eel, it's got to be at least 5 feet long."

Jonno spun around sharply, like a dog who'd just heard the word 'walkies' or 'cat'—it didn't take much to get his attention.

As the two men fumbled with their rods, reels and camera equipment, Kaihautu looked up the slope, and a smile almost managed to crack the ice of his hard-set jaw. If only they knew how close they were, if only they knew what was hidden there. If they did, they'd have the show to end all shows—and they'd return to Christchurch as TV heroes. But these pricks were too stupid and too arrogant to see what was right in front of them, and Kaihautu consoled his own self-loathing, by knowing that he'd prevented the Pākehā from discovering his secret.

'They'll be gone soon anyway,' he told himself, and the money that he'd accepted for bringing them here, would go a long way to clearing his debt; a mortgage on the land that was already his, by birthright.

He looked back again at the two men, still fumbling with their equipment, and he scowled. *'Fucking idiots.'*

Chapter 3

'Beep beep beep!'

Jenny Sunley smiled at the now-familiar sound as the Christchurch tram sped past. She'd been living in the city for just over three weeks now, after arriving from England with her new husband, Owen.

At 40 years old, she was seven years older than he was, but he'd swept her off her feet, and after years of rejection she felt like a teenager again. Jenny, an ex-glamour model, had been in a bad place after her career had started to dry up. And when Owen dropped the bombshell of a job offer in New Zealand, she'd jumped at the chance to marry him and return to the country of his birth.

They arrived in Christchurch just before Easter, spending the first few days in bed, adjusting to their jet lag and making good use of their time together. It was a magical week and Jenny had needed little excuse to lay naked in her new husband's arms, touching and exploring each other's bodies. But like all good things it had ended too soon, and after just one short week, she'd been shocked, when he'd left to start his new job in Queenstown, a six-hour drive away.

But Jenny had never been one for moping around, and on the 5th day after Owen's departure, she'd pulled on her tracksuit and headed out for a run.

As she cruised the city streets, the crisp southern air and auburn glow of autumn had filled her senses. This place wasn't just thousands of miles away from her home in London, it was a different world from the grumpy taxi drivers and sweaty tube carriages that had been her life for the past 20 years.

From that very first run along the riverbank towards Hagley Park, she'd been well and truly hooked, and plotting new routes each day, she'd decided to learn as much as she could about her new home down under. The city's red-bricked museum quickly became her favourite place to visit, and there she would spend hours, reading about the story of New Zealand and its chequered history, both good and bad.

She also liked to spend several hours each day, watching tourists and staff in the café of, 'Te Puna o Waiwhetu', the Christchurch Art Gallery. It was a bright, minimalist building, and Jenny loved how the sunlight streamed through the gallery's acid-etched windows, casting shadows on the floor of the reception area. Māori symbols and swirls projected onto the polished granite surface, and Jenny often wondered if they were simply a random design, or something with a deeper, more spiritual meaning.

Her new surroundings of art and history were poles apart from her old life of clubbing and paparazzi. But without Owen there to share it, Jenny's museum visits quickly became monotonous and predictable. Even the tram drivers who beeped at her now seemed to do so out of habit rather than lust, and the once vivacious blonde was starting to feel trapped by the life of mediocrity that she was slipping in to.

She'd been living in the city for less a month, but the repetitive nature of her daytime activities was already starting to affect the narrative of her sleeping hours too. Dreams should be pure, pleasant—rude even, not the magnolia memories of old school friends and going to the shops. The beige lifestyle she was living, was a poor substitute for the adventure that she'd hoped for, and every day she wished that Owen would return with news of a job, somewhere closer to home.

It was late morning on a Friday when Jenny wandered through the art gallery's glass entrance doors and was greeted unexpectedly by a beautiful Māori woman in stunning traditional dress. She was wearing a knee-length flax skirt and a woven top with brightly coloured shell decoration. To Jenny's eyes, she looked to be about 50, but her heavily tattooed face hid many of the wrinkles that would have given away her true age.

The woman walked silently up to Jenny and bowed her head in greeting. Then Jenny—surprising herself—bowed instinctively in return, touching foreheads in a moment of silent respect. Maybe all those trips to the museum had been worth it after all and some knowledge of Māori customs had lodged somewhere in her brain.

As the two women stood quietly—heads still touching—a strange sense of belonging suddenly swept over the bemused Londoner, and when she looked up into the Māori woman's eyes, she caught a reflection of herself, silhouetted against the etched patterns of the windows behind her.

Jenny smiled instinctively as they stepped apart and the other woman returned her gesture with an equally impressive grin. The woman made no attempt to speak however and instead she held out her hand, offering Jenny a small, stapled pamphlet. The glossy paper was decorated with birds, turtles and all manner of sea monsters, along with the title, 'Māori mythology and the seven voyages of colonisation'.

The woman clasped Jenny's hands in her own, before smiling again and then she turned to greet the next visitor walking through the gallery's entrance doors.

Jenny wanted to ask the woman's name, but she was already touching foreheads with the first in a long line of Japanese tourists and the entire group seemed fascinated by the whole affair.

Jenny turned to scan the café at the far end of the glass atrium. She was looking to see if her favourite spot was free, and on seeing a vacant chair she hurried over to stake her claim.

As she sat down her nose picked up the scent of a familiar aftershave, it was Owen's favourite, and she looked around expectantly in search of her husband. Scanning the cavernous space, she suddenly felt the presence of a man standing in front of her, and assuming it was one of the waiters, she looked up to give her order.

"Jennifer Sunley? I was wondering if perhaps we could talk?"

Jenny was confused. The man looked familiar, almost like an older version of Owen, except he was wearing glasses and his hair was greying at the temples.

"I'm sorry, do I know you?" she asked.

"No, we've never met before, Miss Sunley, or is it Mrs? I'm sorry, the information about you on the internet didn't mention that you were married, but I can see now that you are wearing a wedding ring."

The man spoke with a taut, Scandinavian accent, that was both rigid in its structure and cold in its inflection.

"Please let me start again," he said. "My name is Markus Vintersson, I am chief executive of the Channel 9 TV network and I would like to offer you a job."

"Are you sure you've got the right person?" Jenny replied. "I don't have much TV experience I'm afraid, well nothing except those two weeks I spent roughing it in the Australian jungle."

"Yes, I'm quite sure you're the right person," said Markus. "I think you'll find what I have to offer you is very well suited to your… talents, shall we say."

"Erm OK, that sounds interesting I suppose, what's the job?"

The TV executive sat down on the chair facing her and crossed his legs as he leaned back casually. His manner was assured and confident, as if he knew that there was no way Jenny could say no.

"I'm sure that you will already have seen our morning show, 'Breakfast South', yes?"

"Yes, I think I've seen it once or twice," Jenny replied. Though in truth she'd barely watched any TV since arriving in the country.

"Well, it appears that we have a vacancy in our meteorological department. I believe that having you onboard could help to make it a very popular segment of our show."

Jenny raised an eyebrow at the idea, she'd always fancied being a TV weather presenter.

"Tell me more," she said, leaning forward to shake Markus' hand, and at the same time she pushed out her ample chest, a habit that she'd acquired when dealing with men in power.

Chapter 4

One week later…

"Well done Miss Sunley, very good work indeed," said Markus, as she walked from the bright lights of the studio. Jenny resisted the temptation to correct him on her title, but she still reached for her wedding ring as she made the distinction in her head, *'It's Mrs. Sunley, actually.'*

It had been yet another week with no sign of Owen, and she was starting to wonder if she was going to see him at all before their six-month anniversary at the end of the week.

Markus guided her through the gaggle of floor staff that ringed the studio floor and Jenny squirmed as he continued to heap praise on her. She'd never been good at accepting compliments, and she always felt like a fraud when people told her she was doing well.

"Are you sure it was ok?" she asked, looking sheepishly at her new boss. "I'm only reading what it says on the teleprompt after all".

"Yes, yes, I'm quite sure," Markus replied. "You've only been here for a few days, yet you're already far more accomplished than the gentleman you replaced…

…and of course, you must have seen the ratings?"

"Erm yes, I did hear that we're doing quite well at the moment."

"Quite well? Hah... yes, but you are being very modest Jennifer. Your erm... assets, and those wonderful dresses of yours, they have helped to almost double our viewing figures compared to last week".

They had moved into the control room now, and at the other end of the room, a wall of monitors suddenly filled with the show's closing credits. The production team started to pack up their headsets and Jenny squirmed again as Markus ushered her forwards, with a hand placed on the small of her back.

"Wasn't she wonderful," he announced loudly, forcefully garnering the attention of any stragglers who weren't already looking their way. "…And that's exactly why you won't have the pleasure of seeing Miss... I'm sorry, *Mrs.* Sunley, in the studio for tomorrow's show."

Jenny shot a questioning glance at her boss. Surely, she wasn't being sacked already—and for being good at her job?

"Yes, tomorrow Jennifer will be reporting from her very first outdoor assignment, as we have a rather unusual weather event heading our way!"

'Shit', thought Jenny, what did he mean—a weather event?

Markus placed a hand on her shoulder, before sweeping the room with his other arm, to show her off like some trophy wife.

"There is a storm heading across the Tasman Sea, and it's come all the way from the deserts of Australia. I'm told it's going to create something rather spectacular when it hits our west coast."

'Shit, shit, shit,' thought Jenny, as the possibilities of what might happen started to play out in her head.

"Markus, are you sure I'm..."

...but he cut her off.

"Don't worry Jennifer, I'm sure that everyone here would agree that you're more than capable of handling this assignment."

"Don't worry Jen," shouted one of the production crew. "You'll do a great job, I'm sure of it."

"Yeah, you'll kill it, Jen," said a handsome young runner, as he nudged past carrying half a dozen clipboards and several empty coffee cups.

Jenny was touched that the crew were already showing such faith in her, and she nodded her appreciation to the room; in spite of her nagging self-doubt.

"Now then…" continued Markus, as the rest of the room went back to their business, "I'll take you to see our technician in the assets department. He'll sort you out with everything you'll need for your journey. I'm also going to assign you our best cameraman for the job—you can pick him up en-route at our storage lockup in Queenstown."

The TV executive led her out through a side door and into the featureless grey corridor beyond. Jenny followed behind him silently, she was in a somewhat dazed state of panic. The dusty smell of concrete-filled her nostrils and the walls of the corridor felt like they were closing in on her.

But before she knew it, they had entered a large, high-roofed warehouse, with racks lining the sidewalls and docking bay doors that opened to the street outside.

"I'll leave you here Jennifer if that's ok?" said Markus. "I have a rather important meeting to arrange, but I've told our technician to give you everything you'll need for your road trip down south... you do drive, don't you?"

"Yes... yes, I can drive," Jenny replied. "But I don't have a car I'm afraid. Should I just catch a train instead, and claim it on expenses?"

"Oh no," replied Markus, "Your cameraman David, he only has his camera with him down there in Queenstown. You'll need to take our satellite vehicle—so we can broadcast live from Milford Sound."

Markus pointed towards the bay doors where a battered grey van was parked with its rear end flung open.

"You want me to drive that?" stammered Jenny, "All the way to Queenstown?"

"Don't worry," said the Swede. "It's exactly the same length as my Volvo estate car, and square vehicles are much easier to drive than you'd think. Once you learn where the corners are, you can park them with ease."

Markus flashed Jenny a reassuring smile and turned towards the doors where they'd just entered. As he left, he called out into the cavernous room, "Mr Phillips, your attention is needed at once, please. Make sure that Miss Sunley signs for everything you give her and please make sure that she knows how to refill the vehicle. I don't want to have to subtract the money from your wages if she puts petrol in the diesel tank."

Markus looked at Jenny and winked to show that he was joking—"Always good to keep them on their toes," he whispered.

As he left, Jenny couldn't help but think how much he looked like her husband. They shared the same purposeful stride as they walked, and even the shape of his ears was similar to Owen's. But the Swede was more serious than Owen, and she wasn't sure if it was purely an accent thing, or if he really was as cold as he sounded.

---

8 hours later, Jenny pushed her sunglasses up on top of her head, and she guided the broadcast van into the car park at Queenstown Airport.

Apart from a few scrapes while navigating her way out of Christchurch, she'd found the drive surprisingly enjoyable, even with the van's ancient gearbox and lack of air conditioning.

Judging by the ancient map that lay strewn across the dashboard, she was only a few hours away from their final destination at Milford Sound, but she'd been up since 5 am and was already exhausted. Perhaps when this cameraman showed up, she might be able to convince him to stay where they were for the night, instead of pressing on. After all, the storm wasn't due to hit until 11 am, so they'd have more than enough time to make the drive in the morning. It would also give her an opportunity to meet up with Owen for some long overdue husband and wife action, and to say that she was desperate for physical contact, was the understatement of the year.

As she looked down at her phone, contemplating whether to call Owen, a tap on the window made her jump and her sunglasses fell from her head. They landed somewhere in the footwell below her seat and she bent forward to pick them up.

As she tried to gather her composure, the passenger door opened, and a large canvas holdall was flung unceremoniously onto the bench seat beside her. It was swiftly followed by a short, sweaty man, with a greying beard and thick, oily brown hair. He smelled strongly of cheap aftershave and his Hawaiian shirt was so bright that it made Jenny's eyes hurt to look at it.

"Gidday gorgeous," he said. "I'm Dave, your cameraman—sorry I'm late."

"Oh, it's ok," Jenny replied, failing to mention that she'd only just arrived. She probably could have been there an hour earlier, but she'd stopped several times on the way to admire the incredible views.

"Well I'm here now," said Dave, "and we've got a lot of ground to cover, so we'd best get a move on if we're going to make it in time."

"I was going to ask you about that…" said Jenny. "On the map, it only looks like just a few hour's drive to Milford Sound, couldn't we just stay here for the night and then head out first thing in the morning?"

"Hah, you're joking aren't ya? You obviously haven't experienced the roads around these parts."

Jenny found it hard to believe that there was ever any traffic in New Zealand—she'd seen barely 15 cars since her last stop, and that was hours ago at a strange little place called Twizel.

"Surely the roads aren't that bad, are they?" she asked. "We'll be heading out pretty early in the morning—I can't imagine the roads will be that busy."

"Well yeah, most days you'd be correct, but they're doing a lot of roadworks at the moment, so it's best if we make the journey tonight."

'Bugger!' thought Jenny. This guy clearly knew what he was talking about and her romantic night with Owen, was slipping away fast.

"And anyway…" continued Dave "It'll take at least two hours to make the drive from Te Anau in the morning. It's not that far to Milford Sound, but we might have to queue before we can even get through the tunnel."

It looked like Jenny's booty call with Owen would have to wait and she frowned as she stuffed the phone back into her pocket.

"Ok, you win, but you're driving—I've had enough for one day."

As she climbed out of the door, Dave was already shuffling along into the driver's seat, and the weathergirl cringed as he commented on the space that she'd left behind.

"Ooh, thanks love," he said. "You left it nice and toasty for me—I might even take my shorts off, to enjoy the warmth."

Then as she stepped back into the car on the passenger side,

Jenny noticed the cameraman eyeing her legs, and she pulled down on the hem of her skirt, before trapping it under her thighs.

If this was a sign of things to come, it certainly wasn't going to be the most enjoyable 48 hours that she'd ever spent. And as the cameraman turned the key in the ignition, she looked out of the window and prayed that he was wrong about the traffic.

Chapter 5

Even though it was already late afternoon, DS Blunt had only just sat down to eat her lunch of tuna sandwiches and a Greek-style yoghurt. It wasn't unusual for her to skip lunch completely, so it was a rare occurrence for her to be found in the police station canteen. Her colleague, Tony, had already left for the day, and apart from the cleaner—who was busy emptying bins—the only other person in the station was the Desk Sergeant.

Just as she scraped the last morsels from her honey flavoured dessert, a voice came through on her chest-mounted radio.

"Come in Rachael... are you still on duty?"

"Yes, I'm still here," she sighed, "but it looks like we're the only ones who take this job seriously enough to stay past 4 pm."

Over the past year or so, Rachael had started to feel increasingly frustrated by the work-shy attitude of her colleagues. And even though she herself didn't enjoy the job as much she used to, she still made the effort to get to work on time and keep her case files in good order. But her male colleagues seemed to think that policing was just an excuse to drive fast cars and to rough up the local youths.

Rachael's growing malaise was particularly upsetting, as she'd put so much effort into getting to where she was in her career.

She'd originally studied Archaeology at the University of Surrey but had switched to the newly formed Criminology course during her second semester. And when a fast-track detective traineeship arose in Queenstown, she'd packed up her life in England, and had applied for residency as soon as her probation period was complete. But now after just six years in the job, even the homicide of a TV celebrity was doing little to motivate her.

The voice came back on her radio and Rachael braced herself for a boring job, helping a cat down from a tree, or hearing some old lady complaining about kids riding bikes on her lawn.

"Rachael, if you don't need to rush home this evening, the pathology lab has got an update on your murder victim—Bob James is waiting for you now."

"Ok thanks," she replied. "I'll head over there in just a minute."

Even though the fishing celebrity hadn't been seen for over a week, she was secretly hoping that the pathologist would rule him out as her victim. She didn't fancy the press attention it would attract, and she'd also heard rumours about the celebrity that would no doubt make her investigation more complicated than it should have been. A divisive character at best, Jonno Hart was well known for his strong opinions and sexist attitudes, and if he was confirmed as the victim, the list of possible suspects could be very long indeed.

The pathology lab was just across the road, in the basement of the county hospital, and keen to enjoy the dying rays of yet another incredible Queenstown afternoon, Rachael took her time as she strolled across the deserted street. Autumn days like this were exactly the reason why she'd moved half-way around the world to

New Zealand, and she breathed in the clean mountain air as she walked, feeling it cleanse with its bite.

She arrived at the hospital's main entrance and followed the signs towards the morgue; passing the deserted A&E waiting room as she went. Back home in the UK, those chairs would have been filled almost 24hrs a day, but here they only seemed to find a use during the winter months, when the town became a hub for the skiing and snowboarding community.

As she approached the elevator down to the basement level, she saw a girl waiting there too. She was carrying a large, black sports holdall, and she was dressed in a dirty looking tracksuit.

"Oh hi," said the girl, as she gave a nervous wave. "Are you here about the murder victim? I'm Pippa—the assistant pathologist".

"Yes, I'm here for your findings," Rachael replied. "I take it Bob's downstairs in the lab?"

She'd never met Bob James before, but her colleagues at the station had all mentioned that he could be a bit of an arsehole. A 'know-it-all' they'd called him–often throwing in obscure words to prove his intellectual superiority. According to her colleague Tony, the pathologist took particular delight in getting one up on police officers—belittling them whenever he had the opportunity.

"Overall, he's a bit of a dickhead," had been Tony's exact words, and Tony was one of the nicest people she'd ever met, so he wasn't prone to exaggeration.

"Yeah, Bob should be downstairs," said Pippa, as they both stepped into the lift. "As far as I know he hasn't left the lab since the body was brought in. He knew the victim you see, so I suppose he just wants things done right."

Pippa gave one of those shoulder-shrug smiles that was intended to show sympathy for her boss, but if Bob really was the dick head that Rachael's colleagues described, it was most likely just a hollow gesture.

As they rode the elevator downwards, Rachael caught a glimpse of Pippa's face, staring at the ground in awkward silence.

"You've erm, you've got something on your cheek," she said, pointing to a smear of mud just below the lab assistant's eye.

"Oh shit, have I?" she replied. "I've just come from rugby training and I didn't have time to shower—Bob always rants at me if I'm late for the evening shift."

'Rugby training?' thought Rachael. The lab assistant wasn't big and masculine like she imagined a female rugby player to be, but maybe under that baggy tracksuit, she was tougher than she looked?

The elevator reached the basement corridor and Pippa opened the lab doors to reveal a cold, tile clad room. Stainless steel racks lined the back wall, and two autopsy slabs stood in the centre of the room, with bright, movable lights above each one.

"That's Bob over there," whispered Pippa, pointing to a man, at the far end of the room. He was about 6' 4" in height, with white hair, horn-rimmed glasses, and a white goatee beard. He was overweight, but not obese, and he was wearing a white lab coat that stretched tight over his stomach. Looking the as he did, Rachael couldn't help but think that he should be selling fried chicken, and her brain instinctively assigned him a nickname—*'The Colonel'*.

"You'll have to excuse me," said Pippa, "I just need to go and get changed, but I'll be back in a sec."

She walked out through a pair of double doors, and Rachael watched through the frosted glass as she slipped from her dark tracksuit into a white lab coat.

When Pippa returned, she looked like a completely different person. Her raven black hair was now tied back in a high ponytail and stylish black spectacles had changed her look from scruffy young girl into a typical 'sexy secretary'—it was no wonder that her middle-aged boss had employed her. Rachael watched as the girl strolled confidently into the room. She was wearing killer high heels that tapped as she walked, and the clipboard that was clutched against her chest, helped to push her bosom upwards provocatively.

"Ah good, you're here," bellowed Bob from across the room, "Whoever the bastard was that did this, promise me you're going to catch them and make them suffer, won't you."

"Well I'll do my best," Rachael replied. "Doctor… I'm DS Blunt, I understand you've got some news for me, about the body?"

She approached what was left of the corpse and the smell of iodine and fish-filled her nostrils. It made her feel even more queasy than the previous day at the bridge, when she'd pulled the body from the river.

"Are you ok?" whispered Pippa, now standing next to her boss.

"Yes, I'm fine," said Rachael, regaining her composure.

The smell was like a rotting version of her tuna sandwiches, and she knew that she'd never be able to stomach them again.

"Right then," said Bob, "If you girls have quite finished, I have some findings that should point you towards your killer. I'm sure your detectives will need all the help they can get with this one. After all, it's not every day that we have top blokes like Jonno Hart, murdered in a town like this."

Rachael was already getting hints that the pathologist was exactly the type of man her colleagues had described. She was sure that she'd introduced herself as a detective and not just some beat sergeant, only there to take down notes.

"So, you can definitely confirm that it's Mr Hart we're looking at?" she asked. "Jonno Hart—the fishing celebrity?"

Bob took in a deep breath of air before responding. "Yes, I'm afraid so—the poor bastard".

"Doctor, I know it's difficult with the body so mutilated, but at this moment in time, are you able to confirm the cause of death?"

Rachael could pretty much guess what Bob's answer was going to be, but she thought she'd best give him the opportunity to showboat his intellect for a while. She wanted their relationship to start off at a position of mutual respect, instead of the one-sided dominance that the pathologist assumed over her colleagues at the station.

"Well it's strangulation," said Bob, pointing to what was left of the victim's neck. "Strangulation from the bungy cord around his neck, resulting in myocardial infarction, and eventual mortem. However, it's difficult to confirm whether his medulla spinalis was snapped before or during his fall from the bridge; the predation by the local Milvus Migrans has somewhat confused the exact sequence of events.

You know it's a shame the body wasn't discovered a few hours earlier, before the birds got wind of the scent—I would have had a lot more to work with."

'Ok' thought Rachael. *'Well, that's got me no further than I was yesterday morning.'*

"So… you're saying that he was thrown from the bridge with the bungy cord tied around his neck, and the fall may or not have snapped his spinal cord. And to make things worse, the Black Kites that were feeding on his head, have made it difficult to say whether he died of asphyxiation or because of a broken neck—is that correct doctor?"

"Er yes, I think that just about covers it."

Bob seemed somewhat bemused that the policewoman had understood exactly what he'd just said, and he stood there scratching his head, no doubt thinking of some other way to trip her up.

Rachael could see that she'd caught him off guard, so she gave him the opportunity to regain the higher ground once more, "Doctor, you said earlier that you'd made some observations—something that could help lead me to the killer?"

"Yes, yes, I was just getting to that," snapped the pathologist.

He was clearly annoyed that he was being rushed and wasn't able to reveal his findings in his usual grandiose manner.

"A positive indicator we call it in my business, a nugget of truth that is beyond contestation—something that can only lead in one direction."

Bob was already back on form, the ringmaster of his domain, and he seemed keen to drag out his speech for as long as possible.

"Really?" said Rachael, trying to look intrigued. She was happy to give him the stage, but only if his information was going to be better than, '...the killer hung him from the bridge'.

With that, Bob turned around and reached over to a nearby trolley that held a plethora of scalpels, tweezers, and other medical wotnots. When he turned back to Rachael, he held out his hand in triumph, dangling a clear plastic bag in front of her face.

"Voilà!" he exclaimed. "The name and telephone number of your killer."

"Huh… and you found this on the body I presume?"

"It was tucked right in the front pocket of Jonno's shirt—well, what was left of his shirt anyway—those eels made even more of a mess than the birds."

Rachael didn't need any reminding of that, she was the one who'd had to fend off the creatures as she'd dragged the body from the river. And even then, the eels' voracious appetite had led them to climb from the water using their fins, spurred on by a lust for blood that was frightening.

Bob handed the plastic bag to Rachael and she studied the piece of paper inside.

"The phone number…" said Bob, "it's the Māori fella that Jonno hired to help find him some fishing spots. Jonno gave me the number too, but I'm glad I didn't call it now."

Rachael looked down at the paper and she read the phone number, along with the accompanying name, '*Kaihautu Waitaha*'.

Chapter 6

Dave's concerns of possible traffic delays had been well-founded, and just two miles out of Queenstown, the broadcasting van came to a standstill. Jenny sighed as she spotted the traffic backing up in both directions, and the cameraman cursed the accuracy of his own portents.

At first, they didn't move for a full 30 minutes, and when they finally got going, it was little more than a crawl for the next 10 miles. As they sat in traffic, barely moving, Jenny stared out of the window whilst Dave poured scorn on the council's inability to plan ahead. It was 6 pm on a Friday night and everyone was desperate to get home for the long Easter weekend.

Finally, after what felt like an eternity of stop-start crawling, they started to move at a more reasonable pace, and by 7 pm they had passed out of the city limits and on to the open highway.

As their frustrations began to ease, the weathergirl opened the door to conversation, commenting on the incredible sunset and a line of mountains that were reaching up to touch it.

"The mountains?" nodded Dave. "Yes, they're quite *remarkable* aren't they".

But as Jenny turned to look at them again, she heard the cameraman stifling a laugh beside her.

"What?" she said, "What is it, what's so funny?"

"I'm sorry," replied the cameraman, "The mountain range—it's called, 'The Remarkables' — I thought you'd get the joke."

'Oh great,' thought Jenny. *'Another idiot who thinks it's cool to make fun of people when they make an innocent comment.'*

She wished she had the guts to chastise him for his fun at her expense, but instead, she took the higher ground and chose to stare out of the window instead. Gazing aimlessly at the slopes as they drifted past, a blur of scrubland and rocks that looked like nowhere else she'd ever been, she watched as the ridgeline that divided night and day faded to a smudge that glittered like graphite against the night sky. The beauty of this country was something that she'd only thought possible in movies or paintings, and as she stared at the brush strokes of reflected moonlight, she thought back to her 'still life' world in London, and the dirty grey streets that she used to call home.

A swerve in the road, suddenly shook her from her daydream, and she turned to see Dave struggling with the wheel.

"Sorry about that," he said. "There was something in the road."

Jenny looked back to see what it was, but even with the full moon and a galaxy of stars, it was too dark to see anything behind them. They'd left the bright lights of Queenstown hours before, and now the barren landscape was illuminated only by the flickering yellow headlights of their ancient broadcasting van.

In-fact the lights were so dim, that the glare which would usually have bounced back into the cab, was almost non-existent. Instead, it was moonlight that danced through the side window, in a ribbon of silver that sparkled on Jenny's stocking-clad legs.

As she watched the light reflecting on the nylon material, she caught a glimpse of the cameraman also studying her shapely form. She felt the burn of his lascivious gaze as it moved upwards from her ankles, and she shifted in her chair, pulling down on the hem of her skirt. Dave quickly averted his eyes—he'd obviously got the hint that it wasn't appropriate behaviour.

But instead of being embarrassed by his actions or even trying to cover them up, he instead made a comment that was awkwardly unnerving.

"That's a nice skirt love. Is it from one of those fancy shops in Christchurch, or did you bring it with you from England?"

It was an innocent question that caught Jenny off-guard and she mumbled her answer as she shifted in her seat, "Erm yes, I bought in Christchurch last week. Markus told me that I needed to look smart for the cameras."

"Well it suits you," Dave replied. "And with legs like that to show off, I'm surprised Markus didn't ask you to buy a whole wardrobe full of 'em."

Jenny was used to comments like that, but as she'd only just met the cameraman a few hours earlier, he was already proving himself to be the dirty old man that his 'sex-tourist attire' suggested.

Jenny's instinct was to retreat from the conversation before the cameraman thought he'd been given a green light to proceed, and she pulled out the leaflet that was still in her pocket after her last trip to the museum.

"What's that?" asked Dave, "You're not one of those super organised people are you—the ones who prepare their lines long before they're due to go on camera? I'm used to working with a bloke who rolls up whenever he feels like it and makes it up as he goes along—we're gonna get on well, you and I."

'I doubt that,' thought Jenny.

"So, what is it you're reading?" Dave asked, his eyes once again drifting towards her legs.

"Oh. it's just something I picked up at the museum. A leaflet about the Māori colonisation of New Zealand. You don't mind if I turn the light on to read it, do you? I think I might fall asleep if I don't find something to occupy my brain."

"Sure, go ahead.,"

Now that Dave had shown he had a wandering eye, Jenny was keen to keep her wits about her and spreading the leaflet out across her legs, she shielded them from his lustful gaze.

It was just past 9 pm, when they finally arrived at the small town of Te Anau, in New Zealand's Fiordland region. By then, Jenny had been on the road for almost 11 hours and although Dave had taken over the driving since leaving Queenstown, her energy was still well and truly spent.

They hadn't spoken again since Jenny had pulled out the leaflet and she was glad when they finally turned into a motel car park and the van's engine spluttered to a halt.

"I'll just pop in to see Barry and get your room key," said Dave. "He's a friend of mine and knowing him, he's probably put you in the 'penthouse suite'—what with you being the big TV celebrity an' all."

As Dave wandered into the building, Jenny got out of the van to stretch her legs. The driver's cabin smelled like an abandoned lunch box and it felt good to breathe in air that didn't stink of mouldy sandwiches. She also knew that it was going to take several whiskeys to cleanse the taste of diesel from her mouth after it had started wafting through the air vents.

She studied the rundown looking motel and wondered what Dave had meant when he'd mentioned 'the penthouse suite'. The motel was a single-story building, and all the apartments looked to be identical from the outside.

The cameraman returned a few moments later and reached out his hand to offer Jenny her room key; it was attached to a carved wooden Kiwi bird, almost the size of a dinner plate.

"You're lucky," said Dave, "the penthouse was already taken, so you're in the main building with the rest of us plebs. I don't know why Barry calls it the penthouse anyway, they're supposed to be luxurious aren't they, but that place is just creepy."

As the cameraman spoke, he pointed towards the nearby lake where a row of fairy lights led out to a houseboat, anchored some 30 yards from the shore.

"Is that the penthouse?" said Jenny. "What's wrong with that—it looks really nice."

"Ah, but you're seeing it at night-time," said Dave. "With all the lights making it look romantic and pretty. But I can tell you now the inside's a completely different story, and when you see it in the morning, you'll realise that it hasn't seen a lick of paint in nearly 50 years."

"That's a shame, it looks like somewhere I might have brought my husband."

"Ah, but I haven't told you the worst bit yet. There's a hole in the floor—right in the middle of the lounge. Barry thinks it's relaxing to watch the fish, and he's somehow managed to convince his guests that it's worth an extra fifty bucks a night."

"What's wrong with that? It sounds like a good idea—just as long as it doesn't make the room too cold?"

"It's not the cold that's the problem—it's the fish," said Dave. "I've filmed Jonno Hart catching big fish all over the world, but there are things in these waters that would give you the willies."

"Ok, you've convinced me," said Jenny with a shudder. "Come on let's get inside—I'm shattered, and I'd rather dream about my husband than some creepy houseboat."

They quickly reached the steps up to the hotel and Jenny was surprised when the cameraman offered to carry her things.

"I'll probably be up before you in the morning," he said, lifting the heavy suitcase with ease. "I've got to prepare the van for the satellite connection, so get as much sleep as you can eh—we need you looking your best, don't we."

At the top of the stairs, he let Jenny go ahead on her own, and as she made her way along the corridor, dragging her suitcase behind her, she turned back just in time to see him heading for the bar. He may have helped up a few steps, but he really was a pig of a man, and now he was going to stink of beer in the morning as well. Jenny was glad that her husband was nothing like this stereotypical 'Kiwi bloke', and she made a note to text him before she went to sleep.

She found her room at the end of the corridor and opened the door to find it surprisingly well-appointed. Her usual routine with any hotel room stay was to inspect everything in minute detail for dust or hidden nasties. But tonight, she was too exhausted to care, and she dumped her suitcase by the door before collapsing on to the bed.

She had expected to fall asleep instantly, but as she sank into the mattress, her mind suddenly kicked into gear and she knew that sleep wasn't going to come anytime soon. Her thoughts turned to the task that she'd been assigned, and she struggled to understand how driving into the eye of a storm, could be anything but a stupid idea. Markus clearly thought that it would be a ratings winner, but all she could see were the possibilities for death and disaster.

When she finally drifted off to sleep, her dreams were a cyclone of emotions that were bruising and intense, and when she awoke in the middle of the night, her body felt like a boat that had been dashed on the rocks.

What's more, the taste of diesel still lingered in her mouth, and she knew she would never get back to sleep until it was cleansed.

She looked at the clock, and seeing that is was only just after 11, she wandered down to the hotel bar for a whiskey; if Dave could have a drink, then so could she.

When she entered the bar, her cameraman was nowhere to be seen, but his heavy equipment bag sat wedged between the bodies of a wrinkly old Basset Hound and an enormous Great Dane.

As Jenny approached, the Bassett made a groaning sound before burying its nose under its paws. The weathergirl soon realised why, when the Great Dane shifted its position, and released a wave of doggy flatulence that smelled like nothing she'd ever experienced before.

"Sorry about him," said a voice from behind the bar. "He always stinks after eating lamb and he's been chewing on a bone for the past couple of hours".

A bald-headed man with an arm-full of tattoos appeared from behind the bar. He had a wine glass in one hand and a cloth slung over his shoulder.

"Are you looking for Gloria?" he asked.

"Er no, just my cameraman... Dave?"

"Oh yeah right, I forgot, you're with Davey Boy aren't you—well, as far as I know, he's still next door at the pub."

Oh god, thought Jenny, he was going to be more drunk than she'd imagined, and now she was gonna have to do the driving in the morning.

"There's a 'Lady Gloria' show on tonight," said the barman. "Dave probably won't be back for at least a couple more hours."

'Lady Gloria?' thought Jenny. It sounded like a Drag Queen show, but knowing Dave, it was probably a Thai stripper, shooting ping pong balls from between her legs.

The thought of her cameraman and his mates all sweating over her in their Hawaiian shirts, was enough to make her feel sick, and she quickly ordered a whiskey to remove the taste from her mouth.

"The name's Barry…" said the man, handing Jenny her drink. "I own this place. I'm sorry I couldn't give you the penthouse house suite on the lake, but it was already taken, a young couple from Auckland booked it for their honeymoon. I'll make it up to you next time you're in town, I promise."

"Don't worry," Jenny replied. "It's quite alright."

She remembered what Dave had said about the lake house, but she didn't dare mention it to the hotel owner.

"I must say though Barry, it did look quite impressive as we walked up towards to hotel—it's very pretty."

"Yes, it's quite special isn't it, and with the pool in the middle, it's a wonderful place to sit and watch the fish."

Jenny smiled at Barry's obvious passion for his business. He reminded her of her uncle back in England, who ran a small B&B on the Dorset coast with his partner. It always made Jenny chuckle when her mum referred to them as business partners instead of lovers—after 40 years she was still in denial about the whole thing.

"You know, I'm surprised Davey Boy never asked to have the penthouse for himself," said Barry. "But then again, he always was a gentleman—he likes to put the ladies first."

'A gentleman?' thought Jenny, was this guy talking about the same man who'd been perving at her legs for the past three hours? Barry obviously didn't know the cameraman as well as he thought.

"So, have you known him for long?" she asked.

"Who, Davey boy? Well now, it must be about 30 years I suppose."

"Wow, so then you must know all about his work with Jonno Hart, I get the impression that Dave feels a bit erm, undervalued in the relationship?"

"Yeah, I can see where you're coming from I suppose—Jonno's the biggest dickhead this side of the Tasman. But Davey boy, on the other hand, he really is a wonderful man when you get to know him—far more sensitive than he likes to let on."

"Sensitive, and a gentleman?" said Jenny. "Do I detect a little bit of a crush there Barry?"

He may have looked like a Hell's Angel biker, but the hotel owner was clearly not what he seemed. Jenny gave him a wink to let him know that his secret was safe with her.

"Been there and done that already I'm afraid," said Barry, with a sigh.

Jenny choked on her whiskey. Did she really hear that correctly?

"He's a wonderful bloke…" continued Barry "But it just wasn't meant to be".

The weathergirl handed Barry her empty glass and told him to pour another. She may have had a busy schedule for the morning, but this was going to be a very long night indeed.

Chapter 7

"Wakey, wakey beautiful, I've just had a call from the boss man in Christchurch. He wants you to do a live update this morning, so you need to get out of bed and make yourself presentable—but that won't take too long for you now, will it."

'How the hell does this guy do it?' thought Jenny, glancing at the time on her phone. He still hadn't returned from the pub when she'd finally gone to bed at 2am, yet here he was now, bright and cheerful, and it was barely 6.

Perhaps the cameraman had got lucky with one of the 'beefcakes' that Barry had said would be in the pub next door? Or perhaps even Barry had decided to give things another go between them?

'Well at least somebody got laid on this trip,' thought Jenny, as she checked her phone for any missed calls from Owen.

"I've got a ton of things to set up at the van," Dave shouted, from the room next door. "I'll see ya downstairs in 45 minutes—ok love?"

His shouts were swiftly followed by the sound of a flushing toilet, and the image that it conjured in Jenny's head, made her cringe—he'd been talking to her whilst sitting on the toilet and was probably wiping his backside as he spoke.

"Yeah, yeah, I heard you," she replied, flinging her pillow from the bed.

"I hope you've got a soft-focus lens on that camera of yours Davey Boy, I haven't looked in the mirror yet, but I'm pretty sure I look like crap this morning."

"Don't worry beautiful, the whole country's in love with ya. You could rock up in front of a camera with rollers in your hair, and your approval ratings would still be better than that last bloke ever managed—I don't think New Zealand ever expected to have a goddess for a weathergirl."

Jenny had never been called a goddess before—not even by Owen, and even though the thought of the cameraman sitting on the toilet, still lingered in her head, she found herself warming to his cheeky compliments.

It was strange how the hotel's owner's revelations of the previous night, had changed her opinions towards the cameraman. He was no longer the classic male chauvinist, but was instead, a closet gay man hiding his true self from his colleagues.

Jenny even felt a little bit sorry for the man and she scolded herself for jumping to conclusions about him. When he'd complimented her on her new dress, he was simply trying to make polite conversation. He was no more a dirty old pervert than she was a straight-laced librarian, and she felt ashamed that she'd been so quick to judge.

The weathergirl yawned again and stretched out her entire body, before finally summoning the will to get out of bed. Most mornings in Christchurch, she would have completed several lunge repetitions or perhaps even a yoga headstand against the wall, but today after less than four hours of sleep, she could barely walk into the bathroom to brush her teeth.

As she stood looking at her reflection under the glow of a hideous strip light, she noticed yet another white hair, adding to the small brigade that had infiltrated the area just behind her ear. Jenny knew that she was lucky to have such pale blonde locks, otherwise the greys would have stuck out a mile, but still, she made the decision to tie back her hair, keen to hide the unwanted strands.

After a surprisingly invigorating shower, she re-emerged into the bedroom and immediately scolded herself for not unpacking the night before. Apart from her underwear, she'd only packed two dresses and she knew with certainty that the blue one—a pretty, linen number— would be creased beyond all recognition.

She opened her suitcase and her heart sank. Just as she'd expected, the blue dress was a crumpled mess, and it would take her ages to iron out the creases with the pitiful steam iron that waited patiently in the closet. She could almost hear it calling to her, whimpering like an abandoned puppy, longing to be played with.

She flung the blue dress aside to reveal her plan B, a bright yellow number with a figure-hugging pencil skirt and structured panels around the waist. The yellow dress and its matching bolero jacket had cost half the price of the blue one, yet it was secretly her favourite of the two. Unfortunately. however, it also came with a plunging neckline that left little to the imagination, and although Jenny knew it would get Markus' seal of approval, she didn't want to set a precedent that was going to define her as a yet another blonde bimbo weather presenter.

Jenny looked again at the pile of crumpled blue linen now lying on the floor. It really was a mess, and she couldn't be bothered to even try making it look presentable. It looked more like a dishcloth than a designer dress, and even with a power steam iron, it would take her hours to remove the creases.

"Oh well, tits and arse it is then."

Soon after, the weathergirl stood poised and ready for the scariest two minutes of her life. Her cameraman, meanwhile, was shuffling about hurriedly, twisting knobs and tweaking dials in-an-effort to get the best signal possible. He'd pointed the large white satellite dish of the broadcasting van skywards, and a flashing red light at its tip confirmed that the connection was active.

Even after his comments about the 'nasties' that lurked under the lake house, he'd insisted that Jenny should be filmed outside on its wide veranda, and as she stood there shivering above the mist, she couldn't help but think about what might be lurking under her feet.

She shouted over to Dave, now standing at the ready, some 30 feet away on the safety of the shore.

"So, tell me again, what makes this such a good place to film—I thought you hated this building?"

"I didn't say that, I just said I wouldn't like to sleep in it."

"It's dangerous, you said."

"No not dangerous—just creepy that's all. Oh, and er, don't worry about those underwater nasties I mentioned, most of them stay at the bottom during the daytime. You could probably jump in there naked, and the only thing you'd get a reaction from would be me."

Jenny chuckled to herself at Dave's continued charade of potent heterosexuality. She'd thought that Barry might have mentioned their conversation to him, but as a busload of tourists was now pulling into the car park, she realised that the hotel owner probably had more important things on his mind.

"Oh, that's great," Dave huffed. "A busload of nosy parkers, just what we needed."

'Shit,' thought Jenny, she hated it when too many people watched her back in the studio, let alone a bus full of strangers all clicking away on their cameras and smartphones.

"Hey Dave, what time is it?" she shouted anxiously. "I forgot to put on my watch, we must be about to go live, aren't we?"

"Fuck! You're right—we're on in 30 seconds. I hope you've remembered those lines I gave you earlier, but if you do fluff 'em, just stick your tits out, and most of the audience won't even listen to what you're saying."

"Don't worry," laughed Jenny, "I'm one of the best fluffers in the business!"

"I bet you are," said Dave with a grin, before hunkering down behind his camera. Jenny prepared herself as he counted down the final three seconds with his fingers, before pointing in her direction to indicate that she was now live on air.

Jenny looked down at her notes studiously, trying to convey the gravity of the storm that was coming their way. But a sudden gust of wind took her by surprise, and blew the notes out of her hand, sending them spiralling out over the waters of the lake.

She watched helplessly as the notes landed softly on the water, changing quickly from crisp white sheets to a muddy blue mess as the papers soaked up the water and the ink bled out.

Jenny stood frozen in shock—she didn't know what to do.

Fortunately, a sudden cough in her right ear, brought her back to attention, and she heard the voices of her breakfast show colleagues trying to bluff their way through during her moment of distraction.

"Good Morning Jenny—looks like it's blowing a bit of a hoolie out there eh. That's a beautiful lake house, but are you sure it's safe to be standing there?"

"Kia Ora, New Zealand!" Jenny replied, doing her best to sound upbeat. "Not to worry guys, I'm told by my cameraman that this wonderful old building has been here for over a hundred years, so I think it should be pretty safe for now."

"Jenny…It's Dan here. I understand that we've got a rather unusual weather event heading our way this morning—a dust storm, all the way from Australia. Jenny, can you tell us a bit more about what we can expect?"

Jenny wished that she'd had more time to memorise her notes, and as they fanned out on the water below her, she wracked her brain to think of something interesting to say. But a quick thumbs-up from Dave seemed to give her a boost of confidence she needed, and a sudden stream of consciousness freed itself from her lips, surprising her and the cameraman alike.

"Well Dan, the truth is, we don't really know what to expect I'm afraid."

"Really?" came the response from the studio.

Jenny's co-presenter was clearly puzzled as to why Jenny wasn't just regurgitating the information that she had no doubt have been given.

Jenny picked up on his quizzical tone and was quick to back up her last statement, "Well Dan, this is such a rare event for us here in New Zealand, we don't have any other occasions to compare it with. But one thing's for sure, the gust of wind that just took my notes, is definitely an indicator for the rest of the day."

She was in her stride now, and even though she was still winging it, some of the general points in her notes had started to come back to her.

"So, after a calm early start, we can expect heavy bands of rain to travel eastward across the South Island this morning, dragging warmer air behind them from the Tasman Sea. Then just before lunchtime, we'll start to experience the first effects of the dust storm you mentioned earlier Dan.

As I said before, we don't really know if it will be carrying much material by the time it reaches us, but you can probably expect to see a light covering of dust on your cars and windows when you wake up tomorrow morning."

"So then, an eventful day for us South Islanders eh Jenny?"

"Nothing we can't handle I'm sure," she laughed. Although in truth she was becoming increasingly anxious about what was going to unfold over the next few hours.

"Ok thanks, Jenny. That was Jenny Sunshine everybody... and we'll have more from her…"

"Actually, it's Sunley…" blurted the weathergirl, but it was too late, the audio in her earpiece had already cut off.

'Fuck,' whispered Jenny.

'Jenny Sunshine?' —she knew that name was going to stick and now they'd be calling her it every time she was on air. And what made it even worse, was that she'd have to be eternally chirpy just to live up to her new moniker.

'Bollocks!'

Chapter 8

Rachael removed the ignition key from her patrol car, but instead of opening the door to get out she remained seated, waiting for the engine to come to a complete stop. The car had been assigned to her on her first day in the job nearly 6 years previously, and it had always had a life of its own. Sometimes the engine would carry on running for at least another 30 seconds after removing the key, but she'd gotten used to the unusual quirk and now enjoyed the routine of waiting for it to stop. It gave her a chance to gather her thoughts and prepare herself for the task at hand.

In her hand, she held the slip of paper given to her by the town's pathologist. She'd traced the phone number to the old Māori village, located some 5 miles northeast of Queenstown, and the word 'Kai' referred to a man named Kaihautu Waitaha. He was the registered landowner of the village and some 30 acres of surrounding countryside.

It was 8 am on the dot when she finally stepped out of the patrol car and into the morning mist. The air was damp and biting, and she winced as it sucked down onto her skin like a blanket of leeches. She looked about quickly, hoping that nobody had seen her flinch, but the village seemed abandoned—her momentary slip of control had gone unnoticed. She was keenly aware that maintaining her authority as an officer of the law, required the constant appearance of calm and control, and she stood up straight to shrug off the cold. It was a technique that her Police Chief father had taught her on her first day of primary school.

"Stand up straight, and nothing can hurt you—your posture is your shield".

It was a technique the policewoman had used many times during her early career, when she'd walked the beat on the streets of Queenstown, facing down yobbos, and breaking up fights in the local bars.

She looked around at the collection of tired wooden shacks, each one fronted by a black painted door and their shuttered windows closed tight to the elements. Some of the dwellings looked as though they hadn't been maintained for decades, and the corrugated roofs that they all shared had rusted away to look more like lace doilies than structures meant to keep out the weather of the Southern Alps.

Arranged in a circle, the buildings created the impression of a mediaeval fortress, designed to defend against the outside world. But as Rachael stepped into the exposed centre of the village, she wondered if the layout was designed to look inwards rather than out—like a Roman fighting pit, where even victory did not guarantee survival.

A shuffling of feet over to her left caught the policewoman's attention and she turned quickly to face her gladiatorial foe, a young boy, about 14 years of age. The boy's stance was meant to be intimidating, but as he stood swaying with uncertainty, fingers twitching like a trigger ready cowboy, Rachael instead found comedy in his appearance.

"Hello young man," she said, trying to sound both casual yet authoritative, "I'm looking for a man named Kai, do you know where I can find him?"

Rachael's impeccable English accent always seemed at odds with her life here in New Zealand, but never more so than when she was trying to fit in with the local youths.

"He's not here Pākehā, he's gone fishin'—he probably won't be back until tomorrow."

Rachael could sense that this kid was going to be a pain in the ass, but she decided to play along anyway, he was clearly trying to impress the others who had decided to remain hidden.

"Gone fishing huh? Well if you see Kai, can you tell him I've just been speaking to a rather famous fisherman myself. You might know him actually—his name's Jonno Hart."

At that, the boy's poker face crumpled.

"Jonno Hart? Never heard of him," he stammered.

"Are you sure?" Rachael replied. "His show's on TV almost every day of the week."

"Why would I know him, he's just another Pākehā isn't he? All you lot look the same to me."

Rachael wondered if it might be a good idea to remind this little shit that lying to a police officer was a criminal offence, but her note-taking already seemed to be have had the same effect.

"Hey, don't write that down!" shouted the boy, "You can't record what I'm saying, not unless you arrest me… or can you?"

"I'm sorry young man, but I'm afraid I can. I could also take you in for questioning if I find just cause and I can hold you for 72 hours without charge if you continue to withhold information."

"Oh no, that's ok" replied the boy quickly. "I was just messing about that's all. But I really was telling the truth, Dad's gone fishin'."

"So, Kai's your dad huh? Well, not to worry—I believe you. I'm sure you'd be more than happy to tell me where he's gone wouldn't you....?"

Rachael stared hard at the boy and waited for him to give his name.

"Oh right, yeah, it's Eel," said the boy.

"Eel? That's erm... unusual"

"Well it's not really Eel—but that's what it translates to in English."

"OK, well what's your real name?" said the policewoman, trying not to show her frustration at the slow progress of their conversation.

"Nīoreore o Waitaha," announced the boy, standing to attention as he spoke. "It means Little Eel of the Waitaha, or Child of the Ancestors."

Rachael groaned inwardly—she wasn't a fan of cultural traditions.

"So Nī-oh-rey-or-ey...   or should I just call you Eel? Can you tell me where I can find your father?"

"Like I said, dad's gone fishing, up near the dam at Moke Creek."

"Near the dam huh? Doesn't he know that's illegal? At least whilst the construction phase is still underway."

"Not for us Pākehā, we've got rights ya know— we could get that whole project shut down if we wanted to."

'I seriously doubt that, thought Rachael. But then again, it was certainly true that the Waitangi treaty had granted the Māori very specific rights to the country's rivers and lakes. She'd heard of several projects up north being abandoned after interference from the local iwi (tribes).

"Well little Eel, if you see your father before I do, I want you to tell him that Moke Creek is strictly off-limits—at least for the next 18 months. I don't care about him catching a few fish, but I do care about him putting his life in danger by wandering around an active construction site."

The boy looked relieved that his dad wasn't in trouble for his fishing activities, but he also wasn't happy that he was being told what to do.

"Yeah, I'll tell him," he said scowling, before mumbling something else under his breath.

Rachael had a good idea what he'd said, but she decided to ignore it, the boy was still grandstanding to the audience that looked on from behind closed shutters.

"Now then…" she said, "Tell me about this fishing spot that your father likes to visit-exactly how I do I get there?"

Chapter 9

"Gidday," said the waitress, as Jenny and Dave sat down at a table by the window.

After packing Dave's camera equipment safely into the broadcasting van, they had walked across the street to a café for some breakfast. They still had an hour and a half drive north to Milford Sound and there were two more hours after that until the storm was due to hit.

"Can I get you a drink while you're deciding what to eat, or do you already know what you're having?"

"A cup of tea and an English breakfast for me thanks," said Jenny, without bothering to read the menu.

"And I'll have the same thanks gorgeous," said Dave with a wink. He was still trying to maintain the facade of masculine bravado that Jenny knew to be a lie and as the waitress walked away the cameraman commented on the size of her enormous bosom. They were even bigger than Jenny's silicon enhanced assets and although equally impressed by their size, she reacted angrily to Dave's comment.

"You do realise that I'm a woman too?" she snapped.

The cameraman looked taken aback and he barely looked at her as he gingerly apologised.

"I'm sorry," he said. "You're right—that did sound a bit pervy didn't it?"

He looked embarrassed, like a schoolboy chastised by his teacher.

"Ya know what…" he continued, "I think I'll just go and check that that I locked the van correctly."

Then with that he stood up and hurried out of the door, not daring to look back. It was a guilty-looking walk that seemed to apologise with every little shuffle and Jenny desperately wanted to let him know that it wasn't his fault. She realised that Dave's misogyny only came from a desperate attempt to be something that he was not, and she felt sorry for the tubby little man now scurrying across the road.

She looked towards the broadcasting van and saw that Dave had climbed in through the back doors—it looked like he'd found something important to do while he was stewing in his guilt.

Suddenly, as she watched the van bobbing up and down under his weight, a voice came from behind her and she turned to see a man easing into Dave's chair.

"Wow, this is incredible—you're Jenny Sunley, aren't you? I saw you on TV just a few minutes ago."

The man now seated across from her was much bigger than her colleague, not in weight, but in height and build, and as he leaned forward on the table his lumberjack shirt stretched over his broad shoulders. He looked to be about the same age as her husband, but his face was more weathered than Owen's, more rugged, more like Jenny's usual 'type'. The man was incredibly handsome, and she couldn't help but swoon a little when casually leaned back on the chair and his shirt tightening across his chest.

The man's wavy black hair was silver just above the ears and the week-old stubble that covered his chiselled jaw was equally peppered with grey. He looked like a stunt man or an action movie star and Jenny found herself staring into his sparkling blue eyes.

"That's an awesome dress you're wearing there Jen—it's ok if I call you Jen isn't it?"

"What? Oh yes, of course, that's fine," replied the weathergirl.

"You know we don't see many women around here as good looking as you. I bet even in the city, people turn and look when you enter the room huh?"

Jenny was flattered by the man's remarks and she wished Dave was still at the table, to see how complements were meant to be delivered.

"The name's Liam," said the man, holding out a large, bear-like hand for her to shake. His palms were tough and callused. He obviously worked hard for a living—and that made him even more attractive.

"So, Liam… you like my dress huh? You don't think it's a bit over the top, do you?"

"Nah, you're perfect—I mean, it's perfect."

Jenny blushed.

"Where are you heading?" Liam asked. "North to Milford Sound I suppose—to cover the storm? I've heard it's gonna be dicey up there this arvo."

"Well yes, that's what I've been told. I was actually kind of hoping that we could stay here and cover it from a distance."

"Yeah, you should probably stay here with me… I mean… that would probably be the safest thing to do."

Jenny grinned. The guy was outrageous, but it felt good to be chatted up.

"So, Liam… do you live here in Te Anau?"

"Nah, I'm just passing through like you. That's my truck over there—the one parked behind the Volvo."

Liam pointed out through the window to a large articulated lorry, it had red-curtained sides and a white cabin upfront. There was a logo emblazoned across its side and a picture of a Kiwi bird that looked like a soccer ball with legs.

"Ya know I'm heading up to Milford Sound myself," said Liam. "You know you could always ride with me if ya want. It'll be safer than that rickety old van of yours."

"That's tempting," said Jenny. "But only if I can play with the horn," she laughed.

She was intrigued by the forward nature of Liam's suggestion. She'd read that on average, Kiwi women had more affairs than in any other country of the world and she wondered if the truck driver genuinely expected his suggestion to pay off.

"So that bloke you're with…" Liam asked, "I take it he's your cameraman?"

"Yep that's right—good ol' David, 'Davey boy' Norman. He's one of the best there is, or so I'm told."

"But he's gotta be about 60 though isn't he? Are you sure he'll be able to keep up with you? I bet you leave most men gasping."

Jenny thought back to the previous night when Dave had carried her luggage up the hotel steps. And then there was earlier that morning when he'd been up and about whilst she'd struggled to even sit up in bed.

"Oh, I think ol' Davey boy is in better shape than he looks—he certainly runs rings around me."

"Ah, so he's a bit of a dark horse then eh?"

'More than you know', thought Jenny.

She got the feeling that Liam wasn't a particularly sophisticated or complicated man, but his charm and good looks were still attractive in their own way and as he sat there grinning, she couldn't help but smile too.

"So… have you known this Dave fella for long?" Liam asked. "Or does he usually work with somebody else?"

"Oh no, this is our first assignment together—he usually works with some big-shot fishing bloke. I'm sure he's wondering why he got lumbered with me."

"Nah he could never think that—the weather forecast has never looked so good."

Jenny blushed again, but she was starting to feel awkward. It was difficult to tell if Liam was a genuinely nice guy, or if he was a just sleazebag who didn't know when to stop.

"Well I think this Davey boy fella is lucky to have ya," said Liam. "I know if I was a cameraman, I'd rather be pointing a lens at Jenny Sunley the weather goddess, than Jonno Hart the fishing douche."

Just then, the café door swung open and a bell tinkled gently above it. Davey Boy stepped sheepishly back inside and headed towards them.

Liam seemed to sense that his time was up, and he flashed a cheeky smile before heading back to his table. Jenny watched as the waitress deposited an enormous fried breakfast in front of him and she seemed to linger for much longer than was necessary, before returning to the kitchen.

"Made a new friend, have we?" said Dave, as he sat back down.

"Maybe," replied the weathergirl, before turning to look out the window.

The waitress returned shortly after with their food and as she handed the cameraman his plate, Jenny noticed a change in his body language, it suggested that he was still feeling guilty about his earlier remarks.

Jenny couldn't help but feel responsible for Dave's awkwardness and as the waitress left them to their food, she blurted out a comment that she hoped would ease his guilt.

"You've got amazing tits there babe, I wish mine looked that good!"

The waitress looked back over her shoulder and Jenny was relieved when she responded with a wink. "Aw thanks babe, you're not so bad yourself".

Jenny looked back at Dave, he looked dumbfounded by what had just happened.

"Ok, you were right," she said. "Her tits *are* amazing—but don't do it again eh Davey boy."

They'd finally broken the ice and as they both tucked into their enormous breakfasts, Jenny couldn't help but smile.

Chapter 10

An hour later, Jenny leaned forward in her seat and looked up at the clouds. The morning sun had disappeared, and it felt like night-time had come early. Inside the dingy interior of the broadcasting van's cabin, the darkness was stifling.

"Crack open a window if you like," said Dave. "I could use some fresh air."

Jenny reached down and yanked the window handle, but it wouldn't budge.

"Give it a kick," said the cameraman.

Jenny pulled up the hem of her dress and took aim with her stiletto clad foot.

"Are you sure?" she asked.

"Yeah, that'll work. These old vans have been around for years, but sometimes you just need to treat 'em rough."

"Oh, I can definitely do rough," replied the weathergirl as she eyed up the handle once more. "Ok, here goes…"

With that, she slammed down hard onto the window handle, praying that the tip of her stiletto was positioned correctly so she would strike with the ball of her foot instead.

Fortunately for Jenny, her aim was perfect and as her yellow Jimmy Choo's gave a thousand-dollar thud, the handle spun a quarter turn in response. Her kick seemed to work a treat and the window dropped by about an inch, letting a cool, refreshing breeze into the cabin.

"You go girlfriend!" chuckled Dave. "Tell ya what, give it another whack and I'll open my side as well—that'll really get the air flowing."

Jenny raised her leg once more, this time pulling her foot slightly higher for more power.

Again, she kicked and again the window inched down a little further. This time, however, her follow-through wasn't quite so controlled as her first strike and before she could stop her foot it slammed into the dashboard, her stiletto heel piercing the brittle plastic. She hastily pulled back on her shoe, but it was too late—the heal was stuck fast—and as she pulled even harder, the top half of her thousand-dollar shoe parted company with its expensive undercarriage.

"Shit!" cursed the weathergirl. "Shit, shit, shit!"

"Never mind gorgeous," said Dave, with a grin. "At least you got the window open eh."

Jenny scowled as the cameraman raised a hand to stifle his laughter. Her yellow works of art were ruined. A thousand dollars of beautiful handcrafted leather, up in smoke.

She kicked the dashboard again, but this time in anger.

"Ouch!"

They drove in silence for another 10 minutes or so, with the crisp autumn air flooding in through the windows but doing little to cool Jenny's temper. Those stilettos had cost her a fortune and the only other pair she'd brought with her were flat, navy blue pumps; hardly glamorous enough to go with her figure-hugging dress.

"Hey Davey Boy, are we nearly there yet?"

"Oh, I'd say about half an hour until we reach the tunnel and then who knows, it all depends how much traffic needs to get through."

"Ok, so maybe an hour in total then? Well if you don't mind, I'm gonna catch forty winks—I need to get rid of these bags under my eyes."

"Nah don't worry about those," said Dave. "That's why I filmed you out on the lake house this morning. With that panoramic shot, your figure and *that* dress, nobody would have noticed a few wrinkles."

"Oh right… thanks."

"Why are you so tired anyway?" Dave asked. "I thought you went to bed as soon as we checked in."

"Yeah, I did—but I couldn't sleep—so I went and had a drink in the bar with Barry. He's a nice bloke, isn't he?"

Jenny opened one eye. She was hoping to spot a reaction at her mention of the hotel owner. She'd always been a keen poker player and she could tell when a person knew they'd been rumbled.

"Erm, yeah… he's nice enough I suppose."

"He had quite a lot to say about you Davey Boy. He said you've been acquaintances for quite some time."

"Oh right—what else did he say?"

At that point, Jenny knew that she'd got him.

"He told me lots of things actually. Like for instance, how you're much nicer than Jonno Hart. He even called you a gentleman—but of course, I said, he must have you confused with somebody else."

She waited for the cameraman's response to her jibe, but there was none. He just looked straight ahead, staring at the road.

When he finally responded he still didn't look her way, but he did bite his bottom lip first—perhaps to stop himself from saying more.

"So, he mentioned Jonno, did he?"

Jenny wondered if she'd hit on something, but she wasn't sure what it could be.

"Yeah, I get the feeling that he doesn't like Jonno that much huh? Maybe he thinks you could do better for yourself—career-wise of course."

"I should bloody hope you mean career-wise!" scoffed Dave. "Jonno's a prick, who'd wanna wake up to that wrinkly old bastard?"

Jenny winced at the ferocity of the cameraman's retort—she'd obviously hit on a sore point. But Dave's laughter at her ruined stilettos was still grating on her and she couldn't help but push his buttons once more.

"So, what made you call things off with Barry?"

But the cameraman did not reply.

Dave seemed pissed and he turned to look out of the window, hiding his face from view.

Jenny immediately regretted asking the question, but there was nothing she could do now, the cat was out of the bag.

They sat in silence for what felt like an eternity, but the weathergirl couldn't bring herself to talk. She hated confrontation and although they weren't exactly arguing, she didn't want to upset the cameraman further.

Just then, as if the mood in the van wasn't already low enough, it started to rain, and Dave turned on the windscreen wipers.

Through the van's open windows, tiny pinpricks of water darted through into the cabin and they were soon followed by heavier blobs of rain that thudded onto the windshield.

"You'd better wind up that window," said Dave, as he rolled up the glass on his own side.

Jenny reached down to turn the handle, but she wasn't strong enough to make it budge and the rain continued to penetrate through the gap. Her left leg was quickly drenched, and the window handle became too slippery to grip.

"Give it another kick!" shouted Dave, as hailstones began to clatter on the roof.

Jenny's shoe was now completely heel-less, and she began to kick wildly—no longer concerned with stiletto avoiding accuracy.

Her efforts seemed to do the trick and the window closed a few centimetres before sticking fast. She'd raised the glass enough to stop the worst of the rain, but a bend in the road had changed their direction and the water started to penetrate once more, only this time from a slightly different angle.

"What do I do now?" she screamed.

"Just find something to block the gap. This downpour won't last for long."

Jenny looked around for something to use and she grabbed the first thing that came to hand—the bolero jacket that matched her yellow dress. Shoving the jacket into the gap, she breathed a sigh of relief as the rain was finally thwarted. She was cold, soaked to the skin, and she looked down at her sodden dress. How was she ever going to dry off in time for her next piece to camera?

A sudden tapping noise, however, distracted her from her despair and she giggled as Dave started to dance in his seat. He was tapping out the rhythm of a reggae tune that she knew well and they both burst into song, before giving way to fits of laughter.

They drove for the next few miles singing the song over-and-over again and it seemed to warm them both with its energy. And then finally, about 10 miles south of Milford Sound, their singing turned to a gentle hum as they passed a sign for the approaching Homer Tunnel.

"Are you sure we'll get through ok?" Jenny asked. "With the satellite dish up top, is the tunnel roof high enough?"

"Don't worry, we'll be fine," said Dave. "It's one-way traffic, so we can drive in the middle of the road and use of every inch of headroom."

"Well, as long as you're sure? Markus would be pretty pissed if we wrecked one of his vans."

"It's too late now anyway," Dave replied. "We've just passed the final layby and even if we did want to stop, there's a lorry taking up all the space."

Jenny looked in her side mirror and saw a red articulated lorry behind them. It was parked up with its doors wide open, but the driver was nowhere to be seen.

"Looks like we're in luck," said Dave, returning her attention to the road ahead. "The lights are changing green—no going back now eh."

The weathergirl took a deep breath and closed her eyes. She wasn't a fan of tight spaces and the Homer Tunnel looked more like a mine shaft than a tunnel for road traffic.

Chapter 11

Rachael eased her patrol car off the highway, and she thanked Moonlight Track's gravel surface for drowning out the music on her radio. It was a Reggae song that always seemed to stick in her head for hours, even though she hated every note.

The young Māori boy Nīoreore had drawn a map to his father's fishing spot, but as she rolled along the narrowing track, the policewoman began to wonder if she'd been deliberately misled. She crawled along fruitlessly for a couple of miles and was about to turn back when she spied a pick-up truck parked behind an old Totara tree. There were five more of the giant trees heading in a line up the river valley and it reminded Rachael of a driveway, of the kind you might see leading to an English country house.

For the second time that morning she waited as her patrol car's engine shuddered to a stop before gathering her handcuffs and baton from the passenger seat. Her routine for leaving the car also included an obsessive checking and rechecking that it was locked and this time she cursed herself for her paranoia, *'Who the hell is going to steal a police car, you idiot? And out here in the middle of nowhere.'*

But it was no good, no matter how hard she'd tried over the years, there were some habits that she just could not break.

Standing next to the second tree in the line—the tallest of the group—she looked up at canopy looming above her. It was the tallest tree that she'd ever seen on the South Island and she was in no doubt that it was the one Nīoreore had marked on his map.

'Perhaps the kid is more honest than he looks?'

The tree's ancient roots spread out across the ground, climbing over each other in their search for water and they reminded Rachael of the eels back at the bungy bridge—ravenous in their thirst for blood. The murder scene beneath the bridge had been the first that Rachael had attended since her training in Christchurch and thinking of it again now sent chills down her spine.

Leaving her patrol car behind, she fumbled her way down to the river, slipping several times on the smooth green boulders that marched towards the water's edge. She was about to skirt around one of the larger stones when it suddenly moved, and she realised that it wasn't a stone at all.

"Kaihautu Waitaha!" she shouted, at the man who was hunched down by a small rocky pool.

"Stay where you are, please—I've come to ask you a few questions."

But the man ignored her instructions and instead he stood up to remove his hat.

"Can I help you, officer?"

The man was just over 6 feet tall, lightly tanned, and with perfectly sculpted hair that was shaved tightly around the back and sides. With his clean-cut look and athletic physique, he caught

Rachael off-guard amongst the wild and rugged landscape. She was usually nonplussed by the men she met around these parts, but she found herself lost for words in the presence of this handsome stranger.

"Is there something I can help you with officer?" asked the man once more.

"Erm... what was I saying? Oh yes, Kaihautu Waitaha... do you know him? I've been told that he likes to fish around these parts?"

"No, I'm sorry," said the man. "Never heard of him I'm afraid. But he shouldn't be fishing up here anyway, it's not safe with the dam construction still in progress."

Rachael nodded her understanding, although in truth she'd hardly listened to what the man had said—his eyes were incredible.

"I'm sorry," she said. "What did you say your name was? I didn't quite catch it."

"It's Owen—Owen Penney."

"And you work up at the dam?"

"That's right, I'm the Environmental Engineer—here to see that everything is done by the book. This is a world-class energy generation project and it's my job to ensure that we don't have any ecological disasters that could tar its image."

"Wow," said Rachael. "I didn't realise the project was so important."

"Yes, surprising isn't it," beamed Owen. "It's small-scale compared to other projects on the global stage, but it's groundbreaking in many respects."

The policewoman's initial reaction to Owen's good looks had been enhanced by the engineer's undoubted intellect and she was finding it difficult to find something to say.

"You seem to know your way around these parts," she said finally. "Maybe you could show me the easiest route up the valley? I'd love to hear more about the dam project on the way."

"It would be my pleasure," replied Owen, before flashing a smile that made the police officer bite her lip.

The engineer took the lead and Rachael was surprised when he chose to walk on top of the boulders instead of skirting around them. His long, muscular legs stretched effortlessly from boulder to boulder and he encouraged her to do the same.

"Step on top of the rocks," he said, looking back. "They're less slippery than they look, and it'll stop your feet getting wet."

"Are you sure?" Rachael replied, "My legs aren't as long as yours I'm afraid—I'm not sure I could reach."

"You'll be fine," said Owen, looking her up and down. "I can see you're pretty fit, you should have no trouble with legs like that."

Rachael felt herself blush. She wasn't sure if the engineer was being flirtatious or if he was just stating facts—she really did have great legs.

"You know it reminds me of something my father used to say…" said Owen. "The obstacles of the weak, are the stepping-stones of the brave… Confucius I think, or was it the Buddha? Either way, it's helped me over the years."

"My dad used to say exactly the same thing!" exclaimed Rachael. "I didn't really understand what it meant at the time, but it certainly makes a lot of sense now."

They continued to walk along the edge of the river, staying on top of the boulders and occasionally having to jump the larger gaps between them. It was the most fun Rachael had experienced in years and by the time they caught sight of the dam construction site, she was grinning from ear-to-ear.

They pulled up short about 200 metres east of the dam, with Owen taking the opportunity to offer the policewoman a drink from his flask. As she sipped the cold, refreshing water, she looked out across the river valley and surveyed the concrete dam construction.

The dam was long and relatively low compared to others that she'd seen during her travels, and it terminated at the closest end with a control tower, about 40 feet in height. The far end of the dam was less complete however and Rachael could see there was still a lot of work left to be done.

At the centre of the dam—about 5 metres up from its base—a torrent of white water came bursting through a horizontal slit and cascaded down into the river below. It was like a man-made waterfall, but without the prospect of a cave of wonders behind it.

"That's where the magic happens," said Owen, noticing the direction of the policewoman's gaze. "Thousands of watts of potential energy stored in the deep water behind the dam… it comes rushing through that tiny hole and we convert it into enough electricity to power 20 thousand homes."

"Impressive," said Rachael.

"And by holding some of the water in separate ponds, not only can we generate additional power at short notice, we can also hold some back in reserve for periods of drought."

Owen gestured towards two holding ponds that sat on either side of the river, directly in front of the main dam structure.

"And because we've blocked the natural flow of the river, the ponds also give the eel population a way to climb up to the lake."

"Climb?" said Rachael. "Can't they just jump up the waterfall-like salmon?"

"No, it's too high for that I'm afraid. So, we built them a ladder instead."

With that, Owen stood behind Rachael and lead her gaze towards the front of the holding ponds. As he guided her eyes with his finger, she could feel his breath on the side of her neck and the smell of his aftershave filled her nose.

"There, can you see? There's a thin ramp that angles up from the river. It's got a series of steps and the young elvers use it to climb up to the holding pond. From there, a second ramp takes them up to the water level behind the main dam structure."

"Brilliant!" exclaimed Rachael, her heart racing from having the dam engineer standing so close.

"Eels are fascinating creatures," said Owen. "Once they reach the lake, they spend most of their life in there—or in the streams higher up in the mountains. You know, some can live a hundred years before they make their way back out to sea, and by that age they can be up to six or seven feet in length."

"Six or seven feet!" choked Rachael.

After the carnage left by the three footers at the murder scene, she couldn't imagine what a beast that size could do to a person's body.

"You seem to know a lot about eels Owen, do you fish?"

"No not really—well not since I was a kid. Dad used to take me out on his boat, and he'd spend hours telling me about the different species."

"Maybe he'll do the same for his grandchildren?" said the policewoman, looking back over her shoulder.

'Shit, why did I say that?' she thought. It must have sounded like she was trying to find out if he was married with kids, but part of her wanted to know if the dam engineer was single—he wasn't wearing a wedding ring.

"No, I haven't got any kids yet," said Owen. "And I haven't seen dad in nearly 30 years anyway, not since he left mum for another woman."

"I'm sorry to hear that," said Rachael, feeling slightly awkward at the openness of the engineer's response.

But just then something caught her eye and saved her embarrassment. About 10 metres from where the eel ladder met the river, she saw movement that wasn't a sheep or some other form of wildlife. A hooded figure was moving up the slope, towards a stand of flax that ran along the bottom of a near-vertical cliff face. He'd been less than a hundred metres from where they were standing, and she hadn't seen him until he'd decided to move.

"Over there by the eel ladder," said Rachael. "Is that one of your construction guys?"

"No, I don't think so," replied Owen. "We're pretty strict on health and safety, so all my guys wear hard hats and reflective vests."

Rachael hadn't got a good look at the man's face, but she'd caught a glimpse of a tattooed chin and he was carrying a short wooden club over his shoulder—it had to be her Māori suspect, and she turned to the engineer, still standing close behind her.

"Is there a way I can get across the river?" she asked. "I need to ask that man a few questions, but I'll have to ask you to stay here I'm afraid."

"You're joking, aren't you?" said Owen. "There's no way I'm letting you go over there on your own—let me come with you."

"If you're sure that's ok?" said Rachael. The Māori looked enormous and she was grateful for the offer of backup.

"Come on, let's go," said Owen, "I'll take you across the gantry bridge, but we'll have to be careful as they haven't finished welding the balustrade yet."

They walked at a pace, with Rachael keeping an eye on the large clump of flax where she'd last seen her suspect. But she also couldn't help noticing Owen's tight cargo shorts as he lead the way. She should have asked him to fall back for his own safety, but she let him stay in front for now.

Chapter 12

Davey Boy tentatively eased into the maw of the Homer Tunnel and the weathergirl covered her eyes. She'd half expected the van's satellite dish to crunch on the tunnel roof, but the sound of steel against rock never materialised and she breathed a sigh of relief. Even her expectations of a pitch-black tunnel were quashed, as once inside, a series of LED lamps lit the way at near daylight quality and her pulse began to settle.

But her relief didn't last long, as within metres of clearing the tunnel entrance, the overhead lamps suddenly started to flicker. Like a taunting laugh that only teased their gift of illumination—they finally gave way and plunged the broadcasting van into darkness.

"Quick, let's go back!" screamed the weathergirl, consumed by fear.

"Sorry love, but I'd rather not. The tunnel's not wide enough for a three-point-turn, we'll just have to push on ahead."

The tunnel suddenly felt like the stomach of a giant, a monster that had been waiting for its prey and Jenny felt her pulse rising once more.

"Well at least turn the fucking headlights on!" she screeched. "I can't see a thing."

"The headlights *are* on," Dave replied. "But they're not helping much are they—one of the bulbs must be out."

The tunnel angled steeply downwards and as they drove on into the blackness, their already impaired vision was hampered still further by a constant dripping of water from the tunnel roof. The heavy rain they had driven through earlier, was already working its way down through the rocks and it wasn't going to let the TV van stand in its way.

At several points during their descent, horizontal cracks in the roof funnelled the precipitation into great walls of water and the cameraman was forced to drive on almost blind. He pushed on through, not knowing if he would find clear space on the other side, or the taillights of another vehicle just inches ahead. It was like playing Russian roulette and Jenny flinched at every new barrier they faced.

"Damn this fucking tunnel!" Dave cursed—his patience beginning to wear thin. "And can't you block that window a bit more, even I'm getting wet now."

"Just concentrate on the fucking road," snapped Jenny. Her mind was starting to play tricks on her now and she'd cocooned herself away under her jacket's golden shield. Like Perseus advancing on Medusa, she was too scared to look out, for fear of the monster that lurked in the shadows.

Tucked away inside her yellow fortress, the weathergirl listened to the noises from outside; the rumble of the road surface beneath them and the clattering of the van's engine, amplified by the tunnel walls.

And then it all went quiet...

"Well that was fun," said Dave, sarcastically. "Don't worry, we made it through—you can come out now".

Jenny cautiously raised her head from below her jacket and peered out through the window. They had emerged from the darkness of hell and into an ethereal light that now surrounded them on all sides.

As her eyes adjusted to the light, a vista of sunlit mountains spread out in front of her, their craggy tops already dusted with the first snows of winter. It was a world away from the streets of Christchurch that she'd left only 24 hours earlier, where the smells and colours of autumn were still very much in residence.

They drove onwards towards the tourist centre at Milford Sound, and as they drove, Jenny stared in awe at the steep slopes on either side. The morning's black clouds had already moved inland, but the rain they'd wrung out had funnelled into hundreds of tiny waterfalls now flowing down into the valley below. It was a melancholy vision that made the mountains appear as if they were crying, alive and sentient, weeping for the souls who must pass through their gates.

"Here we are," said Dave chirpily, as they pulled into the visitor centre's car park.

His cheery disposition was starkly incongruous to the misty cold fjord that now spread out in front of them and it caught Jenny off guard.

"I'll just go and sort out our ride"—continued the cameraman—"then I'll be back to unload the van."

He swung open the door and jumped out with a spring in his step. It was surprising for a man who'd been driving for the past two hours and as Jenny stepped out herself, she rubbed away the pins and needles from her behind.

"Don't worry Davey Boy, I'll unload the equipment. You've driven all the way here—you deserve a break."

The cameraman looked genuinely surprised at Jenny's offer and he stood hovering for a short while before responding.

"Nah that's ok love, I've got this one. I've been carrying it all on my own for the past 30 years—so why stop now eh?"

"So Jonno never lends you a hand?"

"Lend me a hand? You've gotta be joking right? That old bastard wouldn't wipe his own arse if he could pay somebody else to do it for him."

The weathergirl wrinkled her nose at the image that had popped into her head.

"And anyway…" said Dave. "You'll need the time to change into another pair of shoes, won't you. They won't let ya on the boat wearing those things, even if they aren't as high as they used to be."

And with that, he turned and headed towards the reception area, leaving Jenny staring forlornly at her ruined stilettos.

The cameraman returned just 5 mins later, accompanied by a middle-aged woman with long false eyelashes and bright red lipstick. Her maroon coloured hair was pulled back into a 60's beehive style and a polka dot skirt completed her vintage look.

"This is Wanda," said Dave. "She's kindly arranged for a boat to take us out, so we can film the storm."

"Wow!" said Wanda, looking the weathergirl up and down. "You weren't kidding were you Davey Boy—she's gorgeous isn't she."

Jenny blushed.

"Of course, you're wasted on this old queen," said Wanda. "But I'm sure those fellas on the boat will be excited to have you onboard."

The woman gave a dazzling smile with her ruby red lips and even though Jenny was embarrassed at her compliment, she couldn't help but smile back.

"Davey Boy—you grab your stuff, and *you*—beautiful girl, you can tell me where you bought that fabulous dress!"

They walked down to the water's edge with Wanda and Jenny walking arm in arm and when they arrived at the jetty the weathergirl gasped at the glittering day-cruiser they found waiting for them. The boat was stunning in white and polished chrome, and two equally gorgeous crewmen were busy untying ropes for their departure.

"Ok boys," said Wanda, "I want you fellas on your best behaviour today. You need to get this beautiful girl out to the headland as fast as you can please. I've already called all of the tourist boats back in, so you should have a clear run out."

"Thank you so much for all your help," said Jenny, as she

stepped onto the polished deck. "And it's such a nice boat as well—I thought Dave would have arranged some ropey old thing, with fish guts on the deck and a smell of diesel in the air."

"You've already got the measure of him then?" replied Wanda, as she flashed a playful wink towards the cameraman. "Don't worry beautiful, I only get the best for the nation's favourite weathergirl.

…Oh, and I hope you don't mind, but I told the captain you might pose for a few photos afterward? I said it would be good for business to have a celebrity endorsement on his website."

"Sure, no worries," replied Jenny. Although in truth, she knew that her photo was worth a lot more than a quick boat ride.

15 minutes later, she stood, flanked by her cameraman and the ship's crew as they bobbed up and down at the entrance to Milford Sound. They'd stopped just short of where it's mirror-like surface met the choppy waters of the Tasman Sea and the water lapped rhythmically underneath them.

"In all your travels Davey Boy, have you ever seen anything like that?" said the ship's captain.

"No, I sure haven't," Dave replied. "And I don't think any of us ever will again."

"You're the weather expert," said the captain. "What the hell is it?"

"Hey, don't ask me," said Jenny. "I just read the words on the screen—I've only been a weathergirl for a week!"

"Well you're gonna have to wing it this time I'm afraid," said Dave. "Those notes you dropped earlier at the lake—they were the only copy I had."

"Well that's just great isn't it," said Jenny. "What do I do now? What should I say? It obviously looks like a storm, but the colour… well it looks… evil."

"Well if that's what you think, then that's what you should say," said the cameraman. "But don't forget to mention that it's a dust storm eh—that's probably quite important too."

Jenny shot him a scolding look.

The weathergirl looked down at the luminous pink life jacket that she'd been made to wear, and she cringed at how it clashed against the fabric of her dress.

"Well at least the storm will distract viewers from how I look," she said. "But let's hurry up shall we, I don't fancy getting wet again, do you?"

"You're right… I've got a good signal here captain—let's drop anchor shall we."

With that, the captain switched off the engine and everyone on board went silent as they listened to the sound of distant thunder. The storm was still several miles away, but they could feel its power pulsating through the air. Jenny could feel its energy vibrating inside her chest, and with every breath she took, she could feel it leaving its mark inside her.

"It looks like we're just in time," said Dave, as his phone beeped to say they were about to go on air.

He reached out and grabbed Jenny's wrist and she watched as he slapped on a thin plastic bracelet with a flashing red light. It looked like the fitness tracker that she used to record her workouts and she shot the cameraman a quizzical look.

"It's a tracking device for my new toy," said Dave. "Just look straight at me and this baby's gonna do all the hard work for us."

With that, he flung out his hands and launched a shiny white camera drone into the air. It was about the size of a large pasta bowl and after a couple of seconds moving in all directions, it came to a stop, hovering roughly 10 metres from the boat.

The cameraman's phone bleeped again, signalling the final 30 seconds before they went live to the nation.

"Remember what I said, just look towards me and the drone will do the rest. We only need a quick soundbite from this live link, and after that, we'll record a longer piece for tonight's evening news."

He grabbed Jenny's wrist again and pressed a button on the tracking device. The drone reacted instantly and lifted away into the air, distancing itself from the boat. It was a strange feeling to be staring at a cameraman with no camera and instead, Jenny chose to focus on a point just above Davey Boy's right shoulder.

"Ok 'Jenny Sunshine', here we go…" said the cameraman and he silently counted down on his fingers before signalling they were live on air.

"Hellloooo Newww Zealand!" said the weathergirl, dragging out her words while her brain searched for something else to say.

"As you can see folks, I'm standing on a fabulous looking boat, here in our beautiful Fjordland region. I'm here today to with my cameraman and our brave ship's crew, to bring you something rather special…"

She was already into her stride, and both Dave and the ship's captain looked impressed.

"Behind me, you'll see a huge wall of cloud that's travelled all the way from Australia. And when it hits our west coast in a few hours' time, it'll bring with it something we've not seen in New Zealand for well over a century."

Davey Boy and the captain nodded at each other in approval and it gave Jenny the boost she needed to shake off her remaining nerves.

"It's a dust storm you see, a cocktail of wind and sand, whipped up in the barren deserts of Australia's red centre. But unlike the stuff the Aussies usually send our way, this brew's got a bit more kick to it—and we could be in for a rather messy post-storm hangover."

Jenny had completely forgotten what else she was supposed to say, but a quick thumbs-up from Dave reassured her that she was doing ok.

"So, join me… Jenny Sunshine… tonight at 10 pm, for my exclusive report on this once in a lifetime event. But for now, it's back to you guys in the studio."

With that, the weathergirl brushed the hair away from her face and flashed her trademark smile. It was a routine that she barely realised she was doing, but its effect was instantaneous on the ship's crew and they all stopped breathing for a second.

The male contingent of the boat may have been happy with her performance—but Jenny certainly was not—and the enormity of what she'd just said, suddenly hit home.

"Shit… shit, shit, shit, shit, shit!"

"What's the matter?" said Dave. "That was bloody brilliant, you didn't even need those prompt cards."

"You know what I'm talking about," Jenny replied. "You and your 'Jenny Fucking Sunshine'. It stuck in my head and then it popped out when I was signing off. Now everybody's going to be calling me that—you bastard!"

"Hey, don't blame me gorgeous. You're the one that doesn't seem to know your own name… and I didn't say it first anyway, it was that bloke on the breakfast show this morning."

"And don't call me gorgeous either!" Jenny shouted back.

But she caught a glimpse of surprise on the captain's face and she stopped herself from saying anything more.

"I'm sorry Dave," she said finally. "It's not your fault, but you've got to help me put a stop to this—before it spirals out of control."

"Talking of spirals," said the captain, pointing towards the storm. "I don't like the look of those clouds—they're starting to funnel down."

Jenny looked out to sea and her jaw dropped when she noticed dozens of waterspouts, now forming at the base of the clouds. Glowing fiery red from within, the moisture-rich tornadoes crackled with energy and they seemed to pull the storm along, like the claws of a dragon, chasing its prey.

"I'm sorry folks," said the captain. "I think you're gonna have to film your next report from the safety of dry land."

"Good idea," replied Dave. "I'm sure ol' Jenny Sunshine here can work her magic from the safety of the visitor centre. And perhaps if we get time, she'll pose for a few photos to put on your website."

"What? oh yeah, sure—no worries."

All she'd heard was the word 'safety', but it was enough to make her agree to anything.

Chapter 13

"Hey, you!" shouted Rachael—but the mountainous Māori didn't stop.

In fact, he kept on moving, striding effortlessly over the rocky terrain and it felt to the police officer that he was deliberately picking up the pace to get away.

"HEY STOP... POLICE!" she yelled.

This time the man seemed to hesitate a little, before turning slightly and carrying on for another 30 metres or so. His change of direction had taken him back to the water's edge and with nowhere left to go, he waited for the policewoman and her companion to catch up.

"Why did you run?" said Rachael as she finally came face to face with the man.

"I didn't run," he replied, with a shrug. "I just didn't hear you Pākehā, that's all."

His disdain for the policewoman was obvious.

"Well that's not what it looked like to me," said Rachael, breathing hard. "Why'd you run—have you done something illegal?"

Unlike the boy, Nīoreore, the man kept his poker face.

"Nah, I've just gotta get home for my dinner that's all. The Mrs is making fish 'n' chips tonight."

He was fidgeting as he answered and an almost imperceptible glance back up the hill confirmed to Rachael that he was up to no good.

"What's your name?" she asked. "It's Kaihuatu isn't it?"

"So what if it is?"

"Well, Kaihautu… you head home for your fish 'n' chips if you like, but I'm gonna go back up to the hill and poke in those bushes if you don't mind. I reckon I might find something rather interesting in there don't you—a weapon perhaps?"

But still, the Māori kept his cool.

"I tell ya what…" he said. "I'll come with ya if you like—I've just realised that I left my fishing bag up their anyway."

He'd called her bluff and Rachael wasn't sure how to handle the situation if things turned sour.

She still had Owen for backup of course and that had given her confidence, but Owen was a civilian and she couldn't possibly ask him to put his life in danger.

She looked at the dam engineer—he was standing back just as he had promised—but Rachael now wished that she'd asked him to stay closer. He certainly looked like he was in good shape and he'd be useful if Kaihautu turned nasty.

But her best course of action would be to let the Māori go. After all, she'd tracked him here as part of a murder investigation and now that she'd seen the size of the man, it would be prudent to take things slow. His actions to-date had done nothing but confirm him as her prime suspect, but her colleagues could pick him up later at the Māori village when there was less risk to innocent civilians.

"Ok Kaihautu, I'm going to the let you go this time, but I don't want to see you around here again, is that clear? This place is off-limits until the dam is complete, so you need to find somewhere else to fish."

"Hey, I've got rights Pākehā, I can fish wherever I like."

"Not this time," said Rachael. "Even the Waitangi agreement allows me to overrule those rights in special circumstances, particularly if you're going to do something that could endanger yourself or others."

"That's bullshit," spat Kaihautu. "You lot are all the same—thinking you know what's best for people like me—but you don't know shit. You don't even see what's right in front of your face."

"Well, you're very welcome to take it up with the government in Wellington, if you'd like? But in the meantime, if I see you up here again, I'll be charging you with trespass and public endangerment."

Kaihautu puffed out his chest—he looked like he was about to say something more—but instead, he just turned and walked away.

"Hey, aren't you forgetting something?" shouted Owen, as he came to stand next to Rachael.

He tilted his head towards the stand of flax, further up the slope.

"Huh? Oh yeah, my fishing gear."

Kaihautu turned and walked back towards Rachael, brushing her shoulder as he passed. His manner was still threatening, and the policewoman stiffened as he walked by, she needed to be ready in case he lashed out.

As she watched the Māori striding effortlessly up the hill, she felt the brush of Owen's hand next to hers. Her instinct was to grab it for reassurance, but instead, she pulled her hand away and reached for the comfort of her chest-mounted radio.

"Are you ok?" whispered Owen.

"Yes, I'm fine," she replied. "But thanks for asking."

"He's a big guy," said Owen, "I can't believe they let you come talk to him on your own, without anyone for backup."

"Damn budget cuts," joked Rachael, trying to sound like it was all perfectly normal. But it wasn't normal at all and she was beginning to wonder why she was even bothering.

Even a man like Jonno Hart deserved justice, but cats stuck in trees seemed to be getting more resources than this homicide case. Rachael knew that she was on her own until she had enough evidence to make a formal arrest.

She watched as Kaihautu Waitaha disappeared into the flax bushes, vanishing like the shadowy figure that she'd seen just days earlier at the bungy bridge.

"Owen, I know I shouldn't ask you this, but would you come with me? I need to follow Mr. Waitaha—to see where he's going."

"Yes, of course," Owen replied. "I couldn't let you go on your own now could I."

"Thanks... I know I really shouldn't be asking you to put yourself in danger, but I can't afford to lose him."

"Really, it's no problem. Come on let's go, he's been in those bushes for five minutes now—that's more than enough time to grab his fishing gear."

Owen led the way, striding up the slope with similar ease to the Māori. But as they reached the flax bushes, the dam engineer slowed, and Rachael grabbed his arm to stop him going any further.

"Let me go in first," she said. "I've got a taser with me. If he tries anything, I'll stop him in his tracks."

"Ok, but I'll stay close—just in case you need me."

The handsome engineer gave a reassuring smile and Rachael suddenly realised that she was still holding his arm—gripping it far tighter than was necessary. She quickly let go and turned away as her cheeks flushed red with embarrassment.

She made her way through the first clump of flax with a hand shielding her eyes, and in her other hand she clutched the taser that hung from her belt.

"Go careful," she whispered. "These leaves are sharp."

She couldn't understand how the huge Māori had managed to disappear so easily—his skin must have been like leather to withstand the flax's dagger-like fronds. She'd already been stabbed several times herself and she was barely five feet into the bushes.

"Ouch!" came a cry from behind her and she turned to the dam engineer.

"Owen are you ok? You haven't been stabbed in the eye, have you?"

"No, it's not my eye," replied Owen. "I twisted my ankle—it feels like a pretty bad sprain."

'Shit,' thought Rachael. She was going to lose Kaihautu, but she couldn't put the dam engineer at further risk.

"I'm sorry," said Owen. "I don't think I can keep up, but you really shouldn't face that guy on your own."

They headed back the way they had come in and as they broke through the final clump of flax Rachael scanned the river valley for any sign of Kaihautu. She looked up at the clouds—a storm was coming in and any chance of tracking the Māori would soon be lost.

"Don't worry," said the policewoman. "Let's call it a day shall we. I'll put out an APB on Mr. Waitaha—I'm sure one of our squad cars will pick up him up soon."

In truth, however, she was frustrated at Owen's inability to push on ahead and she was annoyed at herself for letting him tag along in the first place.

"Is that the bungy bridge?" she said suddenly, after spotting its black frame a mile or so down the valley.

"Erm… yeah, I suppose it must be," replied Owen, now resting his ankle.

"You know, I hadn't realised it was so close," said Rachael. "It makes Mr Waitaha's hiding place very convenient indeed, if he really is involved with the murder at the bridge."

"Murder?" said Owen. "You didn't tell me he was a killer—I just thought you wanted to warn him about illegal fishing—maybe it was a good thing that I sprained my ankle after all."

Rachael looked down at Owen, cradling his ankle. He may have been cute, and his intelligence was undoubtedly sexy, but perhaps he wasn't quite the hero that she'd imagined after all.

Her thoughts turned to her boyfriend Liam and she wondered what he would have done in the same situation. She hadn't seen him for over a week and she wondered whether he was thinking about her too.

He may not have been the smartest guy she'd ever met, but she'd never seen him afraid or back away from confrontation. Perhaps that was why they'd clicked? She'd scared everyone else away and Liam was the only man that truly had the balls to stand up to her.

Chapter 14

At the head of Milford Sound, the ship's captain turned the boat sharply and everyone on board braced themselves for a race back to shore.

"What about the drone?" said Jenny "Shouldn't we call it back to the boat?"

"Nah don't worry about her," said Dave. "She'll keep up just fine. It'll make for some good footage anyway if she can capture the storm behind us."

The cameraman's face was full of excitement, like a kid who was about to unwrap their Christmas presents and Jenny couldn't help but admire his passion for the job. Her husband held a similar enthusiasm for his own career and although she didn't share that passion for engineering, she loved to see the enjoyment that it gave him.

"Hold tight folks," said the captain, as he pushed forward on the throttle.

The boat's engines responded instantly and as they roared into life the weathergirl grabbed a handrail, to stop herself from falling backward. The boat skipped along the waves like a stone skimmed from the beach and Jenny clung to the railing, her knuckles white with fear.

"This footage is gonna be bloody awesome!" yelled Dave, over the spray and noise from the engines. "But make sure you hold on to that wristband eh, if that goes overboard it'll be a disaster. The drone will stop where it is and we'll have to wait around underneath it until the battery runs out."

"Well I don't think the captain's going to allow that," shouted Jenny. "And I certainly won't be asking him to make a U-turn for your little toy."

"Toy!" scoffed Dave. "I'll have you know, that's ten grand's worth of start-of-the-art camera technology—but if the boss asks eh, tell him it cost us five, won't ya."

Jenny looked at the GPS tracker on her wrist. She certainly didn't want to be the one to lose a camera that was worth three times her monthly salary, so she checked that the strap was still secure.

It had taken the boat nearly 15 minutes to reach the fringes of the open sea, but coming back into shore, they found the jetty in nearly half that time and Jenny's legs were like jelly as she stepped from the boat.

"Hey gorgeous, we haven't got time for you to stand around rubbing your pins," said Dave. "And do me a favour will ya, press the home button on that wristband—it'll bring the camera down and we can skedaddle outa here."

'Skedaddle', thought Jenny, she hadn't heard that word since she was a kid. Life in New Zealand really was like in England in the 80's and every day small things like 'skedaddle' made the place feel like home.

She pressed the button and the drone flew down in front of her before dropping lightly into Dave's waiting hands. He wrapped it away in a felt blanket and then swiftly tucked it inside his cavernous green holdall.

"Right, let's go!" he said, straightening up. "I'll pack this baby away properly once we get back to the van."

They said goodbye to the captain and his crew and ran to the car park, where their van was now being buffeted by the storm. The near-vertical walls of the fjord were funnelling the wind inwards and they both struggled to open the doors against it.

As they climbed inside, Dave's phone rang and he put the call on speaker, so he could use his hands to upload the footage via his laptop.

"Hello David, are you there?" said a cold Scandinavian voice.

"Yep, I'm here Markus and I'm uploading the footage as we speak."

"Ah that's good, I am very much looking forward to watching it. And Jennifer, are you there too?"

"Yes, I'm here Markus. But we can't hear you very well I'm afraid—the storm is beyond anything we could have imagined."

"Yes, I know… I mean, I'm sure it is. I just watched your link to the studio—it looks like we're in for a rough ride."

"So, the satellite link worked ok?" asked Dave, as he disconnected the drone from his laptop and placed it back into the holdall.

"Yes, yes, everything has gone to plan. All we are waiting for now is to receive Jennifer's piece for tonight's evening news."

"Erm yeah, about that… I'm afraid your editing team might have to be a bit more creative than we'd originally planned. We had to cut things short, so your studio guys might have to pad things out a bit—you don't mind, do ya mate?"

Jenny knew that Markus was going to be furious and she waited for the verbal ear-bashing that was about to come down the phone line.

"Ok, that's fine—I completely understand."

'What? No shouting?'—Jenny was amazed.

"But I'd like you to do one more thing for me please Jennifer, before you return to Christchurch. I need you and David, to drive back to the Queenstown office as soon as possible."

"What for?" asked Dave. "You do know this is supposed to be my weekend off don't ya?"

"Yes, Yes I know. But this is very important, please come as soon as you can—right this minute in fact—and you will be sufficiently rewarded, I promise."

And with that he hung up, leaving Dave's phone sounding a constant beep.

"Prick," mumbled Dave before turning off the phone and clambering into the driver's seat. "Come on, let's go and see what his Swedish Majesty needs us to do. If the traffic's all clear we should be there by 5 o'clock, and hopefully, we can go out for a few beers tonight before you head home in the morning."

Jenny buckled up and as Dave 'raced' the ageing satellite van out of the car park, she looked back at the pink storm clouds that had swamped the end of the fjord.

"Driving back to Queenstown is probably a good shout anyway," said Dave. "That storm's a beast, and if we stay here any longer it'll swallow us whole."

Jenny knew that he was right and the relief that now spread through her, was overwhelming. She also realised that she'd just been given a second chance to meet up with her husband in Queenstown and she was wondering how she could let the cameraman down gently on his offer of a few beers.

They drove at speed up through the valley towards the Homer Tunnel, and they reached it just as the traffic lights were turning green. With no other cars in sight, they entered the tunnel at speed and although the lights inside the tunnel were still not working, Jenny was in no mood to complain about the cameraman's driving. It was also a couple of hours since the earlier rain had passed through and the waterfalls from the tunnel roof had now slowed to a drip.

"I'm glad all that rain's gone," said Dave, "It was pretty hairy on the way down here wasn't it?"

"You're not kidding," Jenny replied. "I just closed my eyes and prayed we weren't going to hit anything."

The lightened mood inside the cab was palpable and Jenny started to hum as the cameraman tapped gently on the steering wheel.

They were about halfway into the tunnel when he suddenly

stopped tapping and leaned forward, peering ahead into the darkness. A pair of headlights had appeared up ahead and the vehicle was bearing down on them.

"Bugger, the lights must have changed," said Dave. "I'll let him know that we're in here."

He slowed to a stop and beeped his horn repeatedly, trying to warn the other vehicle of their presence.

"Shit, it's a truck... he's not stopping!"

The cameraman beeped the horn again, but still, the truck kept on coming.

"He's gonna fucking hit us!" yelled Dave, but Jenny was frozen in her seat and she could not respond.

Giving up on the van's weedy little horn, the cameraman forced the gearbox into reverse and shifted his weight to get a better view from the vehicle's side mirrors.

The box-shaped van lurched backwards sharply, and the engine whined as Dave pushed hard on the accelerator.

All the while, Jenny sat motionless, unable to scream and unable to help—everything seemed to be going in slow motion.

Suddenly a loud crunch reverberated through the van and Jenny was thrown violently from her seat. Her head thudded against the side window of the van and only a last-minute snap of her seat belt prevented her face from connecting with the dashboard. The van had rear-ended into the sidewall of the tunnel and Dave was trying desperately to make it budge. But the TV van was wedged fast under the curved wall of granite, and with the truck still advancing from the other end of the tunnel, they were running out of options for escape.

"Come on, we've gotta get out of here!" Dave yelled as he swung open the driver's side door. "Jen… did you hear me?"

But Jenny was catatonic, she just stared at her lap and the thousands of glass fragments that had fallen from the shattered side window.

"Well you might want to die, but I don't," screamed Dave, and he grabbed the weathergirl by the arm, yanking her out through the driver's door. He then dived back into the cab to snatch up his camera holdall and had barely escaped when the truck came crashing into the front of the TV van.

The sound of the impact seemed to flick on a switch in Jenny's head and she watched as their box on wheels was crushed backwards into the wall, it's sides buckling like a concertina and its satellite dish letting out a pitiful death cry as it collapsed under the roof of the tunnel. And among this scene of blurred headlights and chrome, Jenny saw her cameraman falling backwards like a rag doll, before landing in a heap beside her.

He hit the ground hard, crashing heavily onto his shoulder, but even the force of his impact could not release the holdall from the cameraman's arms. He cradled the bag protectively, like he was nursing a new-born child, and Jenny rushed to his aid.

"Dave are you ok?" she screamed.

"Yeah, I think so," he groaned, as he tried to sit up.

"Do you think we should go and see if the truck driver's ok?"

"Are you fucking joking? - that bastard tried to kill us."

"But what if his brakes just failed?" said the weathegirl.

"And what if he's some sort of murdering lunatic? Nah, we need to get out of here—and fast—before he decides to finish us off."

Jenny helped the cameraman to his feet and holding on to each other for strength, they stumbled back towards the eastern end of the tunnel. But the smoke from the smouldering vehicles quickly filled their lungs, and as they approached the tunnel entrance Dave had to drag the weathergirl to safety.

"Shit!" he cursed. "I left my camera behind, I'm gonna have to go back and get it."

"Wait, you can't!" choked Jenny. But it was too late, he'd already disappeared into the darkness.

"Davey Boy… come back!" she screamed. But instead of her cameraman responding to her pleas, the tunnel replied instead, with a thunderous explosion that sent the weathergirl tumbling onto the tarmac.

And then everything went black.

Chapter 15

Tourist guide, Wanda Everett, jumped into her battered pink hatchback and screeched out of the visitor centre car park. She knew it would have been safer to wait out the storm in the accommodation block at the rear of the complex, but she had to be certain that all the tourists had left the area and the only way to do that was to make the drive out of the valley herself.

As she neared the Homer Tunnel, the gentle valley road turned into a much steeper incline and her tiny vehicle whined as she pushed the engine to its limits. But the car soon made it on to more level ground and the tour guide tapped on the dashboard to thank the car for its efforts.

"Well done Marilyn, I knew you could do it."

However, they weren't out of danger just yet and as they rounded the final bend before the tunnel, the storm finally caught up with them and a wall of rain dropped down onto the roof. The water hit like a hammer blow and Wanda felt the vehicle slow under its weight. Switching on the wipers she prayed that they would hold up—they'd been playing up for weeks.

Now, as she peered through the river of water running down her windscreen, the world outside seemed to turn a strange shade of red and unable to see where she was going, she slammed on the brakes.

The wipers seemed to take this as a sign to finally give up the ghost and a slick of gloopy red sludge began to cover the windscreen. It quickly blocked out the light and the tour guide found herself being cocooned away inside its crimson shell.

Once again, Wanda knew that she should probably stay exactly where she was, but it felt like she was being buried alive and she knew she had to escape.

She opened the car door and stepped out into the 'blood rain'—for she now realised that's what it was. A mixture of desert sand from Australia's red centre, combined with the moisture-rich air that had been gathered above the Tasman Sea.

As she exited the car, the smell of iron-rich dirt, filled Wanda's nose. The metallic air felt like a nosebleed running down her throat and she choked on its deathly portents. Within seconds she was covered from head to toe in a crimson pack of mud and the tour guide lumbered in her steps like a swamp beast from a Hollywood B-Movie.

Gale force winds were whipping up from the valley below and with pink lightning bolts crackling in the sky above, she knew that the safest place to shelter would be the tunnel.

She sprinted around the final bend in the road, desperate to find sanctuary, but instead she was met by a wall of smoke and she choked on its acrid stench. Thick, black plumes were billowing from the tunnel entrance and Wanda stepped back in shock.

Peering through mud-caked eyelashes she tried to work out what had happened and as she surveyed the scene, she spotted an unmistakable flash of yellow lying just metres from the tunnel entrance.

"Jenny!"

She ran to the fallen celebrity and cradled her in her arms. What on earth had happened here she wondered, and where was Davey Boy in this poor girl's moment of need?

She looked around, desperate to find the cameraman, but he was nowhere to be seen. So instead, she turned her attention back to the weathergirl and wiped the mud from her face. Wanda smiled as her touch brought the girl awake and as Jenny looked up towards her, she let the girl know that everything was going to be ok.

"Jenny it's me, Wanda. We met earlier today at the harbour. We talked about your yellow dress—do you remember?"

But the weathergirl didn't react. Her hands shielded her ears, blocking out a sound that the tour guide could not hear.

"Jenny, what happened here, where's Davey Boy? Is he still inside the tunnel?"

The girl tilted her head, the words had broken through her defences.

"Jenny, it looks like there was an accident inside the tunnel, but you're ok now, you're safe. I've got a satellite phone and I'm going to call for some help. Just stay with me Jenny, everything's gonna be ok."

A chink of light burst through into Jenny's terrified mind, '*Davey Boy?*' — she recognised that name. But he'd gone somewhere, he'd left her on her own.

The memories suddenly came flooding back and the weathergirl screamed…

"He's in the tunnel, Davey Boy's inside the tunnel!"

Uncurling from her foetal position on the floor, she stood up to look for her colleague. She couldn't see him anywhere, but a noise to her left spun her around and she saw Wanda, wide-eyed and grinning.

The tour guide's immaculate beehive hairstyle had flopped into a messy bird's nest and her clothes were covered in a strange red mud… she looked a mess.

"Wanda, what on earth happened to you?"

"What happened to me, don't you mean what happened to you?"

"There was an accident… a lorry inside the tunnel… it couldn't stop… and it crashed right into us."

Wanda looked at the tunnel and the thick black smoke that was billowing from its entrance.

"It's alright baby girl," she said, wrapping the younger woman in a motherly hug. "You're ok now, you're safe."

"But what about Dave? He went back for his camera bag."

Wanda looked again at the tunnel, and her heart sank as she pictured the cameraman still trapped inside.

"Davey Boy's gonna be ok," she replied. "He'll come back out, I'm sure of it."

Although in truth, she wasn't sure if anyone could survive that amount of smoke.

But then, as if to defy her scepticism, a coughing sound echoed from the tunnel entrance and the two women spun around.

"We're over here," they both shouted in unison.

The coughing grew louder and suddenly a figure burst through into the daylight—but it wasn't the cameraman.

"Liam?" said Jenny.

It was the truck driver, the one that she'd met earlier at the café. He was dragging the unconscious cameraman behind him and he looked like he was about to collapse as well.

The two women instinctively rushed to help, but as Jenny grabbed Liam's arm he dropped to the ground, coughing and spluttering as he fell. They we're just a few metres from the tunnel entrance and the smoke was going to choke them all if they didn't get clear.

The weathergirl looked down at the truck driver and her stricken colleague. They were both heavy men—although for different reasons—and she realised that she'd have to drag them.

But then suddenly, a great downforce of wind made the weathergirl stagger under its weight and she looked skyward to see a helicopter hovering above. A rescue team had arrived, and its winchman was descending on a wire to save them. Jenny couldn't help but burst into tears as the man landed beside her and she pulled him close as he released his harness from the cable.

"Thank You!" she shouted, over the roar of the helicopter. But the man simply nodded in response, he was too embarrassed to reply.

"If you don't mind..." he said finally, "I'll take these blokes up first, they both look like they're in bad shape—but I'll be back for you ladies as soon as I can."

The women nodded their understanding and they watched in awe as the winchman ascended first with Liam, and then came back with a stretcher for the unconscious cameraman.

On their rescuer's third descent, he called the women in close, shouting over the noise of the helicopter so they could hear his instructions.

"I'm gonna have to take you both up together I'm afraid. The chopper's starting to struggle with all this weird rain we're having. If we don't get out of here fast, the rotor's gonna get clogged up with all sorts of shit."

The rescuer strapped them both into harnesses and as they ascended, the helicopter's downdraft intensified the velocity of the blood coloured rain. It stung as it hit Jenny's face and she looked down to shield her eyes. Below her, she saw what was once beautiful countryside, now smothered under a cloak of thick red mud—they'd had a lucky escape.

They quickly reached the helicopter and the winchman pulled

Jenny inside, passing her a microphone headset as he strapped her into a seat.

"Ya know, it's not often we get to rescue a TV celebrity," he said. "The boss man up front there, well he nearly broke the throttle trying to get us here in time—he's a big fan of your work."

The winchman gave his colleague a pat on the back and winked at Jenny. She felt her cheeks turn an embarrassed shade of pink and she looked to Wanda for backup.

"Well if you don't want him, I'll take him," grinned the tour guide, forgetting that her own headset was also connected with the crew's.

The helicopter swerved in response and Jenny couldn't help but grin when the older woman flushed red herself. Jenny barely knew the woman, but she knew from that moment onwards, they were going to be the best of friends.

Chapter 16

"So, did you hear about the incident down at the bungy bridge?" asked Rachael.

She was driving the dam engineer to hospital after shouldering his weight back to her patrol car. He was heavier than he looked and her back ached from the sideways strain of carrying him.

"Incident at the bungy bridge?" said Owen. "So that's where the murder took place?"

Owen appeared to be completely out of the loop when it came to local gossip, probably because he was so swept up in his work at the dam.

"Yes," Rachael replied. "But I can't tell you anything more I'm afraid."

"That's ok, you're right to keep things close to your chest—at least until you have something concrete to disclose. In my job, people always ask me for on the spot answers, but I just tell them, I'll let *you* know, as soon as *I* know."

Rachael smiled. Owen had just summed up her job in two sentences. Policing wasn't just about solving crimes anymore. It was about telling people what they wanted to hear and trying to manage the public's expectations. It was a bit like her relationship with Liam, where sometimes it was easier to let things slide rather than standing up and saying what she really felt.

When they finally reached the town, the streets were deserted thanks to a match at the rugby club and they made it to the hospital in good time. There were several more games planned over the coming weeks and although Rachael welcomed the quiet streets during match days, she knew it was going to take valuable resources away from her investigation.

She left Owen at the A&E reception desk and headed downstairs to see if Dr. James had any more information about Jonno Hart's body.

As she pressed the elevator button for the basement level, she prayed that Pippa would be downstairs to offer some additional insight. She sensed that the junior pathologist was the real brains of the operation and she would cope just fine if Bob ever decided to retire.

"Can you hold the elevator please!" came a shout from the corridor. It was quickly followed by a blur of black and white as a track-suited body jumped through the closing doors. It was Pippa, and Rachael smiled as she pulled back the hood of her jacket.

"Rugby practice again was it?" she asked, as the brunette unzipped her jacket to reveal a mud streaked vest that clung to her athletic physique.

"Er yeah, and it got pretty rough towards the end—just the way I like it!"

The girl flicked a playful wink at the detective and Rachael smiled in reply.

The elevator opened into the basement corridor and she held the lab doors so that Pippa could squeeze through with her oversized sports holdall.

"I'm just gonna go freshen up," said the lab assistant, dumping her car keys on a stainless-steel trolley as she went. She disappeared into a side office and Rachael watched through the frosted glass as the girl slipped from her mud streaked tracksuit into a crisp white lab coat. Her lean yet feminine curves were clearly visible through the glass and Rachael averted her eyes when she walked back unexpectedly into the lab.

Pippa strode casually in her stilettoes, making imaginary notes on her clipboard as she walked. It gave the impression that she'd already been at work for hours and Rachael chuckled to herself at the girl's bravado. It was a neat trick, and the detective wondered how many of her own colleagues did something similar when they were late for work.

Bob was apparently so engrossed with what he was doing, however, that he'd failed to notice the absence of his assistant and she coughed lightly to draw his attention, both to herself and to their visitor.

"Ah, Sergeant, I'm glad you're here. I was just about to call your commanding officer and tell him that I needed to see you."

"It's actually Detective Sergeant," said Rachael, in no mood to let the pathologist's mistake go uncorrected. Her back was still aching from shouldering Owen's weight and the mention of her boss had immediately rubbed her up the wrong way. It annoyed her when people still treated her like a junior officer, and older men in particular always seemed to emphasise just how far she still had to climb.

"Yes, yes, *Detective*, whatever you say," snapped the pathologist. "You're here now, and I've got something to show you."

He'd dismissed her correction like it was the backchat of a teenage girl and Rachael bit her lip in frustration.

"I've found some evidence that I think you'll find very…um… compelling," said Bob.

Rachael didn't like that word, 'compelling', it implied that what she was about to see, was unequivocal proof, instead of something to support a theory. She knew from experience that evidence was rarely so black and white in its storytelling and she waited cautiously as the pathologist performed his 'big reveal'.

"Ok, so you know already that while performing my preliminary examination, I discovered something in Jonno's shirt pocket. A vestige of paper, with a phone number for a local fishing guide…"

The pathologist paused for dramatic effect.

"You also know that Jonno's body was discovered in a partially consumed state, after a short but intense period of predation by longfin eels and numerous bird species."

Rachael watched as the pathologist strode around the room. His chest was puffed out and he gesticulated wildly as he spoke to help illustrate his words.

'Why can't he just get on with it?', she thought. *'This had better be good or I might have to lock him up for wasting my time'.*

She noticed Pippa staring at her with a quizzical look and she realised that she must have been grinning. The thought of arresting the patronising old man had tickled her and she couldn't help but smile at the thought of putting him in his place. Pippa smiled back at her and they both rolled their eyes as Bob continued to prattle on.

"So, now that I've had more time to perform a thorough autopsy, I can tell you that Jonno Hart was violated in a most foul way before his body was subsequently mutilated by the local wildlife."

"Violated?" said Rachael. The word had snapped her out of her daydream and brought her back to the task at hand. A violation would certainly be karma at work, if the rumours she'd heard about Jonno, did indeed hold any truth. She'd heard stories of Jonno's trips to Vietnam and a specific resort that was renowned for its child prostitution rings.

"Yes, I'm afraid Jonno was abused in the most terrible way," continued Bob. "Before his killer hung him like a maggot on a fishing line."

"Really?" said Rachael in a deadpan voice, convinced that what was about to be revealed, would be nowhere near as graphic as the pathologist had built it up to be.

"I found this…" said Bob, holding up a small plastic evidence bag. "It was embedded in his scrotum and the cord was wrapped tightly around his phallus. It's a shame the killer didn't use that knot around his neck—as it wouldn't have held. It looks like he was trying to tie a clinch knot, but he tied a Highwayman's Hitch instead."

Rachael took the evidence bag from the pathologist and she

raised an eyebrow at what she saw. Inside was a jade fishing hook, it's surface intricately carved, and with a cord attached, that was made of leather.

"Is that what I think it is?" asked Pippa, leaning in, to take a look. "It looks like a necklace—of the type worn by Māori men—and many tribal leaders throughout the Pacific Islands."

"And you say this was embedded in the victim's penis?" said Rachael, testing the fishing hook's sharpness as she talked.

"In his scrotum," corrected Bob, wincing as he spoke the words. "The hook was inserted with such force that it ruptured Jonno's left testis, and overall it looks to have been a particularly vicious assault.

…Sergeant, you need to arrest that Māori fella as soon as possible, he's clearly a very dangerous individual."

Rachael handed the plastic bag back to the doctor and she reached for her walkie talkie to call the station. Although she didn't like being told what to do, Bob was right, and she needed to move quickly before Kaihautu Waitaha disappeared for good.

"Don't worry Doctor," she said. "With this new evidence of yours, I think we'll have this case wrapped up within the next few days. Then you'll be able to say a proper farewell to your friend."

"Jolly good," said Bob. "I'm sure you'll make this Māori bastard pay for what he's done, won't you. Oh, but if erm, if you need anything else at all, just let me know yeah. I might be able to rustle up some more evidence that'll seal the case."

Chapter 17

Jenny sat nervously in the corridor, just outside the intensive care unit of Queenstown's central hospital. The rescue helicopter had dropped them off several hours earlier, and after being given the all-clear herself, she was now waiting on news of her colleague.

Wanda had been amazing, offering to stay for as long as Jenny needed her, but Jenny could tell that the woman was keen to get home to her family. So, she'd convinced the tour guide that she'd be fine on her own and she'd been left to her own thoughts for the past hour.

They'd all been through a terrifying experience and now as Jenny sat on the first of five plastic chairs, a wave of physical and emotional exhaustion swept over her. She'd only known Dave Norman for 48 hours, but she was already more concerned for his well-being than any of her colleagues back in Christchurch. Perhaps it was because they'd been through so much together in just a short space of time, but she'd already grown fond of Davey Boy, the bearded wonder.

She'd even become accustomed to his childish innuendo, a coping device that he'd so often used to break the silence. The hour that she'd already spent on that uncomfortable blue chair would have been helped no end by one of Dave's jokes about her backside offering more cushioning than most.

Davey Boy was a technical guru who'd managed to make her look good, even when she felt ugly and exhausted, and the confidence that he'd shown in her over the past few days had made Jenny believe that she really could make a go of this TV lark.

Just as she was raising a leg to rub the pins and needles from her backside, the door to her left suddenly swung open and she looked up to see a doctor, his eye's sparkling blue, above a beard of pure white. He looked caring and wise, and the weathergirl knew instinctively that her friend was in good hands.

"Miss Sunley, I presume?"

Jenny nodded and then corrected herself.

"It's Mrs actually, not Miss… but Sunley, isn't my husband's surname, so I never know if I should be Miss, Mrs or Ms? I couldn't bring myself to take his name you see—which is Penny—and that would sound weird, wouldn't it… you know… Jenny Penny?"

The doctor just smiled in response and Jenny realised that she was waffling. She'd been sat in silence for over an hour and her emotions had come bursting out in a jumble of words.

"*Ms.* Sunley, I'm Doctor Forbes, I've been handling Davey Boy's treatment since he arrived."

"Davey Boy?" said Jenny, confused by the doctor's casual turn of phrase.

"Oh yes, I'm sorry, I should probably call him Mr Norman, shouldn't I? But it's difficult when I've known the man for nearly 30 years."

Jenny smiled. Davey Boy was clearly just popular here in Queenstown as he was back in Te Anau.

"Well, he's had one hell of a knock," continued the doctor. "But it looks like he's gonna be ok. He's a tough old bird, that Davey Boy"

"Oh. thank goodness for that," said Jenny, as the weight of concern lifted from her shoulders.

"He's still going to be in here for a while yet, mind you. But apart from not being able to lift a camera bag for a few months, he should make a full recovery."

"That's wonderful news!" replied the weathergirl. "When do you think I might be able to see him?"

"Oh, it won't be until tomorrow I'm afraid. He's still heavily sedated right now and I don't want him moving about for at the least next 24 hours. He's got a broken scapula and several cracked ribs, so he'll need somebody to look after him when he's eventually discharged."

"Oh right, erm…"

"Do you know if Dave's got anyone who could take care of him?" asked the doctor. "I haven't seen much of him these past few years, so I don't know if he's still living on his own?"

"I really can't help you there I'm afraid," said Jenny, "I've only known him for a few days myself. But if you like, I can call my boss in Christchurch, to see if he can help?"

"Help with what?" said a voice from the far end of the corridor.

Jenny turned quickly and she was surprised to see Markus, walking towards her. As the TV executive strode confidently down the bright pink corridor, the strip lights overhead reflected in his spectacles and it seemed to exaggerate the speed at which he walked.

"I was just telling the Doctor that you might be able to offer some help with Dave," said Jenny.

Markus stopped and shook the physician's hand.

"Yes… yes of course doctor, whatever you need. But what about you Jennifer—are you ok?"

"Oh yes, I'm fine," she replied. "But Doctor Forbes was just saying that Dave will probably need some help at home. I don't suppose you know if he's got a partner, do you?"

"I'm afraid not Jennifer. I believe that very much like Jonno Hart, David is quite the bachelor, so I doubt if there's anyone who can look after him."

"Ok, well I'll see if we can keep him in for few days longer," said the doctor, before he shook Markus' hand once more and headed towards the reception desk.

Markus sat down on a chair next Jenny and took off his glasses. As he placed them methodically into the inside pocket of his jacket, he leaned back against the wall and stretched out his legs.

"So, Jennifer, are you sure you're ok? When I heard about the accident in the tunnel, I must admit, I feared the worst."

"Oh yes, I'm fine," she replied. "I've just got a bit of a sore head, that's all."

"Ah, that's good. Well, I'm very glad that the nation's favourite weather presenter is well enough to come back to work next week."

He tapped Jenny's knee as if to comfort her and then stood up abruptly.

"I'm just going to go find the good Doctor Forbes again—there's something else I need to ask him. But I'll be back in a minute and we'll talk about getting you home to Christchurch."

Jenny watched as he marched up the corridor, before sliding silently through the double doors at the end. Markus may have looked like her husband from behind, but he shared none of the warmth and humour that made Owen the only man she'd ever loved. Even Dave, with his crude compliments, was more likeable than the Swede and if only he could stop hiding behind a wall of machismo, he'd probably be quite a sweet guy.

Jenny was thinking more on that, when a tap on her shoulder made her jump.

"Excuse me, Miss Sunley, I've brought your bag—we found it at the tunnel when we went back after the storm."

It was the helicopter pilot who had rescued them earlier that day and he stood there fidgeting, like a nervous schoolboy.

"Oh right… thank you," she replied, not knowing what else to say.

"Are you ok, Miss Sunley? I can pull a few strings, if there's anything you need, anything at all."

"No, no, I'm fine—thank you—and for earlier too, you saved my life, well, Dave's life anyway."

"That's ok, it's all in a day's work. And the winch guys are the ones that you should really thank. I just press a few buttons that's all."

"Well, you're my hero anyway," said Jenny, before standing up to kiss the man on the cheek.

As she did so, a great cheer echoed from the end of the corridor and they both turned to see the rest of the helicopter crew, standing in the doorway, all grinning from ear-to-ear. Both Jenny and her rescuer flushed bright red and the pilot quickly made his excuses to leave. He was greeted by his team him with a round of handshakes and macho pats on the back, and the weathergirl smiled as he was bundled out of the door.

She sat back down on the chair grinning to herself, pleased that she could still have that effect on men, even though she looked rough as hell. At that moment though, she needed comfort more than adulation and she reached instinctively for her phone. She had an urge to call Owen, to hear his voice, telling her that she was safe, and they would soon be together.

As she waited for the signal to connect, Jenny realised that she hadn't even told him she was on an assignment. In fact, she hadn't talked to him since her first live broadcast back in Christchurch—and that was nearly a week ago.

"Hey gorgeous, I hope you're not calling your boyfriend," said a voice.

"What do you mean?" said Jenny, shifting the phone against her ear. Owen's voice sounded echoey like he was inside a cave… or a corridor!

She spun around quickly, flushed with excitement.

"Owen!" she screamed, as she ran into his waiting arms. "But what are you doing here at the hospital?"

"Oh, it's nothing serious, I just twisted my ankle that's all. I'm fine now."

"Thank goodness for that," Jenny replied. "I'm not sure I could cope with another man in my life getting hurt."

"Another man? Is there something I should know about?"

"No, no, it's nothing like that, I meant my cameraman—Dave. We were in an accident on our way back from Milford Sound. I was calling to tell you about it just now."

"So that was you? In the tunnel crash?"

"You heard about that?"

"It's all over the news. I saw it on the TV screens while I was waiting in A&E. Are you sure you're ok?"

"Yeah, I'm fine," said Jenny, as she looked up into Owen's pale blue eyes. "Just a few scratches, that's all."

"You know I also saw some video of you standing on a boat," said Owen. "That was a dangerous-looking storm you covered. Is that something else you were going to tell me about?"

"Yeah, I'm sorry about that. I meant to call you yesterday, but everything's been such a rush you know. It's hard to believe that this time last week, I was sitting in a gallery with a relaxing cup of… cup of hot chocolate… and reading a leaflet about… about…"

And with that, Jenny burst into tears.

The enormity of what she'd been through had suddenly hit home and she collapsed into Owen's arms.

"Hey, hey, it's ok, don't worry. You're safe now and that's all that matters."

Owen rubbed her back and Jenny felt the warmth of his body wrapping around her like a protective blanket. It was a feeling like no other and as she sunk into his chest the barrier that she'd erected to keep out the memories of the crash, suddenly began to crumble. Her emotions came flooding out and Owen's shirt was soon wet with tears.

"Look…" said Owen. "Why don't you come back to my hotel room and I'll run you a bath. We can order in some room service and then catch up properly, if you know what I mean?"

Just then, footsteps in the corridor interrupted their reunion and Jenny lifted her head to see Markus striding towards them.

"Ah, so I take it you're the lucky man who managed to tame this wonderful girl—it's Owen isn't it?"

"Yes, that's right… have we met before? You look familiar?"

Jenny thought she'd better introduce the two men and she

stepped back as they shook hands.

"Owen, this is Markus—my boss at the station. He came all the way from Christchurch when he heard about the accident."

"Well that's not strictly correct," said TV executive. "You see, I was already here in Queenstown when I saw the news and I was already on my way to the hospital when I heard you were being brought here."

"Oh, really?" said Jenny, somewhat miffed that her boss hadn't really made the effort that she'd imagined.

"Well you see, there is a news story here in Queenstown—a very big one actually—and we need to cover it, Jennifer, before the other networks are catching the wind of it."

His accented English was being further distorted by his obvious excitement and Jenny was intrigued to know what had got Markus so pumped.

"A story?" she asked. "What kind of story Markus?"

"I think I might know," said Owen. "There was an incident down at Moke Creek. The police have started a murder investigation—their prime suspect is a local Māori man."

"Wonderful!" exclaimed Markus.

"But how do you know about all this?" said Jenny "I've never known you to be interested in local gossip?"

"It's not gossip…" said Owen. "I heard it from a police officer this morning."

"Jennifer, you must help me," said Markus. "My field reporter isn't going to be here for at least another four hours, but by then it could be too late. We must get something on camera before the other networks descend on the town."

"But how can I help?" Jenny replied. "I'm just a weathergirl, that's all—and look at the state of me—I can't do an interview looking like this."

Jenny looked down at her stained dress and muddied shoes, she looked like an orphaned child from a dust-ridden war zone.

"Don't worry Jennifer, you look fine," said Markus. "And you're a meteorological correspondent, not a weathergirl, please do not sell yourself short."

"He's right," said Owen. "You look amazing Jen, and you'll be…"

But Owen stopped short, his phone was beeping, and he looked down to read an incoming text message.

"I'm sorry, I've got to go," he said, looking up. "There's something I need to sort out at the dam, something's happened."

"But Owen…."

"I just need to go and sort this out, but I'll be back in a couple of hours, I promise. Why don't you go film this piece for Markus, and we'll catch up later—It's only 5 pm, so we'll have plenty of time for what we talked about earlier."

"Good, that's agreed then," said Markus. "I already have a script prepared for your introduction Jennifer, and then it's just a few short questions, that's all."

"Look I've really got to go," said Owen. "I'll meet you at the hotel around seven, ok? And don't worry, you'll be great… Jenny Sunshine!"

And with that, he left.

Jenny watched as he walked up the corridor then through the doors towards reception—she already missed his smile and his smell.

She also knew that she should've felt buoyed by Owen's confidence in her, but instead she felt like a ship being blown out to sea, just as she had reached the safety of harbour.

"Ah very good," said Markus, interrupting her thoughts. "I see you've still got David's bag with you. I brought a small camera in my car, but David's will be much better for your interview with Doctor James."

'Shit', thought Jenny, as she looked down at the bag. It wasn't her own suitcase that the helicopter pilot had recovered, it was Davey Boy's tattered green holdall. She had no clothes, no shoes and no make-up. How on earth was she going to make herself look presentable when all she had was a mud-stained dress and hair that looked like she'd been dragged through a hedge backwards?

It was all she could do to stop herself from crying and then she saw Markus tapping his watch impatiently—she'd have to pull herself together—and fast.

Chapter 18

DS Blunt stepped out of the toilet cubicle just as her phone started to ring, it was Tony, her colleague at the station.

"Hi Rachael, it's Tony. I've got a call for you from the pathology lab. Should I patch it through, or have you clocked off for the night?"

'Bugger,' thought Rachael. *'What does that pompous old fart want now?'*

She'd worked late for the past 10 days straight and she was keen to get home for a date night with her boyfriend Liam. She'd barely seen him over the past six months and even with a murder still to solve, she needed to see him, if only to keep things on track for another few months.

'If I keep Bob hanging on the phone long enough, perhaps he'll get tired of waiting?', she considered.

It was a tempting thought, but the professional in her knew that he was probably calling with good reason and she should listen to what he had to say.

"Alright Tony," she replied. "Patch it through to my mobile."

As Rachael waited to hear the pathologist's booming voice, she wondered if it was too late to change her mind. She could always hang up and pretend that something had gone wrong with the call transfer. But to her disappointment she heard the line connect and so she jumped in first, to make the conversation as short as possible.

"Good afternoon Doctor, what can I do for you?" she said.

"I'm sorry Detective, it's not Dr James… it's me… Pippa."

Rachael could barely hear the girl—it almost sounded like she was whispering.

"Oh right," she replied, somewhat confused as to why Bob's lab assistant was calling her.

"I know you've probably finished for the day, but I just had to call you."

"Don't worry, it's fine—I can come back down to the lab if you like?"

She didn't normally offer up her free time like that, but there was something interesting about Pippa and she felt like she should probably get to know the girl better. After all, the lab assistant could be a valuable ally if she ever found herself at odds with her boss.

"That fishing hook…" said Pippa, "It wasn't there before—I'm sure of it."

"Ok…" said Rachael, surprised by the suggestion. "And I take it Bob wasn't prepared to listen to you huh—and that's why you're calling me now? How can you be sure that you're right?"

"Well I'm not, at least not one hundred percent, but I thought you should know that I had concerns."

'Shit,' thought Rachael, *'there goes my case closed celebration'*

But she still wanted Kaihautu brought in, just in case.

"Wait a second…" she said suddenly. "Did you just say… Dr James?"

"Yes, that's right… why?"

'Dr Robert James, of course!' why she hadn't made the connection before she'd never know.

"Is Bob related to Scotty James by any chance—he's the owner of the Moke Creek Bungy Company?"

"Sure," replied Pippa. "He's Scotty's dad. Scotty was here last night actually—I think it was about 10 pm."

"Really? And why was he there?"

"Oh, he often drops in on his way home from work, but this was the first time I've known him to stop by so late."

"And did he stay long?"

"No, he was only here for a few minutes. His dad had already left for the night, so he said he'd pop back in the morning."

"Ok, well that's very helpful, thank y…."

The exit door had swung open and Rachael suddenly realised that she was standing in the middle of the ladies' restroom.

A woman had walked in through the door and Rachael just

managed to catch sight of her dress, before she slid into a cubicle, slamming the door behind her. The woman's dress was yellow, but it was covered in what looked like blood and a quick glance at floor level showed that the woman's feet were bare and were also stained a deep red colour.

"Listen, Pippa, I have to hang up now," said Rachael, "But thank you for the information—it's been very helpful."

"No worries," said the junior pathologist. "Let me know if you need anything else, anything at all."

Rachael hung up and then tapped on the cubicle door.

"Hello, are you ok in there? I noticed your dress, are you injured?"

"Oh no, I'm fine thanks," replied the woman. "I'm just having a really shitty day that's all."

The woman's voice sounded English like Rachael's, but with a London accent, *'or Essex perhaps?'*

"You know, I've had quite a tough day myself," said the policewoman. "Almost makes me wish I was back home in Guildford."

But there was no response.

"Well, if you're sure you're ok?" said Rachael, looking at her watch.

It was already 5:30 pm and she didn't want to be the one that was late for date night. She also wanted to jump in the shower before Liam made it home; she knew that she smelt pretty rank after her hike up the river valley with Owen.

"Hey, before you go…" said the woman in the cubicle. "I don't suppose you've got any makeup I could borrow—just some lipstick would help?"

"No, I'm sorry. Police officers aren't allowed to wear makeup I'm afraid."

It was a statement of fact, although, in truth, Rachael had stopped wearing makeup long before she'd joined the force.

"I thought I had some in my bag you see, but it turns out it's not my bag at all. It's Dave's bag and it's probably just full of batteries and lenses and stuff."

'Who the hell is Dave?' thought Rachael. This woman was clearly unbalanced, and she had better things to be getting on with than talking to some random bimbo about makeup.

"Look I'm sorry, but I've got to go now. I hope your day gets better, but I've got more important things to worry about than your lack of lipstick."

Rachael didn't really want the woman to answer, and she certainly didn't want to wait around for her to emerge from the cubicle. So, she tiptoed towards the door instead and exited without looking back.

'What a weirdo,' she thought, as she sped away along the corridor. It had been a tiring day all round and she was grateful that she'd managed to make her escape.

'What a bitch,' thought Jenny, as she heard the restroom door slam shut. She may have been a busy police officer, but that was no excuse for being rude.

The weathergirl sat perched on the cheap plastic toilet seat and looked down at her ruined dress. Its once bright yellow fabric was now covered in reddish-brown streaks and she'd given up hope that they might somehow come out in the wash.

'Come on you… stupid cow… you can do this. It's just an interview that's all—and you don't even have to think about what to say.'

Markus had already done most of the hard work by preparing a list of questions, and he'd even made notes on how she should follow up if a response went a certain way.

Jenny slapped herself around the face and then straightened the creases in her dress as she stood up. She could be the most confident presenter in the world, but if she looked like crap, that's all anybody was ever going to remember.

If only she had some lipstick, or maybe just some foundation to hide her wrinkles…

"That's it!" she said out loud. Dave had called Jonno, a wrinkly old bastard, hadn't he? Perhaps good ol' Davey Boy kept some foundation powder stashed away for the fishing celebrity? And if Jonno was as much of a diva as Dave had made out, there could be all sorts of beauty products hidden away in that gigantic sports holdall.

Jenny rushed out of the restroom and sprinted up the corridor. She'd left the bag next to Dave's bed after a nurse had said it would be safe there.

As she rounded the corner, a door up ahead was swinging shut and she caught a glimpse of two men, exiting towards the car park.

It was Owen and another man, a man with dark wavy hair…

'Liam?'

Did her husband know the truck driver somehow, or were they just heading in the same direction? She made a mental note to check with Owen at dinner.

Reaching Dave's room, the weathergirl tentatively opened the door and peeked inside. The cameraman was out cold on a cocktail of painkillers, and she didn't want to wake him.

As Jenny crept quietly in, she whispered her thanks to her colleague in advance.

"Davey Boy, if you've got any slap hidden away in this green holdall of yours, I'm gonna kiss you, you know that—you short, fat, hairy bastard."

She squatted down next to the bed and unzipped the bag, preparing herself for the smell of old socks. It was something that she'd learned from being married to Owen and several other long-term relationships over the years. Men seemed to leave dirty socks in every place imaginable and they always ended up stinking out the place—like deadly cotton assassins.

Jenny foraged amongst the jumble of t-shirts and baggy shorts, and then through to the camera equipment that was stowed underneath. The battered holdall was cavernous, like an Edwardian nanny's carpet bag, and Jenny was beginning to wonder if she might somehow pull out a six-foot standard lamp.

But then suddenly there it was, a small silver compact, and Jenny raised it triumphantly in the air. Springing open the lid to reveal its cargo of flesh coloured powder, the weathergirl let out a small sigh of disappointment. It was more orange than her usual shade, but it would have to do. and she proceeded to apply it on her face, using the compact's tiny mirror to guide her movements.

"You star!" she whispered to the sleeping cameraman. "I knew you'd come good Davey Boy, I bet you were a boy scout when you were younger weren't you—always prepared for anything".

'Now then' she thought, *'are you going to go one better, and have some skin tightening cream as well?'*.

She dived back in—her confidence renewed that she might look presentable after all. This time, however, she was less restrained with her probing and she pulled Dave's crumpled t-shirts straight out onto the floor.

"What the hell?" she exclaimed, as a shock of neon caught her eye.

A shiny, pink wig lay spread out on top of the clothing, its bright colour incongruous to the general palette of khaki and beige. It was then that a eureka moment suddenly hit the weathergirl and she instinctively rubbed Dave's leg in protective reassurance. He hadn't just gone to watch the 'Lady Gloria' show back in Te Anau,

Davey Boy *was* Lady Gloria!

It was a revelation that made Jenny smile and the cameraman's fascination with her shoes and dresses suddenly made sense. *'Poor man'*, she thought, as the realisation of what he probably had to endure, began to form in her head.

Even though New Zealand was progressive in its approach to topics like conservation and the environment, the views of many of its residents were still conservative compared to other parts of the world. What's more, Jonno Hart was notorious for his outdated comments and his daily onslaught of macho banter must have felt like torture.

'I wonder if Jonno knows about Lady Gloria?' thought Jenny. It would certainly be ammunition for the man if he did.

"Don't worry Davey Boy…" she whispered. "Your secret's safe with me."

She leaned down and kissed him on the cheek, before dashing outside to catch up with Markus. She'd left him standing at the lift to the pathology lab and she knew he wouldn't have waited long.

Jenny wasn't looking forward to going back underground, and as she pushed the lift button to go down, a nervous twitch in her eye made her blink uncontrollably.

'Oh, that's just fucking great…' she thought. *'Not only do I look like crap, but now I'm gonna look like a madwoman as well.'*

The lift arrived and as the doors opened, she caught a glimpse of herself in the mirrored interior. It was better than she'd imagined, but she was still hoping that the lab would be dark enough to hide the worst of it.

Chapter 19

The lift opened into the basement corridor and Jenny's nostrils filled with the smell of concrete dust and disinfectant. She spotted a pair of swing doors just a few feet away and she walked towards them tentatively. A small sign mounted on the wall above read, 'Doctor Robert James MD - Head of Pathology.'

"In here please Jennifer," came the sound of Markus' voice.

She pushed through the doors and squinted into the relative darkness within.

"Quickly please young lady, you're not really supposed to be in here, so we need to get this done as fast as possible."

It was a different voice this time and Jenny scanned the room, trying to find its source.

She didn't have to search for long, as a man stepped into the spotlight that had been set up in the centre of the room.

"Miss Sunley, I presume?"

The man leaned forward to kiss Jenny's hand and his lips lingered on her skin for slightly longer than was comfortable. When he straightened up to await her reply, the weathergirl felt her eyelid start to twitch once more.

"And you must be... Dr James?"

"That's right little lady, Dr Robert James at your service. Hey Markus, you weren't kidding were you, she's quite something isn't she."

Jenny faked a smile as the doctor stood there grinning. But his lascivious gaze quickly dropped to her bosom and she nervously pulled up on the neckline of her dress.

"Pippa!" bellowed the doctor. "Fix me a coffee would you, my mouth has gone quite dry in the presence of this beautiful young lady."

"Yes of course doctor—right away."

The response came from behind her and Jenny turned to see a young woman step briefly into the light before disappearing into a side room. The hem of the girl's lab coat gently skimmed her toned thighs and her black stiletto shoes tapped on the concrete floor as she walked.

'Hmm, nice shoes.'

"Can I get you anything Miss Sunley?" said the girl, popping her head back through the door. "A cup of tea perhaps?"

"No, I'm fine thank you, unless you're having one yourself?"

"Oh, I don't drink tea—at least not when it's from a bag—it's a bit old fashioned for me."

'Did she just call me an old bag?'

A roaring sound had started up in the side room and Jenny had struggled to hear what the girl was saying.

"What on earth is that noise?" she asked the Doctor, who was grinning at her bemusement.

"Oh, that's Bertha," he replied. "She's just an old Bunsen burner that I tweaked a while back when the suits upstairs refused to buy me a kettle."

"Oh right… sounds like a good idea. We could probably do with one of those back at the studio, couldn't we Markus?"

"No, I don't think so," replied the TV executive, seemingly unaware that Jenny was only trying to make small talk with the doctor.

The pathologist's assistant walked back into the room and she handed the doctor his coffee. She'd made it in a glass medical beaker, with a handle made from a pair of tongs that were secured by some sort of wire.

"That's a nifty idea," said Jenny, as the girl turned to face her.

"Yeah, it's pretty cool, isn't it. The bunsen heats the water much faster than a kettle, and a separate glass tube forces steam through the cream and coffee beans—it was all Doctor James' idea."

"Ingenious," replied the weathergirl. "And the beaker… I like the way you've used tongs for a handle—but how have you secured it?"

"It's suture wire," said Bob, interrupting their conversation. "The kind I use to stitch up after I've had a good poke around inside a body. It's pretty strong stuff—a bit like fishing wire."

"So, you're good with your hands then Doctor?" said Jenny, flashing a smile that made the doctor choke on his coffee.

She'd encountered men like Doctor James before and she knew that the best way to get them onside, was to always stay one step ahead with the compliments and innuendo. It was a tactic that made the weathergirl's skin crawl, but at the same time, it gave her a feeling of power that she'd always enjoyed.

"Do please call me Bob," said the pathologist, as he wiped foam from his beard. "We're all friends here… aren't we Markus."

"What? Oh yes… yes we are," replied the distracted Swede. He was busy making some final adjustments to his camera set up and he locked the tripod arm into place before turning to join the conversation.

"I'm sorry it's taken so long Doctor, but I think we can commence the filming now."

"Wonderful," Bob replied, before placing his beaker on a trolley. "How do you want me, Miss Sunley? Up against the wall, or right here on the cold hard slab?"

It was an obvious return of serve to Jenny's previous innuendo, but she let the doctor take the point instead of continuing the rally.

"Right where you are is fine please Doctor," said Markus, coming to Jenny's aid as umpire. "Jennifer," he continued, "If you could stand right there please, I will film over your shoulder towards the good doctor."

"So, you're not going to see my face?" asked Jenny, secretly pleased that she wouldn't be in shot.

"Not today I'm afraid Jennifer. I appreciate your efforts to look presentable, but I think perhaps the crash at the tunnel has made you look… not your best, shall we say."

'What the actual fuck?' thought the weathergirl.

He was right of course, but did he really just say that?

"Ok Jennifer, just ask the questions as they are written on the paper, please. Our news anchors back at the studio will then add the required introduction."

Although the spotlight was now on the doctor, the weathergirl immediately felt the pressure shift towards her, and she coughed lightly to clear her throat.

"Are you sure I can't get you a drink?" said the lab assistant in the white coat. She seemed amused by Jenny's discomfort.

"No, no, I'm fine thank you," she replied, before turning her back on the girl.

"Ok," said Markus. "Please start in 5, 4, 3, 2, 1…"

"Doctor James… you're helping the Otago Police Force, following the discovery of a body at a local bungy jumping bridge—have you completed your autopsy and are you able to disclose the cause of death?"

'Phew,' thought Jenny, she'd got through all it without any mistakes. Maybe this wasn't going to be so bad after all.

"Yes," replied the doctor. "I've now completed my examination and I've confirmed to the police a verdict of death by strangulation. It's not a nice way to go, and in this instance, it probably would have taken several hours due to the composition of the rope."

'So, Owen was right,' thought Jenny, but would the doctor say anything more when the police were still yet to hold a press conference?

"And erm, do you think we're looking at a murder investigation Doctor James—rather than a suicide?"

"Just stick to the questions on the sheet please Jennifer," interrupted Markus. "We have very little time here and I need you to get the facts, rather than the Doctor's supposition."

"Oh no," said Bob. "Miss Sunley is quite correct. This is most definitely a case of homicide, there's no way Jonno would have killed himself."

Jenny didn't know what to do. She had a feeling that this story was much bigger than Markus had alluded to, but if he wasn't going to let her probe the doctor for information, how was she ever going to get the full story?

Markus leaned in close behind her and whispered in her ear, "I'm sorry for cutting you off Jennifer, but we need to let the story tell itself. If you simply ask the questions in the order they are written, the good Doctor will… what is it you say in England? …he will spill the beans."

Jenny felt stupid, Markus clearly knew what he was doing and who was she to question his methods anyway—she was just a weathergirl after all, not a serious journalist.

"Ok Doctor…" she said. "Let's continue with another question shall we."

"Oh yes, please do," replied the pathologist, clearly agitated that he'd been interrupted mid-flow.

Jenny stared at her piece of paper, wondering how Markus had devised the exact order of the questions. He'd structured the words in a way that could never have been answered with a simple Yes or No, yet each question seemed to anticipate what the previous response would be.

Wait a second, she thought, suddenly absorbing what the doctor had just said. *'There's no way Jonno would have killed himself? He couldn't possibly have meant Jonno Hart, could he?'.* She looked down again at her question sheet, searching for something that would push the doctor to reveal the victim's name, but there was nothing.

She looked over her shoulder towards Markus, hoping that he could read her mind and offer some telepathic advice.

"Next question please Jennifer," said the TV executive, noticing her gaze.

Jenny turned back to the Doctor and she could see that he was also growing impatient.

"Doctor James… The Otago police have given hints that the victim wasn't necessarily well-liked in the area. Did you find any evidence in your investigation that would corroborate that statement?"

The doctor took a deep breath, pausing slightly before giving his answer. A tense look had crossed his face and Jenny realised that she'd upset him somehow.

"Listen to me carefully," he replied angrily. "Jonno Hart was a top bloke… and the person who did this to him… well, they're some sort of psychopath. The way he was strung up like… like some sort maggot on a hook… well, it's sickening. And if the police don't arrest the Māori bastard that did it—after all the evidence I gave them—well then they need hanging as well!"

And there it was—Jonno Hart—he really was the murder victim. The doctor had revealed it all without Jenny even having to ask the question.

"Well done," whispered Markus, as the weathergirl stood dumbfounded by the revelation.

"I think that should just about cover things," he said louder, before shaking the doctor's hand. Bob seemed almost as stunned as Jenny by what he'd just revealed, and he accepted the handshake without even looking up.

"Come on Jennifer," said Markus. "We need to get this footage to the editing team right away. We're running out of time if we want to make the evening news."

He grabbed Jenny by the arm and before she could even say thank you to the doctor, he had whisked her out of the room and into the basement corridor.

"But there were more questions to ask?" stammered the weathergirl as Markus removed the camera's memory card and handed her the device.

"Jennifer, I've got to go and upload this footage, but can I leave you with the camera? You can take it back to Christchurch with you—David won't be needing it now."

"Erm... ok," she replied, but she was still confused as to why the interview had ended so abruptly.

"Jennifer, I think you should spend the rest of the weekend here with your husband and then make your way back to Christchurch on Monday. You can come back into to work on Tuesday, refreshed and ready to shine."

"Are you sure?" replied the weathergirl. "I really don't mind."

Although in truth, she was quietly ecstatic at the thought of an extra day with Owen.

"Here... take my credit card," said Markus. "Go buy yourself some new clothes—I assume all of your things were destroyed in the tunnel crash, yes?"

Jenny nodded silently; the thought of her once beautiful shoes still raw. If anyone deserved a splurge on the company's finances, it was her.

"Buy yourself some essentials and a few nice dresses," said Markus, as he handed over a platinum coloured card. "But please make sure they are suitable for work—and remember to keep the receipts won't you. We're a very small TV station Jennifer, and what is it they say? Money doesn't grow on trees."

He stared at her over the top of his spectacles and Jenny could tell that he wasn't joking.

"Jennifer, you did very well today. Your work at Milford Sound this morning was exemplary, and just now with the Doctor, you did everything that I asked—I'm very pleased."

He was difficult to read sometimes and just as Jenny was thinking that she had him figured out, he'd caught her off guard. She was surprised at just how good it made her feel and she wondered if perhaps there was a heartbeat after all inside that cold, Scandinavian exterior.

On the flip side, however, Markus hadn't seemed the slightest bit upset about the death of Jonno Hart, and Jenny wondered what made the fishing celebrity so different? Was it simply because he was a freelancer, or had his diva-like attitude ruffled the Swede's feathers on one too many occasions?

The lift door opened, and Markus turned to face her once more.

"And don't worry about David—I'll go break the news to him. I'm sure you're keen to get to the shops anyway. But don't forget what I said… keep the receipts."

Jenny looked at her watch, it was nearly 6 pm and she wouldn't have long before the shops closed. She wanted to find something special for her dinner date with Owen, something that would keep his imagination going until he finally returned home to Christchurch.

Chapter 20

Rachael waited patiently for the patrol car's engine to stop and then stepped out into the rain. It was days like this that she thanked God she lived such a short distance from the police station, and she hurried to the back of the car park where a gate stood hidden under the trees.

Most people would say that living so close to work couldn't possibly be healthy, but Rachael liked the convenience it offered as she would often pop home during her breaks.

As the gate swung open, the policewoman looked up towards her modernist abode.

"Home sweet home," she whispered, before making her way through the garden. Just like the house itself, it was immaculate in its presentation, a work of art that had taken hundreds of hours to manipulate and sculpt—or at least it would have done, if it were real.

It gave Rachael enormous satisfaction when visitors commented on how beautiful the garden looked, saying how proud she should be of all her hard work. But in reality—it was just a few hundred dollars worth of fake grass, plastic ferns, and silk leaved acers. The irony certainly wasn't lost on her, that a person so invested in discovering the deception of others, had manufactured such a blatant lie on her own doorstep.

Putting her key into the front door, she looked down the side of the building and noticed that her car was missing from its spot.

'Where's he gone with that?' she thought, realising that Liam had probably taken the car. He must have been desperate, as he hated driving the little green hatchback.

She stepped inside the house and took off her heavy police issue jacket, before hanging it on a peg next to the door.

She caught a glimpse of herself in the hallway mirror and what she saw stopped her in her tracks. Blood red streaks ran down her face and under her chin, before pooling in the small depression at the base of her throat. It reminded her of the eels' feeding bowl, back at the bungy bridge, and she wiped away the red liquid with a trembling hand.

Was she injured? She certainly felt ok, but then again, the cold of the rain could have numbed her senses. She looked at her hand and watched as the red slick ran down her fingers, travelling slowly from the tips to her knuckles. It wasn't blood, but it certainly tasted like it—she could feel it working its way in from the sides of her mouth and on to her tongue.

She looked down at the floor and saw spots of red dotted across her beautiful porcelain tiles and she cursed herself for not shaking her coat outside.

It looked like the spatter from a murder scene and she knew it would take ages to clean up. She kicked off her shoes and hurried to the kitchen to find a cloth, turning on the counter-top TV as she passed.

As she wiped the floor tiles clean, she listened to a news story of an accident at the Homer Tunnel and the strange red mud that was hampering the recovery process.

She looked over her shoulder at the TV screen and saw footage of a truck being pulled from the tunnel mouth. Apparently, it had collided with a smaller vehicle inside the tunnel and a fireball had engulfed them both.

As the driver's cab came into view, the unmistakable logo of a two-headed Kiwi bird, caught Rachael's eye, and she rushed to the TV for a closer look.

'Liam!'

She immediately reached for her phone and dialled his number.

"Hey, you're through to Liam's phone, please leave a message and I'll call you back."

"Hi, it's me. Call me as soon as you can will you. I saw your truck on TV—let me know you're ok."

She hung up and looked at the TV screen again. The front of Liam's truck had been completely smashed in and what was left at the back had been destroyed by fire.

She called Liam's number again, hoping that this time he would pick up.

"Hey, you're through to Liam's phone, please leave a message…"

Rachael hung up.

'*Shit*'

*W*here was he?

She'd never felt worried about him before and her usual calm demeanour lay discarded on the floor, along with the cleaning cloth that now looked like a blood-soaked rag.

She picked up her phone again, but this time she called the station. Maybe Tony could call the guys down at Te Anau and find out what had happened.

Jenny opened her eyes and stared up at the ceiling. She'd been lying in the bath for over an hour and she was bored of counting the tiles. She'd been waiting for Owen to come home and 'surprise' her with a kiss on the lips—or anywhere else that he fancied. But he was nowhere to be seen and now the tepid water had quenched any fire that was left within her.

She pulled herself out of the water and reached for a towel, noticing the chips to her nail polish as she did so.

"Well, it looks you've missed your chance," she said, stepping out of the bath and onto the mat. "I was all set to let you ravish me, but now there's something more important that demands my attention."

She walked into the bedroom and picked up the case of makeup that she'd purchased earlier using Markus' credit card. As she sat down on the bed, she looked around at the hoard of shopping bags that lay scattered about the room; perhaps she'd pushed things a bit too far? She could justify the expense on most of the items, but the luxury underwear and silk stockings would be difficult to explain if Markus ever questioned her receipts. But she'd bought them as a 'present' for Owen, and now she was wondering if it had been worth the effort.

She sat on the edge of the bed and started to remove the remains of her nail polish, glancing down regularly at her phone, just in case Owen decided to call.

"Where are you, Mr Penny?" she mumbled, as the minutes continued to tick by. But before she had a chance to find out, she fell asleep on the bed and her freshly buffed nails, grabbed only the bedsheets, instead of Owen's toned backside.

Chapter 21

Jenny woke from the best night's sleep she'd had in years and even though refreshed, she rolled reluctantly from her slumber like a 'parent nagged' teenager.

The exhausting schedule of the past few days had been forgotten in a night of dreams—dreams where storms and explosions had been replaced with passion and sweat. As with most dreams of that sort, the face of her lover had remained hidden in shadow, but Jenny knew it was Owen, for there was no doubting the feel his kiss and the method of his stroke.

She opened her eyes slowly, praying that he'd snuck in during the night and the tingle between her legs wasn't entirely the product of her imagination. But he wasn't there, and she saw only the stained cotton wool that she'd used to remove her nail polish.

After a leisurely shower in the suite's marble-clad wet room, she headed downstairs for breakfast, frustrated at having spent yet another night away from her husband.

When he finally rang—just as she was exiting the lift—she ignored the call and let it switch to voice mail instead. If she couldn't give Owen the silent treatment in person, a digital silence would have to suffice. But she called up the voicemail anyway and listened as he apologised for not turning up, before promising to meet her for lunch. He also spared her no blushes as he described what he was going to give her for dessert—she wasn't sure yet if she'd let him, but she decided to let fate make the final decision. If the English breakfast was good, she'd let him ravish her, but if the bacon was cold and stringy, she'd make him wait.

It was a stupid bargain of course, as she wanted him just as much as he wanted her. But she had to lay down some ground rules if their marriage was ever going to survive the long periods of separation that Owen's job demanded.

As she entered through the doors of the restaurant, she was greeted by a raft of cheers and laddish banter. It was incongruous to the quiet formality of the hotel and she looked about to see where the noise had come from. The room was filled with the distinctive red and white tracksuits of the England rugby team and Jenny flushed with embarrassment as the players wolf-whistled her walk to the buffet.

'*Shit,*' she thought, as memories of drunken nights out in Twickenham, came flooding back.

'*God, I hope there's no one here that I've met before.*'

"Hey look," came a shout from the far corner of the room. "It's that weathergirl from the telly. Hey love, fancy sticking your pins on my map sometime?"

The room broke out into a chorus of jeers and whistles, and once again Jenny's cheeks flushed red. They were all a bunch of dicks, but the play on words was quite amusing.

She quickly circled the buffet table of food, gathering up a healthy selection of yogurt, muesli and apple juice. She'd really wanted that full English breakfast, but with the rugby team's leering eyes and the prospect of a long lunch with Owen, she decided that self-discipline was required.

She found a spare table tucked conveniently behind a pillar and had just managed to raise a spoon to her lips when a man slid into the chair across from her.

"You must be tired?" he said. "You've been running through my head all night!"

If it had been anyone else, she probably would have told them to get lost, but on this occasion, the cheesy pick up line made her smile and she offered the man a spoonful of yogurt.

"You too handsome, but I thought we weren't meeting until lunchtime?"

Owen leaned forward and greedily popped the spoon into his mouth.

"What's the matter?" he said, licking the spoon clean. "Can't a husband surprise his wife these days? Or would you rather I left you alone with all these rugby blokes?"

"You know I should probably say yes to that, you did stand me up after all. But fortunately for you Mr. Penny, my dreams are more forgiving than my daytime mood and the two of us actually spent quite an enjoyable night together."

"Really?" said Owen, clearly intrigued.

Jenny smiled as she watched the cogs in Owen's brain assimilating what she'd just said. He liked to project a roguish confidence, but it wasn't difficult to embarrass him, and he quickly reverted to his natural state of 'shy geek'. This was the Owen that she loved the most, the man who'd swept her off her feet, simply by assuming that he never stood a chance. It was strange really because was incredibly handsome and it was surprising that he'd never learned to capitalise on his good looks.

"Look, Jen, I know I stood you up last night and I promised to take you out for lunch, but I think we're gonna have to take a rain check on that as well—I'm really sorry."

"You've got to be kidding me right—what is it now?"

The weathergirl had responded a little too loudly and she scanned the room to see if anyone had noticed—but they were all staring at a TV screen on the wall.

"You know I said we're at a crucial stage of the build?" said Owen, reaching over to hold her hand.

He spoke quickly, trying to explain his situation, but the weathergirl looked on with deadpan eyes. She was annoyed that yet again a concrete dam was holding back her love life as well as the water behind it.

"Well we had some problems with yesterday's detonations," continued Owen. "We've had to reschedule for this afternoon instead."

"Oh right…" huffed Jenny, struggling to sound gracious in defeat.

"But hey, at least we've got this morning huh. Why don't we eat some breakfast and then head back upstairs for some… dessert?"

It wasn't quite the romantic day that Jenny had been hoping for, but it was better than a kick in the teeth and she responded by rubbing Owen's leg under the table with her foot.

"Ok…" she purred playfully. "But there'll be no more talk about dams or hydro-electricity—got it? The only electricity I care about is the sparks we're gonna be making—and you owe me a full recharge!"

Owen had swiped some of her orange juice and he nearly choked as Jenny's toes moved skillfully between his legs. She could feel that he was getting aroused, so she offered to go fetch his breakfast, to save him the embarrassment of standing up.

She slipped her shoes back on and then quickly circled the buffet cart once more, smiling this time at the group of rugby players who were watching her every move. She could hear them whispering about her body as she walked, so she made a big show of presenting Owen his breakfast, kissing him seductively on the lips as he took the plate from her hands.

She wanted Owen to feel like he was the luckiest guy in the room, but she also wanted to remind him that there were plenty of other men who would like to be in his place.

The rugby players may have been taller, more muscular, and more overtly masculine than her husband, but Owen was the first man who had ever managed to completely satisfy her.

Jenny's thoughts were already turning to what they might get up to once back in Owen's suite and she had to force herself to concentrate as he started to tell her about his night at the dam.

"Like I said, I'm sorry about last night, but we had some trouble with a saboteur. He booby-trapped some of our equipment and it put a couple of my guys in the hospital."

"Oh wow, really?"

"It's all ok now though," said Owen. "Thanks to one of my mates, we caught the fella and now we're just waiting for the police to come and pick him up."

"Oh, that's good news," Jenny replied, before placing a spoonful of muesli in her mouth. The 'dessert' that Owen had mentioned, had better be worth it she thought because this stuff tasted like crap.

"Ya know, I'm surprised the cops didn't skedaddle up there as soon as we called," said Owen. "It's that Māori guy you see—the one I was telling you about yesterday—the murder suspect."

Jenny nearly choked on her cereal.

"The murder suspect—and you guys tackled him on your own?"

"Yeah, it was a bit of a risk I suppose, but we couldn't have him booby-trapping our equipment, could we? Although I'm not sure we could have handled him without Liam there to help, that Māori fella's built like a tank."

"Liam?" asked Jenny. "He's a truck driver, right? With long dark hair?"

"Yeah that's right, but how…?"

"You should know, my cameraman Dave, thinks he tried to kill us."

"Oh really? Well, your cameraman's wrong I'm afraid. Liam's a top bloke, and he's already told me about what happened at the tunnel."

Owen's defensive rebuke was a shock to Jenny. She'd never heard even a flicker of anger in his voice before, but he was clearly upset at Davey Boy's accusation.

"So, does Liam remember crashing into us?" she asked. "He looked ok once we were in the helicopter and…"

"Look," said Owen, cutting her off short. "He said he can't remember anything that happened, ok?"

Jenny was confused, she couldn't understand why Owen was being so abrasive. He usually listened to what she had to say, but he wasn't even giving her the chance to talk.

They sat in silence for a minute or two before Owen spoke again; this time with a softer, more measured tone.

"So, your cameraman… you said he's called Dave?"

"Yeah, that's what I said."

"What's he like?"

"He's erm, he's complicated."

Jenny didn't understand why they were talking about the cameraman; it was Liam they should be discussing, and why Owen had been so dismissive of Davey Boy's concerns.

"Look, I've only known him for a couple of days," she said. "And now he's in hospital because of your mate—whether he meant to do it or not."

Jenny immediately regretted her snappy remark, but it was too late to take it back, so they sat there in silence, both staring at their food.

"Well if our lunch date is cancelled…" said Jenny finally. "I should probably go and see if Dave's ok."

"Why?" asked Owen. "Like you said, you've only known him for a couple of days, and you'll be heading home to Christchurch tomorrow. You'll probably never see him again."

Owen's irrational dislike of the cameraman was really starting to get on Jenny's nerves, she couldn't understand why was he being so mean to a man that he'd never met?

"Well I think he deserves a bit of company," she said. "I know I wouldn't want to wake up in a hospital bed, with no idea of how I got there, and nobody to explain what had happened."

She waited for Owen to react, but nothing came, maybe he realised that he'd already overstepped the mark?

"So, is the dam nearly complete?" Jenny asked; desperate to lighten the mood.

"Yes, it's almost finished," smiled Owen, seemingly relieved that she'd changed the subject. "We've just got today's explosions, and then it's a straight-forward build to the finished elevation. They don't need me for that part of the project, so I'll be heading back to Christchurch in a few days.

Owen reached out across the table and took Jenny's hands; his palms were rougher than she remembered, and she suddenly realised how hard he must have been working. He was only contracted in an advisory role, but in the short time they'd known each other, she'd learned that he never missed an opportunity to get out from behind his desk.

"Hey, your hands are all calloused," she whispered. "Are you sure you haven't missed me more than you're letting on?"

She flashed a cheeky wink and then lifted her foot once more between his legs, kneading the inside of his thighs with her toes.

Owen quickly closed his legs, clamping her foot between them so she couldn't move, and he moved his hand beneath the table to tickle her.

Now that was the Owen she knew and loved, and the weathergirl wriggled in her seat as she tried to release her foot. They were both acting like love-struck teenagers, and the loneliness of the past few weeks quickly dissolved away in a fit of giggles.

But suddenly, their playful banter was interrupted, when a loud cheer erupted from the other side of the room and Jenny looked over to see what was causing the commotion. The rugby players, when they saw her, guided her eyes towards the wall-mounted TV and she gasped when she saw herself on the screen.

She was standing next to a mortuary slab, and she looked like she was about to throw up. Watching herself on the TV, Jenny once again remembered the smell of iodine and bleach, and she struggled to hold down her gag reflex.

"Is that your interview?" said Owen, leaning forward for a better look.

"Oh no, don't watch it," Jenny replied, as she hid her face in her hands.

"So, who was the murder victim?" asked Owen.

"Jonno Hart—the fishing guy?"

"Oh shit," said Owen. "Really?"

"When I left the hospital last night, Markus said he going to give Davey Boy the bad news—they've all known each other for years."

"Christ, I bet he was devastated."

Owen looked away, and Jenny wondered if he was feeling a little guilty for his earlier remarks towards the cameraman.

"Apparently Jonno Hart was quite a big fish around these parts," said Jenny. "Do you remember anything about him, from when you were growing up here in Queenstown?"

"No, not really," replied Owen. "But don't forget, I was only 12 when mum took me to England."

"I just thought that maybe you might remem..."

"No, I really don't," Owen snapped; his bad mood seemingly returned.

Just then, Jenny felt somebody standing next to her and she looked up to see a man, grinning from ear-to-ear. He was enormous and he towered over her like a mountain.

"Do you mind if the team gets a photo with you luv? We're all big fans of your work."

"Erm... ok," Jenny replied, before mouthing a silent apology to her husband.

As she stood up, Owen flashed her a smile, but she could tell that he wasn't exactly happy about all the attention she was getting. She knew that Owen wasn't usually the jealous type, but their conversation over the past few minutes had shown a side to him that she hadn't known existed.

She spent the next few minutes surrounded by wall of muscle, with some players displaying biceps that were as big as her thighs, and shoulders that were so broad, they could probably have stopped a truck—if only they'd been there at the Homer Tunnel!

When Jenny finally returned to the table, she half expected Owen to be in a jealous sulk, but instead, he smiled at her with what seemed to be a look of glowing pride.

"Babe, I know your cameraman's still in the hospital, but do you have access to his equipment?"

"Sure, it's in your suite upstairs, why?"—Jenny wondered if the attention from the other men had put Owen in a kinky frame of mind and she bit her lip seductively as she waited for him to answer.

"Well…" said Owen. "Now that you've moved on from smiley-faced weathergirl to hard-hitting journalist, how would you like a scoop that will really make your boss proud of you?"

"Hmmm, sounds interesting."

Jenny liked the thought of herself as a 'hard-hitting journalist'.

"Why don't you finish your breakfast, " she said. "You can tell me more about it in the shower".

"Haven't you already had one this morning?" Owen replied, before running his hand up her thigh.

"Sure, of course I have… but you know what, sitting here with you, it's made me feel all dirty again – VERY dirty indeed."

Chapter 22

Blunt and her colleague Tony stood in the bungy bridge gift shop. She was in a foul mood as Liam had failed to come home and he hadn't even bothered to call. All she'd received was a simple text to say that he was ok, and he would see her in the morning—that was 12 hours earlier and still there was no sign of him.

As the two police officers waited for Scotty James to appear, Rachael re-read the truck driver's message on her phone.

"I'm ok babe, just a few scrapes that's all, but I won't be home until the morning – sorry."

She'd called the hospital after receiving the message, but Liam had apparently disappeared. If he wasn't injured, why hadn't he come home?

She thrust the phone back into her jacket pocket, ripping the seams with the force of her frustration. This was going to be a long day and she was in no mood for the current holdup.

Scotty James was showing a group of Japanese tourists out on to the bridge and Rachael watched through the window as he helped to secure the first jumper into a harness. She was an overweight lady in her late forties or early fifties, and she appeared to be having second thoughts.

Rachael looked on as Scotty and his assistant, expertly bound the woman's ankles. Using a thick blue belt, they circled around the woman's chunky legs several times, before tucking the final few inches between her feet. Next, Scotty attached a steel carabiner to a ring at the back of the belt and then appeared to double-check the woman's weight against a chart that hung on the wall beside them.

Rachael watched as the two men whispered behind the woman's back, before attaching another bungy cord—just to be safe.

Tony seemed to notice it too, and Rachael's bad mood lifted a little when he let out a long trailing whistle, followed by a cheek swelling, "booooom!"

As they continued to wait, Tony pointed out the crappy souvenirs that the tourists were gleefully shelling out for. There was everything from pencil erasers, to sweatshirts, and gold panning kits; all emblazoned with the logo of Scotty's latest idea, 'Swing to Riches!'.

They both raised an eyebrow as a family of Americans tried on matching black and white jackets, before skipping out of the store—they looked like a pod of orca whales bouncing up and down on the waves.

Tony was the only officer on the force that Rachael seemed to get along with, and she was glad that he'd come along to assist. It was supposed to be his day off, but he'd offered to help after hearing that she'd cancelled her APB on Kaihautu Waitaha.

Pippa's suspicions about the necklace found on Jonno's body had made Rachael question her thoughts on the Māori, and she was now considering Scotty James as her prime suspect instead.

"Sorry about that," said Scotty as he came back inside, closing the door behind him.

It was cold outside, and his words hung in the frosty air. Rachael wished that it could tell her what else he was thinking.

"Mr James," she said abruptly. "We've got a few questions if you don't mind, we're just tying up a few loose ends, that's all."

"Oh yeah right, sure, whatever you need…

Can I get you anything detective, tea perhaps, and maybe a beer for you eh Tony—you're not still drinking that pale ale crap are you mate?"

"Erm no, we're ok thanks," Tony replied. He was clearly familiar with the man and Rachael was annoyed that he hadn't mentioned it.

"Mr James," Rachael said loudly. "Could you remind me of where you were on the night of the 15th, the night that Jonno Hart was thrown to his death from your bridge?"

"Shush, not so loud eh."

Scotty looked about to see if anyone else had heard what was said.

"I'm sure I told you all that last time, didn't I?"

Rachael had asked him something similar when she'd first arrived at the murder scene, but she wanted to see if his story had remained consistent.

"I was out on a date," said Scotty. "I took this chick out for dinner, and then we went to a nightclub."

"And apart from this girl you say you were with, is there anyone else who can corroborate your story? Someone at the nightclub perhaps?"

"I'm not sure," Scotty replied. "We must have drunk quite a bit—I don't remember much after we left the restaurant."

It was a plausible explanation given what she'd heard about Scotty's 'play hard' lifestyle, and it was consistent with his hungover appearance when she'd first arrived at the murder scene.

Rachael toyed with the handcuffs clipped to her belt and her brain replayed the scene when Scotty had first led her to Jonno's remains. She'd arrived at the bungy bridge just after 8 am, and his call had been logged barely an hour earlier. If Scotty really was Jonno's killer, he probably would have waited for as long as possible before contacting the police. He would have let the birds and eels destroy any evidence, before calling to say he'd found a body. A man who had been drinking would never have been that patient, that calculating.

The method of Jonno's demise was also a problem—it didn't fit with an act of drunken rage. Other than Jonno's friendship with Scotty's father, there was no apparent connection between the two men and no motive for Scotty to kill the man.

Jonno Hart was in his 60's so he wasn't an obvious love rival. It had to be down to money, and the gold that Scotty had mentioned during their previous conversation.

And even if there was some unknown history between the two men, the fishing hook through Jonno's testicles was a punishment that would have required a clear head to enact, especially in the precise manner that Bob had described.

Rachael looked out of the window, hoping that the steep walls of the valley would somehow channel her thoughts.

In the distance, she spotted the line of Totara trees, where she'd parked her patrol car the previous day. Owen's truck was gone now—he must have returned to pick it up—at least it meant that his ankle was ok.

Rachael realised now that she'd been unfair to judge him. She'd had no right in expecting him to risk his own life for her investigation. And his ankle injury might even have saved her own life too if Kaihautu had indeed been the killer she was looking for.

As she stared out through the window, Rachael's attention turned to the rickety old bridge, and her eyes began to follow the twists and curls of its ornate ironwork. For the first time, she began to realise that it wasn't just some random pattern and instead there was a clear message woven into its design. There were regular verticals that took the weight of the heavy, wooden walkway, but there were also long, sinuous lines, that ran horizontally from one end of the bridge to the other. They were thicker at one end and narrowed along their length towards a diamond-shaped tip. Some of the lines circled around each other, with the longer lines seeming to dominate their smaller counterparts—banishing them downwards towards the lower section of railing.

Perhaps it was just the vibrations as the overweight tourist plummeted from the bridge, but as Rachael stared harder at the lines, they seemed to move and pulse, like living, breathing creatures. She realised then that they weren't just decorative swirls at all—they were eels—hundreds of wicked-looking animals, immortalised like gods of iron, each with golden eyes, all staring at her with ravenous intent.

Suddenly everything seemed to blur, and just as her legs started to buckle underneath her, she felt an arm wrap around her waist, hoisting her back up.

"Are you ok?" said Tony, staring into her eyes.

"Er, yes, yes I'm fine," she snapped.

Rachael was embarrassed at her momentary lapse of control, and even more so that her colleague still had his arm around her waist.

"I think we're done here," she said; stepping away and regaining her space.

"We'll call you Mr James, if we need to ask any more questions. But in the meantime, I'd appreciate it if you could stay away from the pathology lab in future. They have sensitive casework to get on with, and we can't have visitors popping in an out on a whim, even if you are the doctor's son."

"Oh yeah, yeah of course," Scotty replied, looking like he'd just dodged a bullet.

"Just for my notes though Mr. James, why did you go to see your father, two nights ago at the pathology lab?"

"Oh, it was nothing really. He's a silent partner in one of my other businesses, and I just needed him to sign some paperwork, that's all."

"It must have been pretty urgent?" said Rachael. "I heard it was nearly 10 pm when you arrived?"

"Oh yeah, I erm, I'm buying some new equipment, and I needed dad to sign off on the loan agreement, he's the guarantor."

Rachael studied Scotty's face as he stood there fidgeting; he was like a nervous schoolboy waiting to be dismissed. She savoured her moment of power, before folding her notebook and placing it inside her jacket pocket.

"Ok Mr James, that'll be all for now. Thank you for your time."

She then turned and headed for the exit, trying to maintain a long, commanding stride. Tony hurried along behind her, but still too slow for her liking, and she berated him when he finally caught up.

"What the hell was that?" she shouted. "Why didn't you warn me that you and Scotty are old drinking buddies? You undermined any semblance of authority that we had over him."

"What can I say," Tony replied. "I'm sorry, I'll take myself off the case straight away."

Rachael was seething. She was tired from her lack of sleep, annoyed with herself for being so shit at her job, and more than anything else, she was frustrated with Liam for being such a crappy boyfriend; all things she realised, that were no fault of Tony's.

"No, no it's ok," she replied. "Apart from me, you're the only person who seems interested in solving this case—I'm glad you came."

"No worries," said Tony. "Ya know, I really don't understand it either. From what I've heard about Jonno Hart, he probably deserved everything he got, but it doesn't mean we should ignore our job, even if there is an important game this weekend."

"Oh, that's right. You were supposed to be at the rugby match today, weren't you?"

"Yeah, but it's ok. That England squad have been playing well, so we're probably gonna lose anyway."

Rachael had never been much of a rugby fan, but she knew that if Tony was anything like Liam, he'd soon be getting the shakes if he couldn't at least find out the score.

"Why don't you go," she said, trying to put on her best smile. "Without fingerprints to tie Scotty to that fishing hook necklace, this lead is dead in the water anyway, so there's not much else we can do today."

"But what about Kaihautu Waitaha?" Tony replied. "We could always see if he's turned up at the Māori village?"

"No… he'll stay hidden, at least for the next few weeks."

"Yeah, I suppose so. A guy like that, he probably knows hundreds of places to hide out."

Tony was right of course, and it frustrated Rachael that even with modern maps and satellite imagery, a suspect could easily disappear into the mountains around Queenstown.

"Look, Tony," she said, "It's only 9:30, why don't you go to the game, and if you really feel the need to help me out, I'll meet you back at the station this afternoon."

"Are you sure?"

"Yes, it's fine. I've got plenty of paperwork that I need to catch up on anyway, and documents to sign."

'That's it', she thought. *'Documents to sign.'*

"Hey Tony, didn't Scotty say he was buying some equipment for his other business?"

"Yeah, that's right, he said his dad was a guarantor"

"Ok, that's something you can help me with. After the match, I want you to find out what that other business is. If Bob James is a silent partner, there might well be others, perhaps even Jonno Hart."

"Good thinking," said Tony as they both stepped into the patrol car. "I never would have made that connection. Ya know, you hide it well, but you're a clever-clogs really aren't ya."

Rachael hated it when people called her that, but she couldn't help but smile in agreement.

'Yep, you're not too shabby DS Blunt.'

Chapter 23

Jenny and Owen emerged from the steam of the bathroom, both red-faced and exhausted. It was the weathergirl's second shower of the morning, but she could already taste the sweat on her lips as she struggled to cool down.

"I think I'm gonna go back in on my own," she said, "I'm sweating buckets here thanks to you."

"Well you'll just have to wait," laughed Owen, as he sprinted back into the bathroom with his electric shaver. "I won't be long," he shouted, as the door slammed behind him.

"Ok, I suppose you deserve it," Jenny replied. "I'm not as slim as I used to be, so you did have to do most of the work."

The bathroom door swung open and Owen popped his head out through the gap. "Hey, you're as slim as you need to be. And I'd much rather have a girl with curves than some stick-thin catwalk model, who looks like she's sucking on a lemon."

"Are you sure? I must have put on at least four or five pounds since you last saw me."

"I haven't exactly been a good boy either," Owen replied, pointing to his waist. "All that room service is starting to add up ya know. If I'm not careful, I'll end up with a 'dad bod', and we can't have that now, can we?"

Jenny looked at his chiselled abs and replied sarcastically, "Well if that's what the dads look like in your family, I say bring on the parenthood!"

She waited for Owen to respond, but then suddenly realised what she'd just said.

They'd never discussed the possibility of having children, and in truth, it had rarely crossed her mind. She'd already made it to the age 40 without even thinking about getting hitched, but now as a married woman, with middle age fast approaching, the chances for having a baby were becoming slimmer by the day.

She looked nervously at Owen to see if he was thinking the same, but he'd already shut the bathroom door, effectively closing down the conversation, whether intentional or not.

'Well that answers that then', thought Jenny, as she sat down on the bed.

Laying back on the freshly changed sheets, she tried not to think about her life choices to date, and her eyes searched the room for a distraction. Stacked neatly next to the TV, she spotted a pile of tourist information leaflets and she picked them up to see what else they could do, once they were finished at the dam.

Among the various flyers for wine tasting, bungy jumping, and jetboat companies, Jenny was surprised to find the same stapled pamphlet that she'd been given back at the Christchurch art gallery. Lifting it from the pile, she read the title aloud to herself, "Māori mythology and the seven voyages of colonisation".

She thumbed through the pages and settled upon the story of a great waka, named 'Takitimu', a giant canoe that had brought some of the very first settlers to Aotearoa, the Māori name for New Zealand.

Apparently, the Takitimu was a warship, and it had lived many lives, before it finally came to Tupe, a Māori chieftain who eventually brought it south from Tauranga, on the country's North Island.

"…and then the waka came to Tupe who felt sorry for the once-great vessel. It had become brittle and dry during its years of neglect, and nobody was interested in sailing in it."

Jenny certainly new that feeling, it had been well over a month since Owen and she had last made love, and she was sore from their bathroom activities.

"With his brothers and 20 other men, Tupe pulled the waka up from the beach and through the forest to a pool of tar that was black as night. They pushed the waka into the tar and there they left it for many years, soaking up the oil to become water-tight once more.

When Tupe finally returned to pull the waka from the tar, he gave it a new name and carved a figurehead that he attached to its prow. The great canoe was rejuvenated and went on to achieve great success in many more battles and sea voyages."

Looks like I could do with some of that rejuvenating tar myself, thought Jenny, as she glanced down at her feet. After years of wearing high, uncomfortable heels they were dry and sore, and the weathergirl winced as she prodded one of the cracks.

"Well that ends today," she said aloud, before reaching down to retrieve one of her shopping bags. Thanks to Markus' credit card, she now had a brand-new pair of sports pumps. They were smart enough for work, yet soft and comfortable like a pair of slippers.

"What ends today?" said Owen as he finally emerged from the bathroom. "I hope you're not talking about us," he joked. "I may be a bit out of practice, but I wasn't *that* bad, was I?"

"Oh, don't you worry Mr. Penny, I'm not done with you just yet. But if you *ever* stand me up again, you'll be getting one of these shoes on your backside."

"Is that a promise or a threat?" laughed Owen, as he teased her with a glimpse of his perfectly formed behind.

"Oh, it's definitely a promise," Jenny replied seriously, before giving way to a fit of giggles.

"But speaking of promises," she finally continued. "This scoop you promised me, shouldn't we get a move on if we're going to make it to the dam in time?"

"Shit, you're right!" said Owen, looking at his watch. "Come on sexy lady, put on some of those fancy clothes you've bought, and let me introduce you to the wonders of civil engineering!"

---

45 minutes later they finally arrived at the construction site and as Owen eased his truck to a stop, he gestured towards the main

dam structure.

"As you can see, we've come quite a long way since those photos I showed you when we first met."

"Yes, I can see," Jenny replied, stroking Owen's leg to show her approval. "And when we first met, I never realised quite how big it was gonna be!"

"Haha, very funny," said Owen, as he moved her hand from his crotch.

"What are those two mini-dams used for—the ones at the bottom of the main structure? Are they the backups you spoke about—in case the town needs an extra boost of energy?"

"So, you *have* been listening to me during our phone calls," said Owen, smiling. "Or was it just a lucky guess?"

He gave the weathergirl a playful nudge and she grabbed his arm, leaning in close to smell his aftershave.

"Hey, I may be blonde, but you didn't just marry some random bimbo ya know. I'll have you know Owen Penny, that I got two A's for Science in my GCSE exams, and an A-Level in History."

Jenny knew that it was nothing compared to Owen's Ph.D., but it was still more than most of her school friends had achieved and she was proud of that.

"So…," continued Owen. "As I said on the drive up here, today's goal is to demolish that large overhang of rock, just up there on the northern slopes – can you see it?"

"Yep, I can see it".

"Once we've carved out that section, we'll build another tower there and stitch the dam into the mountain. The water behind the dam is already at forty feet, but once we've completed this phase, we can raise the level by another thirty."

Jenny looked up as Owen explained the process, and she couldn't help but smile at the obvious pleasure it gave him. She'd never been particularly interested in the engineering side of his work, but she could listen to him talking about it all day long.

"Right," said Owen. "You wait here, and I'll go tell the foreman that we'll be filming the detonations. They might need me to help keep an eye on our Māori saboteur, so if I'm not back in five minutes you'll just have to start filming without me. There'll be a loud siren one minute before the first explosion, and another one to give the all-clear at the end."

Owen leaned in close and gave Jenny a long, lingering kiss. It sent goosebumps down her neck and she had to force herself to let go of him as he turned away.

She watched as he jogged towards the site office; his chino trousers clinging to his backside as he ran, and his shirt emphasising the toned muscles of his back and shoulders.

The site office was formed from a stacked pair of shipping containers, with metal steps that ran up the side, and Owen sprinted up them effortlessly before disappearing through a doorway at the top.

Once he was out of sight, Jenny turned to the back seat of the truck and lifted out Dave's camera holdall. It was heavy to lift, and she swore as one of her fingernails snagged on the rough fabric.

"Shit!" she cursed, before inspecting the damage to her nail. Couldn't she just have one day without something going wrong?

She turned her attention back to the bag and found a memory card amongst the jumble of batteries and lenses. The card didn't seem to have an obvious front or back, but she managed to slot it in first-time and the camera beeped to indicate that it was ready.

"Not just an airhead weathergirl after all, eh Davey Boy."

Feeling buoyed by her unexpected competence with the cameraman's pride and joy, Jenny wondered if she should call the hospital to see how he was getting on. But realising that Markus might not have had a chance to break the news of Jonno's death, she quickly stuffed her phone back into her pocket.

She scolded herself for being such a coward, but Owen was right, wasn't he? She'd only known Dave for a few days, so it wasn't really her job to break the news about his now deceased colleague.

Thinking again about Markus, Jenny realised that she should probably text and let him know what was going on. She was using company equipment after all, and she didn't want to be held responsible if something happened to Davey Boy's camera.

'Hi Markus, it's Jenny. Hope you don't mind, but I'm using Dave's camera to film something up at Moke Creek dam. Owen has given me the scoop on an important part of the build, and I think it will make a good filler piece if we're short on content later in the week – X x."

She usually ended her messages with a kiss or two, but it didn't feel right in a text to her boss, so she removed them before pressing send.

"Right then Davey Boy…" she said. "Let's see what this little beauty of yours can do shall we, in the hands of an ex-model, turned weathergirl, turned roving reporter."

She wasn't expecting it to be very much, but she desperately hoped that it would be good enough to avoid a drumming from Markus.

She stepped out of the truck and slowly panned the camera across the construction site, practicing a rough commentary in her head as she played with the camera's focusing ring.

As she turned the camera towards the two ponds at the foot of the dam, she spotted a figure, standing on one of the structures. Zooming in with the camera, she could see that it was a boy, roughly 14 or 15 years of age, and he was dressed all in black. Like most teenagers, his baggy tracksuit bottoms seemed like they could fall down at any minute, and he wore his hood pulled up so that it covered most of his face. Jenny could tell that he was up to no good, and she placed the camera on the bonnet of the truck before shouting out to him.

"Hey, you… What are you doing down there?"

But the boy just ignored her, or perhaps he was just too far away to hear. She shouted again, this time with a warning about the detonations that were about to commence.

"Hey, you down there… You need to get out of there fast, they're gonna blow up the mountainside in a minute!"

Jenny pulled out her phone and tried to call Owen, but the phone line wouldn't connect, the steep mountain valley was blocking the signal. But then she remembered Dave's satellite phone—was it in the camera bag?

She rummaged through the holdall, but she couldn't find the phone. Again, she tried to reach Owen on her mobile, but there was nothing.

Whether the boy was there by mistake or even if he was there to cause trouble, Jenny knew that she had to warn him about the pending explosions.

She looked back for Owen one more time and then scrambled down the slope, heading straight for the nearest mini dam at its base. A thin metal gantry bridge spanned the two ponds and Jenny walked tentatively across, trying not to look down as she went. She was only a few feet above the water, but the inky blackness of its depths made her feel like she was standing over an abyss.

When she finally reached the northern side of the river, she scanned the slopes to see where the boy had gone. She caught sight of him heading towards a large clump of flax and she shouted again for him to stop. This time the boy paused and turned to look straight at her, but then he turned away again and ran at speed into the flax.

Realising just how far she had come from Owen and the safety of the truck, Jenny screamed after the boy.

"Get back here you little shit, I'm only trying to help you."

She waited for what seemed like an eternity, but no answer came, and she realised that she'd have to go into the bushes to find him.

Pushing her way through the first line of flax, the sharp, waxy leaves stabbed and scratched at her legs. And as she moved in deeper, the ground underneath her feet started to rise sharply, making her even more nervous about her separation from Owen and the safety of the truck.

"Hey boy… if you're still there and you can hear me, can't you just come out? There's really no need to run away from me."

She stood still and listened out for a reply, but the roar of the dam's waterfall was all that she could hear. She decided to push in just for just a few more feet, and then shouted again, pleading for the boy to come out. From somewhere upfront, she heard the noise of rocks tumbling, followed by a splash of water and she suddenly realised there must be a cave up ahead.

"Shit!" she exclaimed. The boy had probably gone inside and now she'd have to go in too.

It was a prospect that would have been disagreeable at the best of times, but less than 24 hours after the Homer Tunnel crash, it was something that now filled her with genuine fear.

"Please come out," she begged, as the cave finally came into view. The entrance was smaller than she'd imagined and if she hadn't heard the splash, it would have been easy to miss.

Once again, no reply came and Jenny looked to her phone, desperate to find some signal bars so she could phone for help, but the signal was dead.

The cave entrance was around eight feet high, but barely two feet across, and the buxom weathergirl held her breath as she squeezed in sideways between the mossy walls. The floor was wet and slippery, and several times within her first few steps, her feet slipped on the rain weathered rocks.

She was less than 5 metres into the tunnel when the light from the entrance began to fade and so once again, she reached for her phone. In the narrowing gap, she struggled to pass the device to her leading hand, but once there, she switched it into torch mode and held it out in front. Illuminating both sides of the tunnel, the phone's harsh LED light bounced off the moisture-rich walls and Jenny was quickly blinded by its glare.

"For fuck sake," she swore—her potty mouth now in full flow. If the boy didn't get killed by the coming explosions, she was just about ready to kill him herself.

But just as she was about to turn back and leave the boy to his own fate, the walls of the tunnel began to widen, and she found that she had space to breathe again.

Once more, she raised her phone to scan the tunnel up ahead, but this time the walls were far enough apart to embrace the light instead of throwing it back at her, and as she moved the torchlight along the rock she gasped as mad staring eyes emerged from the darkness. Carved into the walls at regular intervals, lined faces with sharp, pointed tongues, lashed out at her, and she instinctively stepped backwards, before stumbling on the slippery floor.

"Watch it, lady," came a voice from behind her. "You nearly knocked me into the water then."

Jenny spun around and her light illuminated the face of the boy that she'd been chasing.

"You shouldn't be in here," shouted the boy as he tried to push the weathergirl back the way she'd came.

But her feet managed to gain purchase between two rocks, and she pushed back against the stroppy teenager.

"Hey, you're the one that lured me in here, I was just trying to stop you from getting blown up, that's all."

"Don't worry about me lady, I can look after myself. Why don't you just piss off back to your Pākehā friends and leave me and my dad alone."

"You and your dad?" said Jenny. "Is he the man that sabotaged the explosives. You do know he put a man in the hospital, don't you?"

The boy said nothing, but he looked angry at the accusation—or was it ashamed—Jenny couldn't tell.

"Listen to me," she said, "We've got to get out of here, this cave could collapse when they set off the explosives."

"But they can't do that," shouted the boy; his voice echoing around the cave.

"Oh, I'm afraid they can, and those carved faces I just saw on the way in here… they're not gonna protect either of us."

"But what about the waka?" said the boy, pointing into the darkness behind him.

'Waka?', thought Jenny. What the hell was he talking about?

Then she remembered the museum pamphlet and the story of the Takitimu, one of the giant canoes that had brought the first settlers to New Zealand.

"By waka…" she asked. "Do you mean a canoe?"

"Of course, I mean a canoe," said the boy. "Are you fucking stupid or something?"

"Hey, there's no need for that language," Jenny snapped, fighting her urge to give the boy a slap. She'd never been good with teenagers and it was probably why she'd never had kids of her own.

"You've gotta stop 'em," said the boy, "That's all my dad was trying to do, he didn't mean to hurt anyone, I promise."

The boy slumped down against the wall, hugging his knees as he started to cry. If Jenny had more of a maternal instinct in her she probably would have given him a hug, but she felt awkward when holding her own nieces and nephews, let alone some strange teenage boy.

"Look, why don't you start at the beginning and tell me your name, then maybe we can see about getting your dad released."

The boy looked up and his angry frown eased slightly, revealing the child that he really was.

"Really? You think they'll let him go?"

"Well I can't promise anything," Jenny replied. "But you never know. If there's something here that needs to be protected, I'm sure the police will be reasonable…. So then, what's your name?"

"Nīoreore…" said the boy. "But most people call me Eel."

"Well I'm pleased to meet you Eel," said the weathergirl, offering her hand to shake.

"I'm Jenny," she said, pulling the boy his feet. "So, what did you mean, when you mentioned 'the waka'—is there another picture somewhere in here on the walls—of a canoe perhaps?"

She was guessing that he probably meant another rock carving, something that she hadn't already seen, something different from the faces that were intended to ward off evil spirits.

"It's over there," said Eel, pointing over her shoulder.

Jenny turned around, expecting to see only blackness, but her eyes had adjusted to the low light and she gasped at what she saw. Released from the darkness and now glittering like a precious jewel, the full extent of the subterranean chamber enfolded before her.

The stunned weathergirl could clearly make out the walls of the chamber, and they arched up like a great underground cathedral to a roof that was perforated with holes. Pinpricks of sunlight streaked downwards through the cavern, in tiny columns of gold, illuminating specs of dust in the air.

And beginning just a few feet away from where she stood, an enormous lake stretched out into the distance, it's mirror-black surface rippling gently, reflecting sparkles of sunlight that danced on walls of the cave.

"It's incredible," said Jenny, marvelling at the waves of sunshine that covered the walls and ceiling. The ripples of light ran diagonally across the granite surface, like froth on a sunset beach, and the whole cavern felt warmed by its glow.

But then a sudden realisation hit home, and it was enough to make the weathergirl feel giddy, with her heart seeming to stop mid-beat in her chest.

"What the fuck" she exclaimed, momentarily forgetting about the young boy standing next to her. "Wait a second," she stammered. "That's not just sunlight, is it? That's gold, that's real fucking gold!"

"Yep, pretty cool isn't it," said Eel, moving forward to stand beside her. "But you can't tell anyone… promise you won't."

"But why?" Jenny stammered. "It's incredible".

"Because of the waka, that's why".

With that, the boy pointed out across the water and Jenny turned to follow the direction of his finger. Before she'd seen only shadows as her eyes had struggled to adjust, but this time she finally saw it and her heart stopped, with her jaw dropping in disbelief. Resting in front of her, perhaps 30 or 40 feet from where she stood, an enormous Māori canoe glittered under a sparkling column of sunlight. Sitting at the centre of the lake, it had been right under her nose, but her disbelief at seeing all that gold had blinded her to its existence.

Perched, on a rocky island just inches above the water, the enormous Māori waka lay majestically like some sleeping beauty put under a spell. It was like a scene from a movie, and Jenny half expected to see a camera crew and producers filming the scene.

"It's beautiful," she whispered, the words somehow feeling right to describe what she was seeing, for this wasn't just some dug out old tree trunk. Instead, the canoe was delicately carved, with a figurehead rising up from its prow, standing fierce and erect, and along the vessel's flanks, the wood was carved with intricate patterns, polished smooth to a sparkling sheen.

Even though she was about 30 metres from the canoe, Jenny could tell that it was a breath-taking work of art and she gasped as her eyes followed its length from prow to stern.

But once again, she realised that she wasn't quite seeing the whole picture—the giant waka wasn't sparking because of its smooth surface—in fact, it wasn't smooth at all. Every inch of the ancient canoe's surface was covered in tiny crystals, and they glittered like diamonds under the sunlight from above.

Jenny looked up to the roof where sunlight was now flooding in. The grey morning sky had cleared to an azure blue and it was clearly visible through a wide, circular oculus, some 20 metres above the surface of the lake. Water droplets from the morning rain were still dripping from the opening, and Jenny watched as they fell on to waka below.

"That's it!" she exclaimed, suddenly remembering her school science homework. The waka looked just like the one at the museum back in Christchurch, and that example was hundreds of years old. If this canoe was the same age or possibly older, it should have rotted away with all that water falling on top of it. But instead, the rain had protected it, preserving the wood in minerals that it carried from the rocks up above. In effect, the canoe had been fossilised in stone and it now looked like a giant Swarovski crystal.

"Hey lady," said Eel, interrupting the weathergirl's thoughts. "Are we going or what?"

"Er yes, yes of course," Jenny replied, barely able to turn her head from the incredible sight. The gold alone had to be worth many millions of dollars, but with the canoe at its centre, this cave was an incredible discovery and she knew it had to be protected.

Chapter 24

"You know, sometimes I really don't know why I bother!" shouted Rachael, as Liam pulled himself up from the sofa.

She'd popped home to grab her fleece jacket and had found him lying on the sofa, snoring like a dog.

Not only had he come home without any word since the previous night, he was also filthy dirty, like he'd been wrestling in the mud.

"Oh, hi babe," he said, sitting up.

Rachael could see the muddy brown marks that he'd left on the sofa, and it was all that she could do not to push him back down.

"Where the hell have you been?" she screamed, her police officer's restraint thoroughly abandoned at the door.

"Didn't you get my text?" Liam replied sheepishly.

"Yes, I got the fucking text, but do you really think that was enough? You were in a car crash, Liam!"

"Oh right, so you know about that?"

"Yes, of course I fucking know about that—it was all over the TV," Rachael screamed. "I saw your truck being pulled from the tunnel Liam, and all I got was a one-line text—what kind of boyfriend does that?"

"Yeah, you're right… I'm sorry… I should have phoned. But I thought you'd be busy with that murder case—there was no point worrying ya."

"That's not the point," Rachael pressed. "All I knew about the crash, was what I saw on the news. They said casualties had been flown to the hospital, but when I checked, your name wasn't even on their records. You could have been dead for all I knew!"

Liam stared at the floor, he looked like a child being scolded by his teacher—but Rachael didn't let up on her reprimand.

"And you must have seen the news yourself… otherwise, you wouldn't have known about Jonno Hart."

"What about Jonno Hart?" Liam asked.

"The murder—Jonno was the victim."

"What the fuck?"

Liam looked stunned.

"I thought you knew?" said Rachael.

"Well yeah, I heard somebody had been murdered, but not him, not Jonno Hart. Are you sure you've got it right?"

Rachael looked into Liam's eyes—he was devastated. She'd never seen him cry before.

"Look, I know you liked the guy and you enjoyed his TV shows, but I've heard some pretty nasty stories over the past few days. He probably had quite a long list of enemies.

Liam stared back at her with a look of disbelief; she was slating his hero and he had obviously taken offence.

Apart from Bob James, the policewoman's boyfriend was the only other person she'd heard praise the TV celebrity, and she wondered if she actually knew Liam at all. From what she'd learned about Jonno Hart over the past 48 hours, he was a womaniser, a drunk, and possibly even a paedophile. So, if Liam was happy to worship a man like that, maybe it was time to rethink their relationship?

"Look, babe," said Liam. "I'm sorry I didn't call ya—I should have known you'd be worried."

His acceptance of blame was what she'd been aiming for, but his reaction to Jonno Heart's death somehow made it feel like a hollow victory. She desperately wanted to let things slide, but she'd done that too many times already, and something needed to change if their relationship was ever going to get back on track.

Rachael didn't understand why they always had to do battle like this, boats jostling in the wind for some sort of inside track to happiness. When she'd first met Liam, their relationship had been carried along at great speed, as the excitement of her new life and her new career made anything seem possible. Back then, she'd barely noticed the small things that niggled at her now, and she'd intentionally given Liam the space to be his own man. But now as the winds of romance dropped to nothing, their sails were floundering, and she feared the storm that was needed to blow them back to shore.

Liam stood there scratching the back of his neck, his gaze off somewhere in thought. But was he really thinking about anything? Was he really the sensitive soul that Rachael had made herself believe, or was he just a mindless truck driver, whose only thought was where he could stop for his next bacon sandwich or 'bit on the side'?

Rachael wasn't sure anymore, and as she watched him picking at a scab on the back of his neck, her frustration boiled over again.

"Stop picking that flaming scab, will you! What the hell is it anyway, a mosquito bite or something else?"

"Huh?" said Liam, barely acknowledging the ferocity of her words. "Oh yeah the scab, I don't know what it is—a Sandfly bite I suppose."

Rachael watched as he rubbed the area frantically and she momentarily let out some slack from the rope she'd been winding.

"Let me take-a-look at it for you," she said, leaning in closer. He may have looked dirty and unwashed, but Liam's musky aftershave still wafted up her nose, and she suddenly realised how much she'd missed him. It had been well over a fortnight since they'd last seen each other, and she'd been lonelier than she'd cared to admit.

"I think you're right," she said, running a finger over the raised lump on Liam's neck. "It definitely looks like some sort of bite—you've got a puncture mark right there."

"Hey! Go easy," said Liam, flinching away from her prodding finger. "I bet it's one of those Asian Tiger Mosquitoes. That shipment of pineapples I was delivering to Milford Sound, I think it came from Thailand."

"Pineapples huh?" said Rachael. "It's probably for all those smoothies the tourists drink; I've never liked them much myself."

"Liked what?" said Liam with a grin. "Smoothies or tourists?"

"Both".

They looked at each other, both smiling, and for a second Rachael felt like she was seeing him again for the first time. It was his cheeky grin that had first caught her attention at the nightclub in town, and now seeing it again for the first time in what felt like years, the memories of their first night together suddenly came flooding back.

Rachael had been out partying with a friend from work, and they were dancing in the corner of a crowded nightclub. Liam had come in with a group of his mates, and he'd spent most of the night staring at her, before building up the courage to come and say hello.

He still maintained of course that he'd come over as soon as he'd spotted her, but Rachael knew better—she'd been watching him too. And not only that, she'd carefully repositioned herself in his line of sight, every time one of his mates had blocked the view.

'His mates!', thought Rachael; suddenly remembering the group of four or five blokes that Liam used to hang around with. She'd only met them on that first night, and even then, it had been brief—Liam had seemed keen to keep them at a distance.

"Your mates at the nightclub," Rachael blurted, just as Liam was leaning in to kiss her.

"Huh?" he replied. "What about them?"

"I only met them the once, but wasn't one of them Scotty James, the bungy bridge owner?"

"Yeah, that's right… why, what's that prick done now?"

Rachael wasn't sure if the word 'prick' was just friendly banter, or if it implied some friction between the two men.

"What's he like?" she asked, before watching Liam's reaction in the same way that she might study a case witness.

"He's a prick," Liam replied. "Just like his ol' man."

"Really? So, you're no longer mates?"

"Nah, we haven't spoken for ages—probably not since that night when we first met."

"That's a shame," probed Rachael. "I hope it's not anything to do with me?"

"Nah, you're all right… we just had a bit of a bust-up that's all. He wanted me to do something for him and I said no."

Now that sounded dodgy, and Rachael's police officer brain suddenly kicked into gear.

"Was it something illegal?" she asked.

"Can't we just leave it?" said Liam, clearly not wanting to talk about it.

"Why won't you discuss it?" asked Rachael. "If Scotty's into something that he shouldn't be, then it's my job to put him in handcuffs."

"That's the problem," Liam replied. "And that's why I told him to fuck off."

"Huh?" – Rachael was confused.

"Listen," said Liam. "Scotty's a dirty bastard—just like his dad. That night when we first met, and you were with your mate from work… what was her name again? It doesn't matter now anyway. Well, Scotty said that we should try and get you both into a foursome, so I told him to go fuck himself."

Rachael was stunned, she'd never heard this story before and although she was pleased that Liam had reacted the way he did, she was revolted by the revelation that he'd been friends with a man like that.

"I'm sorry I never told you," said Liam. "But it really doesn't matter now does it."

Rachael didn't know what to say, and she stood there dumbfounded as Liam stepped forward to hug her.

"Scotty said he could make it easier to get you both into bed, and although I never asked how, I knew what he meant. He was into all sorts of drugs at that time, and I knew he often swiped things from his dad's office—ya know, sedatives and stuff."

'Of course,' thought Rachael, remembering that Bob James was a GP before moving into pathology.

"And that's why you don't speak to him anymore?" she asked.

Liam nodded.

"And you never took any drugs with Scotty before that night, or anytime since then?"

Rachael stared at her boyfriend as she waited for him to answer. She felt like a judge instead of his lover and she hated every minute of it.

"No, never—I promise. I've never been into that sort of shit. I'm a beer and pizza kinda guy, you know that."

Rachael did know that, but hearing it from Liam's own lips was still comforting and she relaxed into his bear-like hug.

They stayed like that for ages, not talking, just…being, and the chill in the atmosphere slowly melted with every shared heartbeat between their chests.

Then suddenly, before Rachael could protest on grounds of professionalism and being on duty, Liam lifted her off her feet and carried her to the bedroom. He kicked the door shut behind him and as Rachael landed on the bed with a bounce, she hoped that the beep in her pocket, wasn't her radio being turned on by mistake.

Chapter 25

Rachael's phone rang for what must have been the fifth time and she pushed Liam away so she could answer the call. She'd been ignoring the sound for the past few minutes while Liam had pinned her to the bed. He was a big man, with a rugby player's physique, but he didn't have a sportsman's stamina and as usual, he'd gone at things like a bull in a china shop.

The phone switched to voice mail just as Rachael picked it up, so she decided to wait while the caller left their message.

As she waited for the beep to say the call had ended, she looked over at Liam, who was struggling to catch his breath. He looked back at her and grinned, no doubt convinced that he'd just made the earth move… it hadn't.

Rachael heard the caller hang up and she immediately dialled the voicemail service to hear their message. She desperately hoped it wasn't her boss, or worse still, Tony. If he'd left the rugby match early and found that she wasn't at the station, she'd feel even more guilty about hijacking his day off.

"Rachael, it's Tony – where are you?"

'Shit', thought Rachael, her worst fear confirmed. She'd have to think of an excuse before she called him back.

"Rachael, when you get this message, give me a call will ya. I'm at the station, something big has come up. It's Bob James, the pathologist—he's dead."

Rachael hung up.

"Bob James? What the hell?"

"Huh?" said Liam, still breathing deeply.

"I'm sorry, I've got to go."

Rachael jumped up from the bed and started gathering up her clothes.

"Ok babe, I'll see ya later yeah? I'll cook dinner, shall I?"

"er… yeah… whatever you want," Rachael replied, as she rushed to get dressed.

She dashed out of the house into the biting wind and ran across the car park to the police station's back entrance. Tony was already waiting for her at the door and he handed her a piece of paper as she stepped in from the cold.

"Sorry to interrupt your erm, lunch break," he said. "But I thought you'd want to know as soon as possible."

Rachael looked at the piece of paper, it was a communication from the ambulance team that had discovered Bob's car. It appeared the overweight pathologist had suffered a heart attack at the wheel of his Volvo and had crashed off the road, not far from his home.

Rachael wasn't exactly surprised to read the news, but it was a set back to her case that couldn't have come at a worse time.

"Spicy sausage for lunch was it?" asked Tony, clearly amused that Rachael was so red-faced.

"More of a chipolata" Rachael replied, hoping that would be the end of the conversation.

Tony smirked, he obviously thought he'd been given the green light to continue.

"Ya know, my wife says that sausage for lunch always leaves her feeling…"

"Feeling what?" snapped Rachael, cutting him off mid-flow. She may have felt guilty about hijacking his weekend, but she was still his superior officer and she wasn't about to discuss her sex life with him, especially via some charcuterie themed innuendo.

"Sausage for lunch always leaves her feeling what, Tony?… Unsatisfied? Frustrated? Or sick to the stomach perhaps? It seems to me Tony, that your wife might be better off trying something different for lunch—a muffin perhaps? Maybe the sausages in your kitchen aren't quite what they used to be Tony, or maybe your wife's just gone off sausage?"

Tony stood there speechless and Rachael knew that she'd won the battle, but she immediately regretted the means of her victory.

"You were right to call me," she mumbled finally. "I'll go and give Scotty the bad news, but if you could carry on with the work we discussed earlier, that would be great… thank you, Tony."

She turned to the door and darted across the car park. She didn't look back to see if Tony was still standing there, but he was probably just as confused as she was. She'd snapped at him twice in one day now and even though Tony wasn't exactly the sharpest tool in the box, he'd probably guessed that something was wrong.

Rachael jumped into the patrol car and stared at herself in the rear-view mirror. She wasn't just losing control of the case—she was also losing control of herself. Something was different today and she wasn't sure why.

Chapter 26

Jenny and the boy Nīoreore emerged from the tunnel and made their way through the flax that concealed its entrance. Thankfully this time around, she had the boy on-hand to show her a less prickly route, but the sharp-tipped leaves still scratched through her jeans.

Finally, they stepped out into the crisp mountain air and the weathergirl looked across the valley. Scanning the other side of the river, she spotted Owen pacing around the car park; he looked as if he'd lost something or someone.

"Owen!" she shouted into the buffeting wind, but he didn't react.

She shouted again, but louder this time and Nīoreore joined in as well with a two-fingered whistle that bounced off the valley slopes.

Owen immediately turned around and Jenny waved to catch his attention.

He finally spotted them and pointed to his phone, indicating that he was going to call her.

Fortunately, the phone connected, but before Jenny could explain where she'd been, Owen shouted down the line in panic.

"What are you doing?" he yelled. "You've gotta get out of there, that whole mountainside is about to blow up."

"You've got you stop them!" Jenny screamed. "The explosions need to be called off."

"But I can't," Owen replied. "The guys are already on their way to the control deck."

"Owen, listen to me, you need to stop the explosions NOW. I haven't got time to explain, but please trust me, it's the most important thing you'll ever do in your life."

Owen didn't respond, but even from the other side of the valley, Jenny could tell from his body language that he was annoyed.

"Ok," he said finally. "I'll try and stop them."

Jenny watched as he climbed inside his truck and started to beep the horn. Each series of short bursts echoed around the valley and Jenny quickly realised that it was an SOS—a signal in Morse Code. The message seemed to have the desired effect and Jenny watched as a man emerged from the site office and sprinted over to the truck.

Shortly afterwards, Owen came back on the phone line and Jenny breathed a sigh-of-relief as he explained what was going to happen.

"Ok, I managed to buy you some time. I'll come over there now and you can tell me why I've just authorised a ten-thousand-dollar delay."

"That's great," Jenny replied. "Oh, and can you bring the video camera? I left it on the bonnet of the truck."

Jenny watched as Owen picked up the camera and scrambled down the slope towards the metal gantry. She was about to film one of the greatest discoveries in New Zealand's history, and she couldn't help but picture Markus' face when he saw the footage.

She still couldn't quite believe it herself, but with Owen there to pinch her, she'd know whether it was actually real or just some impossible dream.

Owen finally reached the bottom of the slope and stepped out on to the gantry. It only had a handrail on one side, and he held it tightly as he crossed with the heavy camera on his shoulder.

About halfway across, he suddenly stopped, and Jenny shouted down to ask what was wrong.

"I'm getting a call on my phone," he shouted back. "Just give me a second."

Owen lifted the camera off his shoulder and lowered it down on to the walkway. He was standing directly above the white water of the river and Jenny held her breath as he paced about just inches from the edge.

After a minute or so, he came off the phone and picked up the camera again. He looked up at Jenny and waved, mouthing the word 'sorry' to apologise for his delay.

She waved back with a grin, but her smile quickly turned to dismay when she saw Owen stumble on the slippery metal gantry. After waving at her, he'd gone to put his hand back on the railing, but he'd missed, and he dropped the video camera as he slipped. Everything seemed to move in slow motion as the camera tumbled over the edge of the walkway and then slid down the near-vertical wall of the holding pond. Jenny watched in stunned silence as Owen reached out desperately to save it, but it was too late, the camera had sank without trace.

Jenny was still in shock as Owen clambered up the slope towards her; his head hung in shame.

"I don't know what to say, Jen, I'm sorry, I don't know what happened."

Jenny could hear Owen's apology and she didn't doubt that he meant every word, but she was fuming inside, and it took everything she had not to shout at him for his clumsiness.

"Don't worry about it," she said finally. "Just come and see this cave will you, and then promise me you'll do everything you can to protect it."

"Cave?" Owen replied, appearing confused.

"Owen, this is my friend Eel. You've got his dad tied up in the site office and I promised you'd let him go once you've seen what I've got to show you".

"Ok…" said Owen. "You've got me interested"—but his body language suggested that he had doubts.

With the boy leading the way, they quickly made their way back through the flax and entered the tunnel. Even in the darkness, the boy seemed to know exactly where he was going, but Jenny and Owen both pulled out their phones and switched them into torch mode to illuminate the path ahead.

"You were right," said Owen, as they shuffled past a giant eel carved into the rock. "It's incredible! I can't believe this was here and nobody at the dam ever found it."

"How old do you think it is?" Jenny asked. "The carvings look different to the Māori exhibits that I saw back in Christchurch."

"I think you're right. These definitely look less stylised—more primitive shall we say."

"Who's primitive?" shouted the boy from somewhere up ahead. "You Pākehā are all the same aren't ya—always thinking you're better than us."

"No Eel, that's not what he meant," said Jenny. She was concerned that they'd upset the boy and she turned her light forwards to seek out his face.

"Owen was just saying that the carvings look pretty old, that's all."

"Eel, what do you know about the pictograms?" said Owen. "Are they as old as they look, buddy? Or are they something that you and your father worked on together?"

Owen obviously had doubts about the authenticity of the carvings, but Jenny was glad that he was taking a friendly approach with the boy.

"Oh yeah, they're pretty ancient," Eel replied. "Nearly two thousand years, so my dad says."

"Two thousand years?" Owen stammered.

"That can't be right?" Jenny whispered. "The first settlers only landed in New Zealand about nine hundred years ago; maybe a thousand years at most."

"I think you're right," whispered Owen. "This kid's even crazier than his old man."

"Shush, don't upset him," whispered Jenny. "And anyway, didn't you believe every word that your father told you when you were a kid? I know I did."

"Yes… yes, I did believe him… and that's the problem."

The scowl on Owen's face suggested a hidden anger behind his words, but now wasn't the time for Jenny to question why. She'd noticed hints of that anger before, but she'd never dared ask where it came from. Owen was a calm and gentle man, but if there was something about his father that made him upset, it was up to him to let her know about it.

"Come on, there's still more to see," said the weathergirl, and she forged ahead to catch up with the boy.

Finally, they reached the open space of the cave's main chamber and Jenny turned off her phone's flashlight. She told Owen to do the same and they both waited for their vision to adjust.

Jenny couldn't wait for Owen to see the cave and she listened intently to hear what his reaction would be.

She didn't have to wait long, as Owen let out an approving whistle that echoed around the cave and he pulled her in close for a hug.

"What do you think of the canoe?" she asked. "It's beautiful isn't it."

"Beautiful?" said Owen. "It's the most beautiful thing I've ever seen!   …After you of course."

"That's all right," Jenny giggled. "I don't mind taking second place—I only wish I could look that good after a thousand years."

"TWO thousand years," interrupted Eel, as he appeared by her side.

"But that can't be right Eel," said Jenny. "Everything I've read in museums and books… it all says that the Māori only came to New Zealand about nine hundred years ago—your dad's got to be mistaken."

"Are you calling him a liar?" said the boy as he adopted an angry-looking stance.

"No, we're not calling him a liar," said Owen; stepping forward protectively in front of his wife. "But if your dad *is* correct… well, it changes everything we know about Māori civilisation."

"That's right," said the boy. "It changes everything YOU know about Māori civilisation. You Pākehā, you think you're so clever, but you know fuck all about people like me and my dad. You come in here with your bulldozers and trucks, thinking you can do whatever you like, and we've had enough of it I tell ya."

Even with Owen standing in front of her, the boy's anger was palpable, and Jenny knew that she had to do something to calm him down.

"Then let us help you Eel," she said calmly, before stepping out from behind Owen's protective shield. "Let me film this place and we'll tell the whole world that it exists. The government will never allow this cave to be destroyed, once they know what's inside. Then you and your dad can stop worrying about the canoe and the archaeologists who know about this stuff… they can find a way to preserve it for it the nation."

"There you go again," said the boy. "The archaeologists who know about this stuff? Who do you think we are… some kind of idiots?"

The boy was more animated now and he shook his fist as he paced up and down.

"We're Waitaha," he said fiercely. "We're the first… we're the ancestors. We're not like the iwi up north—the ones who do a Haka for every tourist dollar they can get—or whenever there's a rugby match in town!"

The boy spoke with passion and Jenny didn't doubt that he believed everything he was saying, but his words sounded rehearsed, like a script that his father had forced him to learn.

"Then let me tell your story too," she offered. "You could be the one to set the record straight and put an end to any argument about who owns this land."

The boy stopped pacing, he was assimilating what she'd just said and the anger in his eyes turned to hope.

"Ok, but first you've gotta let my dad go. I'm not saying nothing until he's set free."

"Agreed," said the weathergirl and she held out her hand to seal the deal.

But as the boy accepted her handshake, Jenny looked to Owen for reassurance, and the forced smile that he gave, didn't exactly fill her with confidence. Any dispute over ownership of the mountain would have enormous consequences for Owen's dam project and she could tell from the look on his face that he wasn't pleased.

"You know, there's actually another reason, why we need to protect this cave," said Owen suddenly. "And it's got nothing to do with the carvings, or the gold, or the giant canoe with national, if not global significance."

"What do you mean?" Jenny asked. "What could be more important than the waka?"

"Them!" said Owen, pointing to the lake.

Just at that moment, the water seemed to bubble into life and the weathergirl jumped backwards as hundreds of long, dark bodies, erupted to the surface in a terrifying frenzy.

"What are they?" she screamed in panic.

"Eels," said Owen with a smile. "Beautiful, majestic… and rare, Long Fin Eels."

Chapter 27

"Ya know, I really think it's the right thing to do," said Owen, as they both jumped into his truck.

Jenny felt guilty of course that they'd let the boy down, but she was willing to accept that they couldn't just let his father go. After all, his saboteur antics had put a man in hospital and the last Owen had heard, Kaihautu Waitaha was a suspect in the murder of Jonno Hart.

One positive thing had come out of their meeting though, as they'd managed to secure a further delay on the detonations, with Owen citing animal protection rights; much to the foreman's disgust.

Jenny was just fastening her seat belt when Owen leaned over and kissed her on the cheek.

"Ya know I still can't believe what we've just witnessed. It's truly an amazing discovery."

"I know," said Jenny. "It's incredible, isn't it. And it's going to make the news all around the world."

"You're not kidding, those eels are incredible—truly the find of the century. In fact, some of them could even be a century-old themselves."

"The eels?" said Jenny. "Owen, you've just seen a cave lined with millions of dollars in gold and all you can think about is eels? Not to mention the priceless Māori relic, that could change everything we know about the history of New Zealand – Owen, you're weird."

Jenny smiled as Owen shrugged his shoulders to concede her point, but she wasn't done teasing him just yet.

"And don't think you're off the hook with me just yet Mr Penny. You still owe me one very expensive video camera, remember? How am I supposed to document this amazing discovery we've made, when we've no camera to film it on?"

"Well I've been thinking about that actually and I think I might just have the answer."

---

10 mins later they pulled into the car park at the Moke Creek Bungy Bridge and Jenny stepped out of the truck onto the gravel surface.

At the other end of the car park, a tour bus was about to depart, and a queue of backpackers were filing on board. The mixed group of twenty-somethings were all hyped up on adrenaline and their raucous laughter reminded Jenny of her own good times when she'd travelled around Australia during a gap year.

Suddenly a wolf whistle cut through the noise and Jenny turned to see a group of lads all waving in her direction. Their chanting was brazen, and the weathergirl couldn't help but feel embarrassed when Owen placed a protective arm around her waist. She usually liked it when he asserted his dominance, but this time it was uncalled for as the lads were nearly half her age.

Owen led the way as they entered the reception foyer and Jenny was surprised when his commanding demeanour continued as they approached a young girl sitting at the desk.

"Hi, I wonder if you could help? We're filming a news story up the road, but we had a bit of an accident with our video camera. We were wondering if you guys might have something we could borrow. It would just be for an hour or two, so we can make tonight's evening news?"

"Erm... ok, sure," the girl replied.

It was an unusual request, but Owen's authoritative tone of voice seemed to act like a stage hypnotist's command and Jenny was amazed when the girl simply stood up and walked over to a cupboard on her left.

The girl returned promptly with a small black rucksack and was just about to hand it over when she suddenly seemed to realise what she was doing. She took a step backward and withdrew the camera bag before saying, "You know what, just let me go check with my boss if that's ok—I won't be a second."

The girl hurried out to the bridge with an embarrassed looking shuffle and Jenny watched through the window as she spoke to a tall, athletic-looking man. He was laughing and joking with a group of backpackers and was obviously enjoying being the centre of attention.

The girl returned with the man following close behind and he made a beeline for the weathergirl to introduce himself.

"Hi, pleased to meet ya Miss Sunley—I'm Scotty James—you interviewed my dad at the hospital."

"Oh right," said Jenny, as Scotty leaned in to kiss her on both cheeks. It was unusual for a Kiwi man to greet her in that way, but she got the feeling that it wasn't because he'd spent any time living in France.

"It's Mrs, actually," said Owen; placing a protective arm around Jenny's waist.

"Mrs Actually? That's an unusual surname," joked Scotty, as he flashed Jenny a wink.

Jenny could sense Owen's irritation at the remark, and she realised that Scotty was going to be just as much of a handful as his father.

"Mr James…" she said, flashing her best smile.

"Please… call me Scotty."

"Scotty, I need your equipment… I mean, I need your help"

She'd chosen her words carefully, guessing that a little innuendo would appeal to his sense of humour. And by using 'I' and instead of 'we', it would hopefully make her seem like a damsel in distress.

"Yeah, my receptionist mentioned something about that. You

broke your camera, right?"

"Yes, that's right. And I really need a replacement if I'm going make the deadline for tonight's evening news."

"Sure, no worries—what are you filming?"

He was completely blanking Owen now and Jenny knew that she had him hooked.

"Oh, we're erm, we're filming a news story about the English rugby team. They're visiting the Māori village, before their match later this evening."

"Oh yeah the rugby, of course. Ya know some of those blokes were here yesterday, trying out our new attraction. It's a shame you weren't here to film that too, I could've got 'em all wearing t-shirts with our logo on."

"Really?" said Jenny, "That's a shame. Maybe next time eh."

She looked at Owen and they both nodded in fake agreement.

"I'm surprised the Māori folks were willing to show 'em around though," said Scotty. "They've always been against having outsiders up there."

"Oh, right?" said Jenny, her interest piqued.

"Ya know, I once offered their leader a cut of the profits if he'd let me take some tourists up there. But the crazy bastard refused—said he'd run me through with his grandad's spear if I came near the place."

Jenny felt Owen's hand twitch in response, and she could tell that he was thinking about Jonno Hart's murder.

She was about to respond when she noticed that Scotty's attention had shifted back to her husband.

"Owen... it's Owen, isn't it? You went to my school didn't you, and then you moved away to England?"

"Erm yeah, if you say so."

It was unusual for Owen to be so rude and Jenny felt his grip tighten around her waist.

"You probably don't remember me," said Scotty. "I was in the year below you—in Liam Braithewaite's class."

"Oh, right," said Owen—but his face was devoid of recognition.

"He was a top bloke that Liam, we used to make cover stories for each other and then bunk off school to go gold panning—we were gonna be millionaires."

Jenny tapped Owen's arm at the mention of gold and he gently patted her hand in return.

"Look, Mr James... I mean Scotty. We really hate to rush you," said the weathergirl. "But we really need that camera if you don't mind. It'll just be for a few hours that's all... and who knows... maybe if we get time, we could come back and film this new attraction of yours—what was it called again?"

As Jenny talked, she wound a lock of hair with her fingers and she waited for the bridge owner to take the bait.

"It's called Swing to Riches," said Scotty, as his gaze drifting towards Jenny's cleavage.

"Perfect!" she replied. "I'm sure my producers in Christchurch would love to see how a successful businessman like yourself is bringing fresh ideas to the region."

Scotty nodded in response; the moniker of 'successful businessman', clearly appealed to his ego. He might not have shared his father's beard and rotund belly, but Jenny could tell he was a carbon copy of the pathologist in every other way.

"Just one thing though," said Scotty. "I've got a business meeting this afternoon, so if you want to borrow the video camera, you're gonna have to film the bridge swing right now. It won't take long and it'll be the best thrill you've had in years."

Scotty gave Owen a playful nudge and the engineer faked a smile in response. Jenny could tell that Owen was getting irritated by Scotty's jokes at his expense and she wasn't sure how long he could manage to maintain his cool.

"Ok," she said. "Just one go on this swing of yours and then you'll lend us the camera?"

"You got it…" Scotty replied. "And I get to use the photos in our next email marketing campaign."

'Now you're pushing it,' thought Jenny.

She was more aware than most just how much her image was worth. But they needed the camera and time was running out.

"Ok, it's a deal," she said with a smile. Inside though, she was terrified at what she'd just signed up to and as a scream from the bridge penetrated the large panoramic window, a shudder ran down her spine.

Chapter 28

It was mid-afternoon when Rachael finally pulled into the bungy bridge car park. She wasn't looking forward to seeing Scotty James again and breaking the news of his father's death.

She entered the reception area and watched through a window as Scotty strapped a woman into a bright yellow harness. She was in her late 30's or early forties and looked vaguely familiar.

The harness setup was different from the ankle binding that Rachael had watched Scotty perform earlier that day and he seemed to take particular care when fastening the buckle that sat across the woman's chest. The blonde had massive boobs and although one sharp tug on the strap would have sufficed, Scotty took at least three attempts to get it fastened just right.

He then moved on to the legs straps and as the policewoman watched Scotty's hands reach between the woman's thighs, the sound of a door unlocking spun her around.

Exiting the toilets to Rachael's left was a man, he was wearing a crisp white shirt and a pair of neatly pressed chinos. It was Owen, and he looked—perfect.

"Owen," she blurted; a bit louder than she'd intended.

"Hello again," he said, as he casually walked towards her.

The light from the window sparkled in Owen's icy blue eyes and for a second Rachael forgot to breathe. He was even more handsome than she remembered.

"How's your ankle?" she asked.

"My ankle? Oh yes, of course, my ankle. It's ok thanks—just a slight sprain that's all."

"That's good to hear," said Rachael. "I'm glad there was no permanent damage."

The dam engineer's smile was intoxicating, and she was finding it difficult to look at him.

"So, how's your murder investigation going?" said Owen. "I'm assuming your colleagues are on their way up to the dam?"

"The dam?"

Rachael didn't have a clue what he was talking about.

"The Māori guy, Kaihautu? Aren't you sending somebody to pick him up?"

Rachael still didn't understand what Owen was getting at and her blank expression prodded him to elaborate.

"He tried to sabotage our explosives," Owen continued. "But a group of us managed to corner him and we've now got him detained in the site office—we called the police station hours ago."

'What the fuck?' thought Rachael. Why hadn't she heard about this?

"When was this?" she asked.

"Early this morning—didn't you know?"

"No… no I didn't, but thanks for the heads up. I'm sure somebody's dealing with it."

'They must have called while Tony was at the rugby', she thought, he wouldn't have forgotten something like that.

"So, what are you doing here?" Rachael asked. She was intrigued as to why the dam engineer was visiting the bridge.

"Oh, we're erm, we're just borrowing a video camera that's all. We're filming something up at the dam. It's to do with the next stage of our construction project."

Rachael remembered the eel ladders that Owen had shown her during their hike, and she could see the same look of excitement on his face now.

"Something else to protect your eels huh?"

"Something like that," Owen replied with a smile.

He looked like he was about to say more, but a loud scream from outside caught both their attention and they turned just in time to see the blonde woman dropping from the bridge. She was screaming like a banshee and Rachael struggled to hide her smirk.

They stood side-by-side for a while, both watching as the woman was hauled back up on to the bridge. Even though her hair was a mess and her face red with adrenaline, she was still annoyingly pretty, and Rachael couldn't help but dislike her.

"What did I tell you eh," said Scotty, as he led the woman back into the reception area. "Didn't I say it would be the best thrill you've had in years."

The woman walked over to Owen and draped her arms around him in mock exhaustion. He looked embarrassed at her actions, but he didn't push her away.

'You've got to be kidding me,' thought Rachael, the pairing just didn't make sense.

"You need to watch yourself," said the bungy bridge owner, as he slapped Owen on the shoulder. "This girl's an animal—a beast even—I've never seen anyone hacking away so hard at the gravel. I'm amazed she didn't find any gold though."

'Probably because there isn't any,' thought Rachael, as she lingered in the background.

Scotty leaned over the reception desk and produced a small black rucksack, along with a small strip of paper.

"Here you go beautiful," he said. "One video camera as promised and a small present from me—a time-lapse photo of your jump."

Scotty held up the paper and passed it to the blonde. From where Rachael was standing it looked like roughly 10 to 12 photos, each one slightly different.

"Cool, isn't it?" said Scotty. "It shows everything from the fear in your eyes as you jump, right through to the excitement as you scoop the pan at the bottom of the swing."

Rachael chuckled to herself at the stupidity of Scotty's gold panning idea. It had to be the most ridiculous thing she'd ever heard.

But her laugh must have been louder than she'd intended as Scotty suddenly said loudly, "Detective Blunt, I didn't expect to see you back here so soon. Have you come to try out our bridge swing as well?"

'Not in a million years,' thought the policewoman, but her response was more diplomatic.

"Not this time I'm afraid. Police officers aren't allowed to swing while we're on duty."

"So, it's just at the Christmas party then eh?" joked Scotty, as he flashed another wink towards the blonde.

Thankfully though, Owen must have noticed Rachael's discomfort and he stepped in to save her from further embarrassment.

"Look, we can see you're busy here Scotty—we should probably get going."

"Thanks again for the camera," added the woman, as Owen ushered her towards the exit.

"No worries beautiful…. Oh, and erm… good luck with those rugby fellas eh."

'What's rugby got to do with eels?' thought Rachael, as she watched the couple step out through the door. The blonde still had her arm draped around Owen's shoulders and she was giggling like a stupid schoolgirl.

"So…" said Scotty, interrupting the policewoman's thoughts. "What can I help you with detective? If you wanna have a go at our bungy jump instead of the swing, there's a couple of hours wait I'm afraid—we're busier than ever after last week's shut down."

Scotty was clearly in a good mood and Rachael wasn't looking forward to breaking the news of his father's death, no matter how much of a dickhead he was.

"Mr James," she said slowly. "I have some bad news I'm afraid; you might want to take a…"

But Scotty was already sitting down.

In fact, he'd jumped on the sofa next to the window and was slouching back on its worn leather cushions like a disinterested teenager.

"Mr James…" Rachael continued. "I'm afraid I have to tell you that your father has passed away. His body was found this morning behind the wheel of his car."

It wasn't the most sensitive of deliveries, but she'd said it, and she breathed a sigh-of-relief that she hadn't fluffed her words.

"I'm sorry, what?"

"Your father Mr. James, he's dead."

"Dead?"

The bungy bridge owner seemed confused.

"Was it his heart?"

Rachael nodded to confirm his suspicions.

Scotty looked devastated and stared out of the window.

"Ya know he had a heart attack a couple of years ago as well. I always said he should have retired when he sold his GP surgery, but he wanted to keep on working. It's not like he even needed the money, he's worth a couple of million dollars just in property alone."

'So there'll be plenty of money to inherit?' thought Rachael, before making a note of it in her pad.

"So, your father had a history of ill health?" she asked, trying to sound sympathetic.

"Well no, not really," Scotty replied. "It was just the one heart attack while he was out fishing one day. Jonno Hart saved his life—well him and his cameraman."

"And that would be er…" Rachael checked her notepad. "That would be a Mr David Norman, is that correct?"

Rachael had been trying to get hold of the cameraman for the past few days, but according to his employers in Christchurch he was away on an assignment.

"That's right," said Scotty. "Dave… Davey Boy, Norman— they've all known each other for years. I think dad only puts up with him though because he's Jonno's mate. Dad says he's a bit of a bore, ya know what I mean, a know it all?"

Rachael did know what he meant, but she was tempted to think that she'd quite like this Davey Boy.

She was about to ask something else, but it was then that she finally saw Scotty begin to choke. In her training, she'd been told that news of a death often took time to sink in and Scotty's continued references to his dad in the present tense indicated that he hadn't fully processed the reality of the man's death.

Scotty raised a hand to wipe away the tears and Rachael looked away uncomfortably. For some reason, it seemed worse to see a man cry than a woman and she was reminded of her father when her mum had died suddenly of breast cancer.

Rachael heard Scotty stand up behind her and she turned to see him staring out through the window. He was smiling now; no doubt remembering something good about his father. Rachael wasn't sure what that could possibly be, but Bob couldn't always have been a pompous old misogynist.

"Ya know, dad went to see Dave Norman just yesterday afternoon."

"Really?" said Rachael, wondering if that meant the cameraman was back in town.

"He texted me to say he was gonna break the news about Jonno, but the nurses said Davey Boy's in a bad way himself."

"Nurses?" said Rachael. "He's in the hospital?"

Scotty took a big gulp of air, before placing a hand on the window to steady himself.

"Dad said… he said that Dave had been involved in an accident, down at the Homer Tunnel. Apparently, some truck driver went through the red lights and ploughed straight into them."

'Shit,' thought Rachael, that must have been Liam.

"And now this Dave Norman... he's in the hospital?"

"Yeah, that's right. Dad was also going to tell him about his interview, but he was out cold when he went to see him."

"TV interview?" said Rachael. "What interview?"

She was already fearing the worst and even before Scotty opened his mouth to respond, she knew what he was going to say.

"It was on the telly this morning—didn't you see? Your boss wanted him to give an update on the case."

'That stupid idiot', thought Rachael, struggling to maintain her calm. As usual, her idiot boss in Christchurch had put politics and PR ahead of strategy and now her investigation was going to get a whole lot more complicated.

"Turns out the chick who interviewed him was also involved in the crash," said Scotty. "She reckons the truck driver tried to kill them."

It was an accusation that stopped Rachael in her tracks.

"And do you happen to know where I might find this TV presenter, or what channel she works for?"

"Hah" laughed Scotty. "That was her just now with Owen—she's his wife... lucky bastard."

Chapter 29

Jenny and Owen arrived back at the dam and as they pulled into the car park the weathergirl was surprised to see her boss waiting for them.

"Markus must have got my text and now he's come to check up on me," she whispered.

They pulled in beside the TV exec's Volvo and stepped out onto the gravel as he came to greet them.

"Ah very good Jennifer, I can see that you've purchased some sensible shoes."

The Swede looked her up and down approvingly before his usual stern look returned "But please make sure I get the receipt won't you, so I can record it as a legitimate business expense."

'Shit,' thought Jenny. She hoped that he didn't need a complete itemised breakdown of everything that she'd bought. At the time, she'd felt fully justified in having a bit of a splurge on the boss' credit card, but now she was thinking that $150 just on underwear, was probably a bit excessive.

"I've just been speaking to the site foreman," said Markus. "He said you've made a discovery that could put a stop to the work going on here—something to do with eels?"

Jenny nodded.

"He also mentioned that you had a bit of a mishap with our camera, Jennifer. I do hope that what you've discovered is worth the loss of such an expensive piece of equipment?"

Jenny wasn't sure if he was hinting that she'd have to pay for the camera, but he seemed to be waiting for an answer and he stared at her over the rim of his glasses.

Fortunately for Jenny, however, Owen came to her rescue and he waded in to take the blame.

"I'm sorry Markus, it was all my fault I'm afraid—I'll make sure you're fully refunded for the loss."

"And we've already managed to borrow a replacement," Jenny chipped in, trying to sound upbeat.

"Don't worry Markus," said Owen. "When you see what we've found, you won't care if we lost a hundred cameras trying to film it".

"And if we get a move on, we could probably make tonight's 10 o'clock news," said Jenny.

"Let's not get carried away shall we," said Markus. "First show me what you've discovered, and then we'll talk about what we're going to do about it. We might need to get one of our news reporters down here, if it's as interesting as you say."

Jenny was confused, less than 24 hours earlier he had asked her to go well beyond the boundaries of her usual role to report on a murder victim. But today, he was trying to put her back in her box, as the 'eye-candy' weather presenter, there to do as she was told and look pretty. Jenny was starting to think that maybe Markus' reputation as a control freak wasn't as exaggerated as she'd first thought.

She desperately wanted to tell him about the Māori canoe and the cave that was lined with gold, but she also wanted it to remain a surprise—something that would knock his socks off.

So, she picked up the camera rucksack loaned to them by Scotty James and set off down the slope towards the gantry that bridged the two holding ponds.

"Well come on then!" she shouted back. "These eels aren't going to film themselves are they."

Owen and Markus looked at each other like a couple of soldiers who'd just been given their marching orders and Jenny chuckled as they launched themselves down the rocky slope. Owen led the way with Markus following close behind and once again Jenny couldn't help but notice how similar they were in appearance. It was mainly the way they were dressed, both in chinos and both wearing white shirts. But they also walked in a similar way—both commanding and purposeful in their stride.

The two men caught up with her quickly and Jenny was about to step out on to the metal gantry when she stopped abruptly.

"Don't tell me you're scared of going over," said Owen. "You've already been there and back once already."

"No, it's not that," she replied. "It's just that we haven't tested the camera yet. We should probably check that the battery's charged before we get all the way to the other side."

"Ok," said Owen. "Take it out and we'll check that it works before we go any further – we'll need to film the dam anyway, to give the rest of the footage some context."

Jenny pulled out the camera and pressed the power button. It was a rugged, action model rather than a bulky TV camera and the handheld device did a 360 spin on its gimble mount, before stabilising its focus on the dam.

"Very nice," said Markus; clearly impressed with the fancy little camera.

"Shit," said Jenny, "It says there's no memory card. What are we gonna do Owen? We haven't got time to drive back to the bridge."

"Are you sure you pressed the right button?" said Owen, taking the camera from her hands.

"Yes, I'm fucking sure I pressed the right button," snapped Jenny, forgetting that her boss was standing right next to her.

"OK, let's all just calm down, shall we?" said Markus. "We'll check the rucksack and if there's still no memory card, I'll just have to get a film crew down here tomorrow. You can still show me your discovery and maybe we'll get you on the phone to the studio later."

The two men were handling the situation much better than the weathergirl and she could feel herself turning red with anger and frustration. If Owen hadn't dropped Dave's camera in the first place, they never would have been in this situation. In fact, they probably would have sent the footage to the studio by now.

"No, I am afraid there aren't any memory cards in the rucksack," said Markus. "We shall just have to give the filming a miss and I will assess whether this discovery of yours is newsworthy in the first place."

Jenny could feel her chance at glory being snatched away and she had to fight back the tears that were starting to well in her eyes.

"Get a grip woman," she mumbled to herself, as Owen reached out to comfort her. But he was the last person she wanted to touch her right now and she flinched away from his touch.

"I've got it!" she said suddenly. "Dave's camera bag, it's still in the truck, I bet he's got dozens of memory cards stashed away in there."

And before the two men could respond, she was off, sprinting back up the slope towards the car park. She arrived at Owen's truck sweating, struggling to breathe, and her hands trembled as she put the key in the door.

She quickly found Dave's camera bag and dived in, pulling everything out as she went. Wires, batteries, old t-shirts, and even Lady Gloria's pink wig, were soon spread out on the bonnet of the truck, but there were no camera memory cards.

Jenny could feel the tears welling up in her eyes again as she became delirious with desperation.

She caught a glimpse of herself in the truck's rear-view mirror and shouted at the pathetic wreck she saw staring back.

"Think—stupid woman—think!"

She needed to get into Davey Boy's mindset and think about

where he would keep his spares. The camera bag was big and heavy, so there was no way he could have carried it when scrambling around after Jonno Hart. Perhaps he just kept everything in those horrible cargo shorts that he always seemed to wear?

Jenny searched amongst the pile of detritus that she'd thrown on to the bonnet, and she yelped with joy as she spotted a particularly nasty pair of camouflage shorts. They had zips and pockets all over them and she carefully searched each one in turn. But still, there was no memory card—only snotty tissues and a handful of old till receipts.

"Shit, shit, shit, shit, shit!" she screamed.

Only an hour before, she had discovered one of the archaeological finds of the century, and now the glory of showing it to the world was going to be handed to some jumped up news hack.

Jenny looked at herself in the rear-view mirror and her glowing face stared back at her. An angry vein was throbbing on her forehead and her skin had gone all blotchy.

Remembering Jonno's make-up that she had pilfered the day before, she quickly found the small plastic case and opened it up to steal some of the foundation powder inside.

After a quick dusting of her cheeks and forehead, she was about the close the case when she noticed a corner of plastic sticking out from under the powder tray.

Sliding her fingernail under the tray, she lifted it up carefully, and was surprised to find a small, black memory card hidden underneath.

"You, fucking beauty!" she screamed aloud, before snatching up the card. As she did so a cloud of foundation powder spilled out of the case and onto her jeans. But Jenny didn't care, she finally had her memory card and even if she looked like shit, she was going to film this damn canoe and the cave of gold.

10 minutes later she stood at the entrance to the cave with both Markus and Owen beside her, and she gathered her thoughts before leading the way in. They were about to make history and she wanted to make sure that it wasn't all just a dream.

"Pinch me," she whispered, as Owen moved in close behind her. "I want to make sure that I'm not imagining all of this."

"Don't worry," said Owen. "You're not the only one who thinks it's just too incredible to be real… and you know what, I think you're incredible too."

Jenny could feel his warm breath on her neck and she suddenly had a flashback to their steamy bathroom antics, earlier that morning.

"Oh, and by the way," she purred. "If you manage to make me look good on camera, I might just let you film something else when we get back to the hotel room later!"

Owen pinched her waist in response, and she let out a giggle that echoed in the cave up ahead.

"Whenever you're ready Miss Sunley," said Markus impatiently. "It was you, after all, that wanted to show me this cave of eels."

"Yes, come on slow coach," said Owen, in mock reprimand. "We haven't got all day you know and it's not like those eels are gonna wait around for a thousand years!"

"Or TWO thousand years," whispered Jenny.

They made their way into the darkness of the cave with the weathergirl leading the way. Owen followed closely behind, and Markus took up the rear. All three had their mobile phones out to illuminate the passageway and now with three torch lights to brighten the gloom, even more of the incredible carvings became visible-to-the-eye. Jenny's eyes followed the walls of the cave upwards to a ceiling where hundreds of stalactites clung to the roof, each one a needle-sharp point of limestone, hanging with deadly intent. If they came crashing down, the three explorers would surely die, so the weathergirl hurried on.

"Fascinating," said Markus, seemingly oblivious to the danger from above.

Jenny looked back at Owen and found him similarly absorbed by the incredible images they were now seeing thanks to the combined light of their smartphone LEDs.

"I have to say," said Owen, "The eels up ahead are pretty impressive, but this one here is outstanding."

He guided Jenny's eyes with his finger, and she gasped at the sight of a long and sinuous giant, erupting from beneath the familiar image of the Māori canoe.

"That must be Te Tunaroa," said Jenny. "It's said that the demi-god Maui defeated him and chopped him up before casting the body parts back into the river. There they transformed and became all the eels of the world that we know today. Te Tunaroa was the first—the alpha."

"Impressive," said Markus, as he caught up behind them.

"Oh, she's not just a pretty face," said Owen. "Jenny's always teaching me new things."

Jenny blushed; if there was one thing that Owen was good at, it was making her feel both respected and embarrassed at the same time.

"Come on you two," she said. "Only a couple of minutes ago you were moaning at me for wasting time. Let's move on shall we."

Jenny pointed her torchlight forward again and they pushed ahead into the gloom. She could tell they were nearly at the lake cavern, as sparkles of reflected light were now finding their way onto the ceiling above.

"Ya know, I never noticed it the last time we came in here," said Owen, "but I think we must have ascended by at least 10 metres since we entered the tunnel. That would put the lake surface several metres above the dam outside—and that's not good news."

"Why's that a problem?" asked Jenny, as she squeezed through the final rock chicane.

"If the cave walls were ever to lose their integrity…" said Owen "The water inside the mountain could flood out and overwhelm the dam."

They were both inside the narrowest part of the tunnel now and a tumbling of small rocks behind them seemed to emphasise Owen's prophecy of doom.

Jenny froze in response and a flashback to the Homer Tunnel rooted her to the spot.

"Are you ok?" Owen asked as he came up behind her. "It was just a couple of loose rocks that's all. It'll take more than the three of us to bring this place down."

"I'm alright," Jenny replied, as she regained her composure. "I just want to get in and then get out, that's all. This place is special, but over the past few days I've seen enough tunnels to last me a lifetime".

Once through into the cavern, Jenny shuffled along the narrow ledge that circled the lake and the two men emerged from the tunnel behind her.

"Oh my," said Markus, as his eyes darted around the chamber. "So, this is what I've been hearing so much about. You were not exaggerating Jennifer, it is indeed, quite spectacular."

"Magnificent isn't she," said Owen, as he reached around Jenny's waist.

"Shush..," whispered the weathergirl. "You're embarrassing me."

But then she realised he was talking about the Māori waka and her face flushed red in the darkness.

"Yes, the canoe is quite special," Markus replied. "But of course, all of this gold is the *real* story here. That's what will really grab the public attention."

He was right of course, but Jenny still felt the need to mention the importance of the waka.

"Yes, you're quite right Markus, all this gold will certainly make for a good bulletin, but that's all it will be. A headline grabber that floats around for a few days, before being buried under a sea of celebrity gossip and presidential gaffs."

"Jenny's right," said Owen. "The waka and the eels are what really matters here, and we need to film them both."

Markus nodded in reply, but even in the darkness of the cave, Jenny could see the dollar signs in his eyes.

"Ok," said the TV executive. "Jennifer, could you please prepare yourself for filming, while I go back outside to make a phone call—there is much that I need to discuss."

The Swede's cold and methodical approach had sprung into action and he quickly disappeared back down the tunnel entrance.

"Listen Jen…" said Owen. "I'm gonna go with him if you don't mind. I need to speak to the site foreman and decide how we're going handle all of this. He's gonna be pretty pissed off, but if we need to shut down for a few months, then so be it."

Owen leaned in close to kiss her on the cheek and Jenny breathed in the scent of his aftershave. But before she could say anything more, he was gone, and she listened to his footsteps as they disappeared down the tunnel. After a minute or so, all that remained was the sound of her heart thumping inside her chest and she turned to study her surroundings.

The light coming in through the cave roof had shifted during the time they'd been away, and it now created a glare that was blinding from almost any angle. Owen was going to have a tough time filming the waka from where Jenny was standing, so she decided to try a few different viewpoints instead. She rehearsed some lines as she shimmied along the ledge that circled the lake; trying to keep her mind off the fact that she was now all alone.

"Good evening everybody—I'm Jenny Sunley. Tonight… I'll be reporting on a discovery that is going to send shockwaves around the world. A discovery that will tell a new story of New Zealand. A story about the Land of the Long White Cloud, and the people who journeyed across the Pacific to make it their home."

'Hey, that wasn't too shabby,' she thought, as she stopped to inspect a particularly shiny vein of gold.

Next to where she stood, a line of rocks projected out into the lake and she raised the borrowed camera to her eye to assess the view.

"Perfect!" she exclaimed, as the viewing screen lit up with an image of the Waka. She could stand right out on the lake, whilst Owen filmed from the edge of the cave. It was just like the set up that Davey Boy had arranged, back at the Lake House in Te Anau.

Once again, a pang of guilt washed over her as she thought about her injured cameraman. He really should have been the one to film this discovery and she winced at the thought of telling him that he'd missed out.

Just then, as Jenny went to fold the viewing screen shut, she must have pressed something, and the onscreen display changed to the view of an angler. She'd accidentally switched the camera into playback mode, and she watched as the familiar face of Jonno Hart cast out his rod in a well-practiced arc. He was standing on a ledge that hovered above an inky black pool, some 10 feet below him.

'Wait a second?', thought Jenny. *'That's not a ledge… it's the gantry, the metal walkway that runs across the holding ponds.'*

Jonno Hart had been there at the dam and he'd used the ponds like he was shooting fish in a barrel. Trapped inside the vertical walls of concrete, the fish inside would have been easy targets and Jenny could see the smug look on Jonno's face as he reeled in an eel.

She also spotted another man in the distance, but he didn't seem quite so impressed with the celebrity's fishing skills.

It was difficult to make out on the video camera's small display, but with his long black hair and chin tattoo, the identity of the man was unmistakable—it was Kaihautu—the Māori saboteur, who was now tied up in the dam's construction office.

Jenny was wondering how Jonno had got permission to film at the dam when the camera suddenly lost focus on the celebrity and instead zoomed in towards Kaihautu's brooding face.

The hint of a smile had broken the ice of his hard-set jaw and his eyes flicked repeatedly away from the fishing action. He was looking up the slope towards a rocky outcrop and a large stand of flax.

'That's here', thought Jenny. *'He's looking at the entrance to this cave and Davey Boy saw him do it!'*

Jenny rewound the tape to make sure that she hadn't imagined it. Jonno Hart's cameraman—her cameraman—had filmed the entrance to the cave, and now he was in hospital, possibly as the result of a murder attempt.

It was a revelation that sent a shiver down the weathergirl's spine and she immediately worried for Owen's safety. He was heading back to the site office—exactly where the Māori was being detained.

Chapter 30

With Scotty now thoroughly consumed by the shock of his father's death, Rachael's discomfort became unbearable and she made her excuses to leave. It was the first time that she'd had to inform somebody of a loved one's passing, and it was something that she never wanted to do again.

Leaving Scotty with his head in his hands she exited through the gift shop and once again she noted the tacky souvenirs that lined the shelves. This time, however, her eyes were drawn towards a carousel of leather thong necklaces, all on sale at heavily discounted prices; Scotty was obviously keen to get rid of them. Amongst the various tribal motifs and New Zealand ferns, she spotted something familiar. It was a carved Māori fishing hook, made to represent the much larger version wielded by Maui, the Polynesian demi-god. Rachael took some photos of the necklace, hoping to compare it with the one that had been discovered on Jonno Hart's body—it certainly looked the same.

But this necklace had a sticker on it, disclosing it as resin instead of bone—something a Māori leader like Kaihautu would never have allowed around his neck. If it was indeed a match for the evidence they had in storage, it would have serious repercussions for Rachael's investigation.

She looked back at Scotty, who was now staring out of the

window. *'Surely he wouldn't have been so stupid as to use a necklace from his very own gift shop—why try to implicate Kaihautu, when all the man had done was to refuse a request to host nosey tourists?'*

There had to be something more to all this that Rachael wasn't seeing, but Scotty had already proven himself to have friends in high places and she needed to be sure, before making any decision to arrest him.

Making use of the bungy centre's free wifi, she quickly emailed the photos to Tony for a comparison, and then stepped out into the drizzle that had swallowed the car park. There was still a taste of iron in the air after the previous day's 'blood rain' and she could feel this latest precipitation gently cleansing the valley's wounds. It was less than a week since the death of Jonno Heart, and already it seemed that the world was wiping away the stain of his existence. He had by all accounts, been a pig of a man, who no doubt deserved everything enacted on him. But Rachael was finally starting to see things more clearly and she needed to apply a similar justice to the man who had murdered the celebrity.

She made her way to her patrol car and radioed Tony to check that he'd received the email.

"This is Romeo Bravo Three Two... Tony are you there?"

After a short delay, the radio crackled briefly and Tony answered.

"Sure boss, I'm here. Hey, guess what... we only went and won it!"

"Sorry, won what?"

"The rugby—we beat the English! Our tiny little club, we beat the fucking Lions!"

Tony had apparently forgotten that she was English herself and more importantly he'd forgotten to mind his language when talking to her on the radio. Rachael decided to let it slide this time, but if he did it again, she'd have to find some way to tell him off without seeming like a tyrant.

"Tony, I've got something I need you to look at please. I emailed you a photo just a moment ago, can you compare it against the evidence that was found on Jonno Hart's body. It looks like a good match to me, but I want your opinion as well, before I decide what to do about it."

"Sure, what is it?" Tony asked.

"It's a fishing hook necklace that they sell here at the Bungy Bridge, I think it matches the one that Bob James found embedded in our victim's penis."

"Ouch," said Tony. "I must have missed that little nugget of information when I booked the evidence into our storage locker."

Rachael pictured Tony in her head, and she smiled at the thought of him crossing his legs in sympathy for Jonno Hart's pain.

"Ya know, I always thought there was something dodgy about that Scotty James," said Tony. "And this fishing hook proves it right? I take it you're gonna arrest the bastard eh?"

"Well, let's just see shall we," cautioned Rachael; although she was pleased that finally, somebody else was keen to wrap up the case.

"Oh, and Tony, while you're analysing the evidence for me with your eagle eyes, could you also chase up some video footage as well please?"

Rachael still had a weird feeling about Liam's account of the tunnel crash, she couldn't help thinking that it might be connected to her case.

"I want you to get hold of the camera footage on the southern side of the Homer Tunnel. I want you to see if it captured anything out of the ordinary in the hour or two before yesterday's tunnel crash."

"Sure thing," Tony replied. "I'll do my best, but don't get your hopes up of receiving anything tonight. It's nearly 4 o'clock already".

The hum from the radio went dead and Rachael sat in silence, staring out across the river.

'Bugger!', she thought. She'd forgotten to ask if anyone had gone to pick up the Māori.

Owen's team had done them a favour by apprehending the man and she didn't want to let the engineer down by not following up on it.

As she sat waiting for Tony to get back to her, she absentmindedly played with the buttons on her phone. Out of habit more than anything else, she sent Liam a text to see what he was up to. She was still furious at him for disappearing after his crash, but she'd barely seen him over the past few weeks and she quickly followed up her first text with a second message.

"Hey you, do you fancy going somewhere for dinner tonight?"

Within seconds a reply came back from Liam; its content was both intriguing and annoying at the same time.

"Yeah, sounds great babe. But can we make it a double date? I want you to meet an old buddy of mine."

Rachael had never met any of Liam's friends before, except Scotty James, and now that he was a potential murder suspect she dreaded to think what secrets this other associate might hide. But a night out with company, was still a night out, so she sent back a text to confirm their date.

"Yes ok, that sounds good—what's this friend's name?"

"His name's Owen. I went to school with him and he wants us to meet his new wife."

'Shit! This is going to be awkward,' thought Rachael, but she couldn't let on that she'd already met Liam's handsome friend. More importantly, she'd have to make an extra special effort if Owen was going to be bringing his trophy wife—the blonde bimbo with incredible tits.

For her whole life, Rachael had been confident of her looks and her abilities. But even she could acknowledge that Owen's wife was stunning. But it just didn't compute that a man like him, could fall in love with an airhead like that. There must have been something she was missing, and she found herself imagining the incredible sex that the couple must have been having, to compensate for the lack of conversation.

Rachael very rarely felt anxious or out of control, but in the space of just a few short days, she'd fallen from the top of her game to the bottom of the heap. Glancing up from her phone she caught sight of her reflection in the rear-view mirror and the face that she saw staring back looked unfamiliar to her. She flinched away sharply from the tired-looking hag and banged her head on the door as she did so.

"You, fucking idiot!" she screamed in frustration.

"I'm sorry, I didn't quite catch that?" came Tony's voice on the radio.

"What?"

"Can you repeat that please boss—I didn't quite catch what you said."

"Oh, it's nothing," she replied, realising the slip of her tongue. "What have you got for me, Tony?"

"You were right boss, the fishing hook's the same. So, you're not just a pretty face after all eh?"

Rachael was Tony's superior officer and it grated on her that he was so casual in his conversation, but the 'pretty face' comment was just what she needed.

"That's brilliant Tony… thank you."

"Oh, and I've got some good news about the footage you wanted," said Tony.

"Really?"

Rachael was amazed that he'd even remembered to look into it, let alone come back with information so quickly.

"The blokes down at Te Anau had already analysed the footage," said Tony. "They reckon the truck that caused the crash was parked up for well over an hour before it went inside the tunnel. Apparently, it's not unusual for trucks to stop there—a lot of them need to remove their roof deflector, so they can fit inside the tunnel."

"But he doesn't even have a roof deflector?" said Rachael, thinking-out-loud.

"So, do you know the fella then boss?"

"What? Oh yeah, maybe—but I'm not sure yet."

'Why would Liam stop for so long if he hadn't need to adjust his vehicle?'

He was always moaning that he never had enough time to make his deliveries, yet the camera footage clearly showed him parked up for far longer than was necessary.

"Were there any other vehicles parked up?" she asked suddenly. A flash of suspicion had entered her head as a memory of her mother surfaced in her mind.

Years before, when she was just a teenager, she'd spotted her mother's car parked in a layby, not far from her school. The school had been closed early that day thanks to a faulty fire alarm and she'd decided to take a stroll instead of going straight home. From a distance of some fifty metres, she'd watched through the car window as her mother had kissed a man that was not her father. It was something that she'd never discussed with her mother and she'd never forgiven the woman for her betrayal. But now with Liam's truck parked in similar circumstances, she wanted more than ever to ask why her mother had done it. They'd never been close, even before the incident, but after witnessing her adultery first-hand, Rachael had retreated to the loyal but disciplined love of her father. It was probably the source of her reluctance to get close to people, or heaven forbid, to fall in love. And now with Liam's loyalty also in question, she was already imagining the worst.

"Yeah, there was another car—how did you know?" said Tony. "It was a black Volvo estate, but I can't make out the license plate—perhaps it's one of our own? I know the traffic cops down there have got a couple of Volvos on trial."

The Swedish cars were unusual in New Zealand, but Rachael knew from experience that they would be a great improvement on the rickety old Holden's that made up their current fleet.

"Hmm, one of our own—you're probably right," she replied.

'And that's probably why Liam didn't want me to find out,' she thought. If he'd been caught speeding even before entering the tunnel, he'd know that she wouldn't have been happy. He'd assume that she'd blamed him for the accident without giving him a chance to state his case.

"Ok Tony, that's all for now thanks. I need to think some more about this fishing hook, but I think we'll probably be making an arrest sometime tomorrow. Why don't you go home, and I'll see you at 6 am?"

"Sure-thing boss. We'll get that bungy bastard before he's even had a chance to pull on his pants eh!"

Rachael could hear the excitement in Tony's voice, and she should have been happy that he was keen to make an arrest, but something still nagged at her about the convenient way things were falling into place. Scotty wasn't the sharpest tool in the box, but he wasn't stupid either. If he was going to plant fake evidence to cover up his own wrongdoing, surely, he wouldn't have picked something from his own gift shop?

Rachael was just about to switch on the patrol car's engine when something caught her eye on the other side of the river.

A line of yellow trucks and excavators was making its way along Moonlight Track, leaving a cloud of dust in its wake. As the cavalcade of vehicles passed the opposite end of the bungy bridge they slowed briefly, and the lead driver waved to Scotty James. He'd pulled himself together and was back outside, strapping another customer into a harness.

Leaning forward over the steering wheel to get a better look, Rachael could just make out a logo that had once been emblazoned on the side of the lead vehicle. The vinyl lettering had been removed, but an outline of rust remained, and the words read, 'Queenstown Gold Mining Company'.

Aside from being a crappy looking logo, it was a piece of the puzzle that had completely slipped her mind and she picked up her CB handset to radio Tony once more.

"Hey Tony, are you still there?"

"Yep, I'm still here boss, how can I help?"

"Scotty's other businesses," Rachael blurted. "You were going to look into them for me weren't you—to see if Jonno Hart was connected in some way?"

"Oh yeah, sorry boss, I forgot to tell you about that didn't I..."

Rachael waited patiently to hear what Tony had to say…

"…and?"

"Well it turns out Scotty's got his fingers in all sorts of pies and you were right, Jonno Hart's named in the company accounts for at least two of those businesses."

'Perfect!' thought Rachael.

"And would one of those businesses happen to be a gold mining company?" she asked.

"Hey, you're pretty good at this, aren't you?" said Tony. "It turns out Jonno Hart was listed as a director for The Queenstown Gold Mining Company, at least until a few weeks ago, when he was replaced by Bob James."

'That's it', thought Rachael. *'That's our link, and that's our motive.'*

She knew that there had to be money involved somewhere, and if she dug a bit further, she'd discover the pay dirt that would finally stratify everything else they'd discovered so far.

Chapter 31

Rachael turned her patrol onto Moonlight Track and sped up the dirt road, leaving a cloud of dust in her wake. She wasn't going to question the truck drivers, but she did want to follow them to find out where they were going. As far as she knew, almost all of the gold in the area was long gone; mined out over a hundred years earlier by the gold rush settlers.

Reaching the line of Totara trees where she'd stopped the previous day, she pulled up in their shadow and watched as the line of yellow rock trucks crossed over the river. She couldn't follow them now even if she wanted to, so she pulled out her binoculars and peered across the valley.

Each truck driver was now out of their vehicle and they stood around chatting with no obvious sense of urgency. *'Perhaps they're about to knock off for the day',* Rachael thought. *'Or maybe they're delivering the vehicles to site, before starting work in the morning?'*

What she was sure of though, was that all the vehicles and equipment must have cost Scotty a fortune and the fuel cost alone would have been enormous. He must have been confident that the river valley still held enough gold to make it worth his while.

But Rachael soon got bored of waiting for something to happen and she turned her binoculars northwest to where she'd tracked Kaihautu, 24 hours earlier.

She spotted the stand of flax bushes where the Māori had disappeared, and she considered what would have happened if Owen's twisted ankle hadn't forced them to turn back. Kaihautu Waitaha was a big man, and an extremely dangerous one if her new line of inquiry with Scotty James turned out to be a dead end.

Scanning the bushes for Kai's possible exit point, Rachael caught sight of a man talking on his mobile phone. She couldn't quite make out his face, but it appeared to be Owen and her heart suddenly skipped a beat. Even from a distance, his stance oozed confidence, and in his crisp white shirt he stood out against the reddish-brown flax.

Rachael decided to go and talk to him, to see if he knew anything about the mining vehicles or Scotty's intentions within the valley. It was a feasible excuse for a conversation, but in reality—she just wanted to be near him.

She turned the key in the patrol car's ignition and headed up towards the dam, praying all the while that Owen's wife had gone back into town.

As she pulled into the construction site car park a man emerged from the site office; he was probably the site foreman she concluded.

"Gidday," he said as Rachael stepped out of the patrol car. "Are you here to take care of our unwanted visitor?"

"Visitor?" she asked.

"You know, the saboteur, the Māori fella, we've got him tied up in our site office."

'Oh great', thought Rachael, nobody had come to pick him up after all.

"I'm sorry, but it's the first I've heard of it," she lied. "But I can certainly take him off your hands."

"You do know it took five of us to get him to the ground?" said the foreman. "Are you sure you wanna take him on your own love?"

'Love?' thought Rachael. Who did this guy think he was talking to? She really hated middle-aged men sometimes.

"Ya know, that fella's had us chasing him around all night," continued the foreman. "It's taken us hours get our pyrotechnics ready again and if it hadn't been for Owen's mate giving us a hand, we never would have caught the bastard at all. Shame Liam had to dash off though, I would have bought him a beer to say thanks."

'So, Liam was here at the dam?' thought Rachael. He hadn't mentioned that either. Something fishy was going on and she didn't like it one bit.

She glanced across the river to see if Owen was still there, but his white shirt was nowhere to be seen. Her disappointment must have been obvious, as the foreman asked if she was ok.

"Are you alright love?" he said. "Were you here to see somebody in particular?"

"Oh, I erm, I just wanted to speak to your environmental engineer that's all. I noticed there's some industrial activity further down the valley, and I was wondering what the erm, what the consequences might be for the local wildlife."

"Oh right," said the foreman. "You'd be looking for Owen then. He's not here I'm afraid—he's over to the other side of the dam with his wife and some TV fella."

"TV fella?" said Rachael, before remembering something that Owen had said earlier. "Oh, that's right, Owen mentioned something about the next stage of the construction project?"

"Yeah, that's right. The bloke turned up about an hour ago, while Owen and his Mrs were at the bungy bridge. Apparently, Owen promised that he could cover the detonations scheduled for this afternoon. So, I gave him a quick tour and showed him the best place to film the action."

"And where's that?" Rachael asked.

"The control deck of course. It's got a clear line of sight, right across the valley towards the detonation area."

"Ok, that makes sense I suppose."

"The guy wasn't too happy though, when I said we might have to cancel for today. He mentioned something about his schedule demanding it."

"Cancel, but why would you cancel if your pyrotechnics have all been rechecked?"

"Don't ask me love, I just do as I'm told. Owen asked us to hold off for a few hours—said it was something to do with eels. Ya know, that bloke's more like his dad than he cares to admit, even if he doesn't talk to Davey Boy anymore."

"So, you know Owen's father, Dave Norman?"

"Yeah, he's a top bloke that Dave… puts on a cracking show. Can't sing for toffee mind you, but he's funny as hell."

"I'm sorry… show… what show?"

"Lady Gloria, he calls himself. I don't usually like drag queens and that sort of stuff, but the Mrs made me go along one time and he was funny as fuck. That fella's got more talent than Jonno Hart ever had."

Rachael made a note in her pad…

- Jonno Hart's cameraman is a drag queen
- Did Jonno know about this?
- Would it have caused tension between them considering Jonno's macho image?

"So, this TV fella…" said Rachael. "He's with Owen and his wife you say?"

She'd suddenly realised that this TV guy might be an acquaintance of both Jonno Hart and his cameraman.

"That's right, they've been gone about half an hour now, I can try calling them if you like?"

"Could you? I'd appreciate that, thanks."

"Ok, just follow me to the site office and I'll grab my radio. You can take-a-look at this Māori fella as well while you're there—you might want to reconsider taking him in on your own."

The foreman lead the way and he took Rachael into the bottom section of the two-story site office.

"Ya know that Owen's a lucky bastard," he said, as they entered the bright yellow cabin. "His wife looks amazing and did ya know she's a TV star? I dunno why he kept that quiet—I'd be showing pictures of her to everyone I met."

Rachael was really starting to hate this woman and she'd only met her for a minute or two.

She looked around the room for Kaihautu, but all she could see was a grubby looking desk, an ancient-looking computer, and stacks of paper that were piled high in no discernible order. The cabin stank of male body odour and the place generally looked like a tip.

"I can you see you run a tight ship," said Rachael.

"Yeah, sorry about that," replied the foreman. "I've been telling the blokes to clean it up for ages, but they never take responsibility for their own mess".

That sounds familiar, thought the policewoman as she stepped over a pile of blueprints on the floor.

They reached the back of the room and the foreman opened a storage cupboard to reveal the Māori sitting on the floor. He was bound by several leather belts and enough rope to hold down an elephant.

"That's a bit over the top don't you think?" said Rachael, as she removed a gag from Kaihautu's mouth. Untying the gag revealed a large bruise on the man's cheek and she shot the foreman a questioning glance.

"You should have seen the bastard," said the foreman defensively. "He got no more than he deserved, I promise."

"Mr Waitaha, you're coming with me I'm afraid, but if you'd like to make a complaint about the way you've been treated, I can take a statement about that once we're at the station."

It was a remark that seemed to please the man, and he flashed a grin towards the foreman in response.

"So, you're really gonna take him on your own?" said the foreman. "Are you sure that's wise love?"

So far, Rachael had been willing to overlook the man's bad language, but the word 'love' was a step too far and she momentarily considered arresting him on suspicion of assault.

"Oh, I think Mr. Waitaha will be quite amenable now, won't you Kai?"

The Māori nodded reluctantly, but it was enough to make Rachael think that he would be complicit.

"After all, you wouldn't want to get locked up now would you Kai, not when you've got a boy to raise and a duty to stop the mining activities out there in the valley."

A look of surprise and recognition suddenly crossed Kai's face and Rachael knew that she was on to something.

"Mining?" said the foreman, but Rachael ignored him—the love comment was still grating on her.

Instead, she helped Kai to his feet and gave him a wide berth as he shuffled out of the cupboard. His feet were bound by a black leather belt, which she instantly recognised as Liam's. The kiwi shaped buckle was a give-away and she remembered the moment when she'd given it to him, on the anniversary of their first date.

Just as she was about to close the door behind Kai's enormous frame, a familiar voice came from inside the cupboard.

"Hey, wait up Pākehā, you're not taking dad anywhere without me."

It was the boy Nīoreore, and Rachael frowned as he stumbled out into the light; his hands and feet bound like his father's.

"You tied up a minor?" she said angrily.

She didn't like the boy but locking him up was a step too far even for her to ignore.

"Hey, don't blame me, he wanted to go in there," said the foreman. "But I wasn't about to risk him untying his old man was I, so he agreed to be tied up."

"Is that correct?" said the policewoman, releasing the boy's bonds. The boy nodded in response, but Rachael wasn't convinced.

"Are they back from the cave?" asked the boy as Rachael untied his ankles.

"Cave? What cave?" she replied.

"The cave with the eels," said the foreman. "I can't understand what the fuss is about myself, but the TV bloke seemed keen to see it too".

Rachael studied both Kai and the boy, but neither seemed willing to offer any further information.

"Tell me about the eels," said Rachael. "Is that why you're trying to stop the dam project? I can probably help you know."

"You don't know anything," spat the boy, before his father shot him a silencing look.

"Listen, Kai," said Rachael. "If you're worried about the boy getting into trouble, you don't need to worry. Even if he did help you to sabotage the pyrotechnics, I'll omit that from my notes if you take all the blame."

Rachael waited for Kai to respond, but his lips remained shut and she could see the tension building in his jaw. She also noticed him flexing his muscles against the strength of his bindings and she started to worry that she might have gotten out of her depth.

Her attempts to sound amenable obviously weren't working, so she reverted to type and handcuffed the boy to see if that would push Kai's button.

"What do you think you're doing?" he shouted, as he struggled to free himself.

The policewoman reached for her taser in response and the boy urged his father to calm down.

"It's alright dad, just tell her about the cave, tell her about the eel—I think we can trust her dad."

It was as if the words had wounded the giant and he slumped back down to the ground, his great strength suddenly drained by the revelation. The boy had apparently mentioned something of great importance—perhaps the real reason for Kai's actions at the dam.

Chapter 32

"That's it!" Jenny exclaimed "It has to be… it's the Takitimu!"

She couldn't believe it, the giant canoe—lying 30 metres from where she stood—was the actual waka that had brought some of the first people to New Zealand.

'Where the hell is Owen?' she thought. She needed to show him what she'd discovered and explain her theory about the waka. She'd been re-reading the museum pamphlet that she'd discovered in Owen's hotel room and suddenly everything had started to make sense.

She re-read the paragraph again, just to be sure.

"…and when Tamatea finally made it back home to Tauranga, he told the story of how the great Takitimu, had been lost. The eel god Te Tunaroa (a huge sea monster) had swallowed the waka whole, before spitting it out onto the mountain tops, where it then turned to stone."

The daylight inside the cave was starting to fade now and they were running out time if they were going to make the evening news. Just then, the weathergirl heard footsteps and unable to wait any longer she shouted out to her husband.

"It's got to be her babe, it's the Takitimu, I'm sure of it!"

"Almost, but not quite," replied a male voice, but it was neither Owen nor Markus.

Jenny raised the torchlight from her phone and stumbled backwards as a giant of a man emerged from the tunnel. She recognised him as the Māori saboteur, but the last time she'd seen him he was tied up in a cupboard and she'd had no idea of his size.

Following quickly behind him, a second figure emerged into the cave and once again Jenny recognised the face from earlier that day.

"I understand you're here to film the cave," said the policewoman, shielding her eyes from the glare of Jenny's torchlight.

"Erm yeah, that's right," Jenny replied, as the woman walked past her.

"So, this is it? This, is why you wanted to stop the dam construction—a cave full of eels?"

Jenny was about to answer, but Kaihautu spoke first and she realised that the policewoman hadn't been speaking to her at all.

"You weren't listening, were you?" said Kai. "I didn't say eels… I said eel… THE Eel in fact."

And with that, he pointed his finger out across the lake.

Jenny watched as the police officer's face turned from smug superiority to wide-eyed disbelief and the weathergirl couldn't help but smile.

"Incredible, isn't it?" she said, as she sidled up next to the policewoman. "I'm Jenny by the way… Jenny Sunley."

She held out her hand and the policewoman shook it briefly, but quickly returned her attention to the spectacle in front of them. It was late afternoon now and the fading sunlight that still trickled through the roof had taken on a pinkish glow. The mineral encrusted canoe at the centre of the lake now sparkled like a giant pink diamond and Jenny grinned as the policewoman gasped in amazement.

Rachael couldn't believe what she was seeing, and she dug her thumbnail into her palm to check that she was still awake. The boy had promised her that she'd be impressed, but she'd taken his assurances with a pinch of salt. She was also glad that Kai had insisted the boy stay behind at the office, otherwise the little shit wouldn't have shut up about being proven right.

The cave was like something from a dream and the policewoman tried desperately to make sense of what she was seeing.

She knew about the Māori legends of course, but she'd never thought that one day she would come face-to-face with one—and to find it so beautiful. She'd chosen to live in New Zealand because she loved its mountains, its rivers, and its forests—she even on occasion, loved its people. But until that moment, she had never loved its history, and she was conflicted about what to do next. She was a typical Pākehā—the Māori slang term for European settlers—and at that moment she was ashamed of the person she had become.

Ever since she'd joined the force as a junior officer in Christchurch, she'd been dismissive of Māori claims to the land and its bounties. Māori rights had seemed overly one-sided in her opinion and they seemed to be based solely on tales of fictitious gods and vague histories of settlement. Yet here was unequivocal proof of an ancient Māori past, one that she'd thought only existed in song.

Kai watched as the two women looked on, they were both in awe of the cave and its walls of gold. As they gawped and fawned over its splendour, he'd made his way across the lake to the waka, silently traversing the line of posts that sat just below the water's surface. He needed to check that 'The Eel' was ok, and that the most recent detonations hadn't damaged it further. He had known the giant canoe all his life and although he may have turned blind to just how beautiful it was, he had never forgotten what the great waka meant to his people or the oath that he'd sworn to protect it.

The pretty blonde had referred to the waka as 'she' like it was a woman with a personality and feelings. But 'Te Tuna Moe Vai' was much more than that—it was a symbol of hope.

In English its name translated to 'The Eel That Slept', and Kai pondered if it was finally time for the canoe to awaken.

His people, the Waitaha, had guarded the waka for nearly two thousand years and he was tired of keeping its secret. Unlike other Māori tribes, the Waitaha Iwi had travelled from much farther west, and after the demi-god Maui had fished the islands of Aotearoa up from the ocean floor, they were the first to call this place home.

Other people had arrived later of course, and their stories had become merged with those of the early Waitaha settlers. The great waka 'Takitimu', had also sailed along the southern coast, just as The Eel' had done nearly a thousand years earlier. And it too had been smashed on the rocks. But the Takitimu had been lost to the waves and so its survivors had adopted the story of 'The Eel That Slept', to keep the memory of their great waka alive.

Then, as the centuries rolled on, The Eel was finally forgotten and only the Takitimu remained alive in memory. The Waitaha people themselves had become just a surname, with little knowledge of where they had come from and only Kai's direct ancestors left to guard the secret of the once-great waka.

Kaihautu thought for a second about what might have happened if the two wakas' fortunes had been reversed, and what it might have meant to the story of his people. They were the first, but they were also the forgotten, and their rightful place in the annals of history had been unwittingly stolen from them by the Takitimu.

He clenched his fist at the injustice of it all and then realised where his son had picked up the habit. Nīoreore was a great kid, and he deserved much more than he could offer him. But the boy also needed to learn that the Pākehā would never change, and once word got out about the gold, 'The Eel That Slept', would never be safe again. People like Scotty James would come crashing in with their bulldozers, and The Eel' would be smashed to pieces, long before the government got around to recognising its importance.

Kai realised that he'd have to put a lid on things soon and his eyes turned to the women, still gawping at the gold streaked walls of the cathedral-like cave.

The blonde one, thought she knew what she was looking at, and Kai listened as she prattled on about the amazing history of the Takitimu. But when her story finally turned to the Takitimu mountain range—named after the great waka—his patience finally buckled.

"It's not the Takitimu you stupid woman. It's 'Te Tuna Moe Vai'—The Eel That Slept. And it's not a she, it's a he… and if HE was a man, he'd tell you two to SHUT THE FUCK UP!"

Kai stopped there, but his words continued to echo around the cave…

"SHUT… SHUT… SHUT… FUCK… FUCK… FUCK… UP… UP… UP…"

He immediately regretted raising his voice and he sighed when a response came echoing back.

"EXPLAIN… PLAIN… PLAIN…"

Bugger,' thought Kai, he'd let the cat out of the bag and now he was going to have to explain what he'd meant, otherwise, the stupid women would never shut up. He was tired from being up all night and he was tired from years of keeping the secret. Finally letting go of things and telling the world about The Eel' was a tempting thought, and he could hear the voice of his wife whispering in his ear to let it go. If only he'd listened to her while she was still alive, then maybe he wouldn't have been in this mess at all.

But the promise to his grandfather was something that he couldn't turn his back on and now he felt ashamed that he'd let the old man down.

"Ok," he said finally, in a quieter voice so as not to create an echo. "But don't question what I say, and I don't want to see you writing any of this down, you understand me, copper?"

"Ok," said the blonde, before the policewoman had a chance to respond. "But like I said to the boy, if this canoe really is what you say it is, you've got to let us help you, Kai."

Kaihautu sat motionless in the dark of his hiding spot; he could hear the shuffling of the women's feet as they waited for him to tell his story. He could sense the ghosts of his ancestors waiting on him too, they were waiting to hear if he still remembered the story, waiting to hear if he'd finally put aside his doubts. It was a story that had been told to him by his grandfather, when Kai was just a child. It was a story that contradicted everything that he'd learned in school about the history of New Zealand. But Kai's grandpapa had insisted that he learned the words anyway, and so he'd practised them, reciting them back to the old man every day for years.

Finally, after several deep breaths, Kaihautu started to tell the story, and amazingly the two women listened, not questioning and not interfering with the flow of his words.

He told them about the story of Kupe, the first man to discover the land of Aotearoa, after it had been fished up from the ocean by the demi-god Maui. He told them of how Kupe had travelled from his homeland of Hawaiki, far away in the islands to the north.

"...but Kupe's waka, The Eel That Slept, was smashed on the rocks after the mariner steered too close to shore. And so, Kupe had his men drag the great canoe inland to repair it, using totara and flax that they found in abundance.

One of the hulls, however, was too damaged to ever be seaworthy again, and so they fashioned a replacement, lashing it with flax to the remaining half of the once-great canoe. This new waka they named 'Matahourua', and although it was a fine vessel, Kupe knew that it would never be as perfect as The Eel', a vessel that he himself had stolen from the people he now used as slaves.

And so, Kupe and his men, returned home to Haiwiki, telling the other tribes about the land that they had discovered

But Kupe was embarrassed that he had lost one half of his ship, so his men embellished the story of the wreck and made it sound as if the waka had been damaged during a fight. They told the story of a great sea monster, an octopus named 'Te Wheke-a-Maturangi', and they told how Kupe had finally defeated the creature after a long battle in the straights between Aotearoa's north and south islands.

But not all of Kupe's crew had returned with him on the Matahourua, half a dozen slaves had escaped into the bush, and when Kupe finally sailed off, they had decided to hide all trace of the great waka that he'd left behind. They were the Waitaha, the first true settlers of New Zealand, and they went into the mountains to hide.

It was the sacred waka, 'Takitimu', that would be next to travel that way, some 900 years after Kupe's great voyage. Captained by Tahu, son of Tamatea, the sacred waka had got caught in a *whirlpool, near to the present-day town of Te Anau, and had broken apart before disappearing under the waves.*

Unable to find suitable trees to build a new ship, Tahu and his men had travelled inland, hoping to find a short cut that would bring them closer to home. But at a great lake circled by mountains, they met a tribe of people who spoke the language of the priests and their jewellery was made of gold and precious greenstone. The people were timid and easily conquered, and Tahu forced them to reveal the secrets of their wealth.

Beaten and bruised, they led Tahu to a cave that was lined with gold and sitting at its centre he found Kupe's great waka, glistening under the sun. 'The Eel That Slept', was a prize far greater than any gold or greenstone could ever be, and Tahu fell to his knees in worship of the great vessel.

Tahu turned to his men and commanded them to move it, hoping to sail it north to his father. But the waka had long since turned to stone and the men slipped into the lake as they tried to lift it. Consumed by the blackness, the men disappeared without trace and only Tahu was left to tell the story of the cave.

After making his escape, Tahu returned to his father in Tauranga with a story concocted to protect his ego. It was a story so impressive that even Tamatea was jealous of his son's great adventure and so he took the story as his own, claiming the battle with the great eel—Te Tunaroa—as one of his greatest achievements..."

Kai left his story there and waited for the women to respond—as they no doubt would—because women could never just accept things as they were.

"Isn't it wonderful?" whispered Jenny.

"Ridiculous more like," replied Rachael.

She'd been listening to the Māori prattle on for what felt like an eternity, but she'd suddenly become aware that she had no idea where he was.

But before either of the women could say anything, a rumble suddenly shook the air and rocks began tumbling from the ceiling, shattering the lake's mirrored surface with the first drop.

The black water responded instantaneously, and it boiled into life as hundreds of giant eels all rose to the surface, scrambling over each other to find the source of the disturbance. And then, before any of the group could say a word, a loud cracking noise whipped through the cavern, silencing the creatures of the lake once more, like a parent scolding its children.

Kai knew that his story had touched a nerve and he feared what would happen next.

Chapter 33

"Kai... Where are you?" Rachael shouted as the cracking sound finally trailed into an echo.

The mountain seemed to have come alive with energy and with the cave's gold streaked walls now glowing pink under the evening sunlight, it felt to Rachael as if she were inside the belly of a beast. The ground was rumbling beneath her feet, and the vibrations in the air shook her body in an unsettling way.

She stood at the edge of the lake and shouted out again.

"Kaihautu Waitaha, if you're thinking of running away, you know we'll find you, don't you? As far as I'm concerned, you've only disconnected a few explosives—don't give me a reason to change my mind. If you don't come out Kai, I'll assume that you've got something else to hide. My team will come in here and tear this place apart for evidence."

The reply she was waiting for came immediately, but thanks to the echoing throughout the cavern, it gave no indication of Kai's whereabouts.

"Don't worry Pākehā I'm not gonna run, I just wanted to check that the waka is still ok. What the fuck are they are doing out there anyway, I thought you told the foreman we were coming over here?"

He was right, thought Rachael. She'd made it crystal-clear that all work on the site must stop until she'd given them the go-ahead to proceed. Yet they appeared to be pressing ahead with the detonations knowing full well that she was still on-site, not to mention the civilians that could be put in danger.

No, it had to be an error, Rachael concluded. Kai's tampering must have backfired spectacularly and instead of disabling the devices, he'd accidentally made one go off.

A devilish cracking sound suddenly filled the cavern and it made the hairs on Rachael's neck stand on end. Kai's mistake still hadn't run its course and the whole mountain was about to implode because of his stupidity.

"What the fuck was that?" screamed the weathergirl. "We need to get out of here fast".

The woman was right, thought Rachael. They couldn't stay there any longer and it was her job to make sure that they all got out alive.

"Kai, we're leaving now…" she shouted. "And that means you too!"

"Go without me…" he replied from the shadows. "And tell my boy that I'm proud of him, no matter what happens."

"Don't be stupid," Rachael yelled. "Nothing's happened yet, and if you come with me now, I'll tell the foreman not to press charges. I can see now that you were only trying to protect the waka."

"The foreman can go fuck himself!" Kai responded. "The Eel's more important than anything you Pākehā can imagine."

"He's not exaggerating," Jenny interrupted. "If his story's correct, it pushes back Māori history in New Zealand by nearly a thousand years. That could have huge consequences for land ownership and settlement rights."

Rachael was irked that she'd been schooled by a silicon Barbie doll, but at the same time, she was impressed by the woman's assessment of the situation.

"She's right Kai, you need to tell the story of the waka. But if you die in here, nobody will ever know what's in your head."

"Listen, Kai…" Jenny interrupted, her voice smooth and less aggressive than Rachael's bark. "You need to come with us now, or the boy will end up without a father, and you know what that's like don't you?"

Her words seemed to strike a chord with the man and he suddenly appeared on the ledge beside them.

"Tell the boy that I'm proud of him," he said. "But I can't come back with you—at least, not yet."

The weathergirl reached out instinctively and touched the man's arm. She could see love in his eyes, but there was also pain. He was a man torn between the conflict of love and duty, and she wished that she had the words to tell him everything would be ok.

But once again, before she could speak, another loud crack whipped through the air, and a shiver ran down her spine.

"Come on," said Rachael as she grabbed the weathergirl's arm, dragging her towards the entrance tunnel. Leading the way, the policewoman squeezed into the gap and shimmied sideways towards the fading sunlight, and she was about halfway when she saw a torchlight coming in from the other end—an angel in a white shirt had come to save them.

But then suddenly, a deluge of rocks fell from the ceiling and she was forced to retreat, as a cloud of dust and debris fell to block the tunnel entrance.

Backing into the weathergirl, Rachael tripped over her feet and stumbled towards the lake. Desperately reaching out to grasp something, she toppled into the water and landed head-first.

Pockets of air, in the rear of her combat vest, acted to stop her sinking, but the heavy metal plates at the front kept her facing downwards, and she found herself unable to breathe.

For what felt like minutes she struggled to right herself, but with no sense of gravity to let her know which way she should be swimming, her kicking was ineffectual, and she ended up going nowhere. It was dark in the water but not completely devoid of light and as she struggled against her liquid chains, she caught glimpses of long shadows circling her, like wolves stalking their prey. The giant eels were preparing to attack, and Rachael knew that they could sense her fear.

Then suddenly she was moving again, but not from her own efforts, and she felt herself being lifted from the water. Hoisted back into the world of physics and gravity, she briefly felt the water draining from her vest before she dumped onto the ground with a thud.

Kaihautu had picked her up with ease and then tossed her aside like a worthless rag doll.

Rachael wasn't sure whether she should thank the Māori for saving her life or shout at him for treating her so roughly. But Kai was clearly even stronger than she'd imagined, and she bit her lip to keep her mouth shut.

She stood up from her soggy heap on the floor and wiped the strands of hair from her face. She had never felt more embarrassed than she did at that moment, and it didn't help when she caught sight of the weathergirl, her hair and makeup still flawless.

The policewoman's uniform suddenly felt even heavier than before and she reached around to unclip her combat vest. It dropped to the floor with a thud and the weight off her shoulders was a welcome relief.

Suddenly, a sharp pain burned on Rachael's left calf and she wondered if the vest had scratched her on its way to the floor. She looked down to see where the pain was coming from and jumped in fright at what she saw.

Attached to her leg was a slippery black eel, about four feet in length and she could feel its teeth sawing into her skin with every movement of its ugly head.

"Get it off!" she screamed, flinging her leg in all directions. But instead of letting go, the eel seemed to bite harder, and it launched itself into a 'death spiral'—a feeding technique designed to tear off mouthfuls of flesh.

As the beast thrashed and shook, the policewoman screamed once more…

"Get the fucking thing off me—before it rips my leg off!"

She had completely lost her cool now and her eyes sought out those of the weathergirl to appeal for help.

The blonde, however, looked just as shocked as she was and she waved her foot in the direction of the eel, as if 'air kicks' from her hideous shoes would somehow scare the beast away.

"What the fuck are you doing?" Rachael screamed in response. "Pull the fucking thing off me."

But the weathergirl just stared, apparently unable to act.

"Don't just stand there—stupid woman—do something!"

Like a stick prodding a dumb animal, Rachael's words seemed to have the desired effect and the weathergirl snapped out of her coma. But before the policewoman could muster the word 'stop', the stupid bitch had picked up her taser from the floor and pointed it at the eel.

As if in slow motion, Rachael saw a flash erupt from the end of the weapon and its metal prongs flew through the air, towards the creature. Trailing behind, fine wire filaments unfurled like a spring, and in an instant, Rachael's head turned into a prison of pain. 50,000 volts of electricity coursed through the body of the eel and straight into her leg. Every muscle in her body spasmed in response and her jaw clamped shut like a magnetic lock.

Once again, the policewoman collapsed to the floor in a heap—but this time she didn't get up.

"Got it!" cheered Jenny as she watched the eel go rigid from the shock.

For a second, the beast went poker straight as the prongs delivered their debilitating charge and then it dropped to the floor like a rubber toy, lifeless and limp.

"Now that's what you call an electric eel!" laughed the weathergirl, as she kicked the creature back into the water.

But the policewoman didn't answer, and instead she lay motionless on the floor.

"Oh, that's just great," said Kai as he knelt down by the detective. "You fucking killed her you idiot, what the hell did you think you were doing?"

"Killed her?" said Jenny. "I didn't... did I? Tell me you're joking... please, Kai, tell me you're joking?"

But Kai just looked away.

"Kai!" screamed Jenny. "Tell me you're joking Kai... tell me I didn't kill her... please Kai, tell me she's still alive."

Jenny threw the taser on the floor in disgust. She'd somehow managed to kill a human being, a woman that she barely knew. She was struggling to breathe under the guilt that was crushing her chest, and she dropped to the floor in a heap.

Sobbing and unable to control her emotions she wailed, not only at the loss of the policewoman, but also at the loss of her own life too. She was sure that she'd be put in prison for the rest of her life and she would never see Owen again.

Suddenly, the weathergirl felt something grab her ankle and she spun around, thinking that the eel had returned for another bite. But it wasn't the eel, it was the policewoman, and she looked pissed as hell when she said through gritted teeth, "It's ok, I'm fine. Now just shut up and don't ever… EVER… touch my taser again!"

The look of relief on Jenny's face must have been obvious as the cavern suddenly erupted to the sound of laughter. Kai's trick had been revealed and he revelled in his deception.

"You bastard!" Jenny shouted as she pulled herself to her feet.

"Hey, it's not my fault you're stupid," replied the Māori, as he wiped a tear from his eye. "And that's exactly why you Pākehā have got no right to be here. You think ya know everything, but ya don't. And now the tunnel's collapsed, and you're both gonna die in here with me… you stupid idiots."

"Well I guess the joke's on you then isn't it!" spat Jenny, still fuming that somebody would lie like that. "You made me think that I killed the poor girl and now you're stuck with both of us, aren't you?"

"Hey… less of '*the girl*'," said Rachael, finding her feet. "And nobody's dying either, not today, not on my watch."

In her head, it had sounded like the right thing to say, but as soon as the words came out of her mouth, she instantly regretted it.

"Not on your watch?" spat Kai. "What kind of bullshit statement is that? You've been watching too many movies love. We ain't goin' nowhere, and there ain't nobody coming through that tunnel anytime soon."

"Oh shit, I forgot… the tunnel!"

A memory had suddenly appeared in the policewoman's mind and she ran to the tunnel entrance.

Scrabbling amongst the fallen rocks, she looked back at her fellow prisoners.

"Just before the roof collapsed, I thought I saw somebody in a white shirt—I think it was Owen!"

The weathergirl looked stunned.

"Well come and help me then!" screamed Rachael, as she started clawing at the boulders.

But Jenny was struck dumb with shock and she stood rooted to the spot.

Rachael continued to dig and Kai stepped up to shift the heavy rocks. He seemed to lift most of them with ease, and even the larger boulders, he somehow managed to roll away into the lake.

"Fucking help us will you!" shouted Rachael, as Jenny got in her way yet again. But the weathergirl was completely lost to them now and she just stood there mumbling, repeating Owen's name, over-and-over again.

Her earlier composure had been crushed by the thought of losing her husband and Rachael knew that if she didn't get them out of there soon, the weathergirl would struggle to control her demons as night-time fell.

"You're stronger than you look," said Kai, as the policewoman rolled another stone into the lake. "You're like that 'Doctor Death', one of the girls at my rugby club."

"Doctor Death?" replied Rachael—what the hell was he talking about?

"Do you mean the pathologist?" she asked, as she stopped to wipe the sweat from her brow. "Pippa Barrett—she plays at your rugby club?"

"Yeah, that's the one."

'Huh', thought Rachael, as she remembered her first encounter with the pretty lab assistant. The girl had been wearing her rugby kit that day and was covered in dirt.

She also remembered how Bob James had tried to embarrass the girl before producing Kai's phone number, but she'd stayed calm and composed in the face of the Doctor's misogyny.

Yes, she certainly was tougher than she looked, and Rachael admired her for that.

"So, then…" said Rachael, trying to sound casual in her conversation. "How was it that Jonno Hart came to have your number, I can't imagine that you openly advertise your services as a fishing guide?"

She waited for Kai to respond, but he just carried on digging.

Finally, he answered, but he continued to shift boulders and didn't look up from his work.

"Doctor Death gave it to him I suppose."

"I'm sorry?" said Rachael, "Pippa Barrett gave your phone number to Jonno Hart—is that what you're saying?"

It was a revelation that stopped her in her tracks. Pippa had supplied Kai's details to Jonno Hart, but she'd kept quiet about it when her boss had produced the Māori's phone number as evidence.

'Surely she would have known how important it was to disclose her connection with the case?'

"So, Pippa gave Jonno Hart your phone number... and then what?"

"And then we went fishing," huffed Kai, but he still refused to look up from his work.

"...and then you went fishing."

The Māori was being deliberately evasive, and Rachael was finding it difficult to keep her frustration in check.

"The fella knew that I had ancestral fishing rights and I was offered money to take him up to the dam. But even at the holding ponds, the prick couldn't catch more than a few tiddlers—and he called himself a fisherman."

"So, you took his money... and then you killed him?" said Rachael.

It was the first time that she'd openly accused Kai of the murder and she quickly realised that she should have been more prepared for his reaction.

"You think I killed that piece of shit? I wouldn't even waste my spit on that dirty old man."

Rachael was aware that she wasn't in the safety of an interrogation room, but she was on a roll, and she couldn't hold back.

"But you *did* take his money? – or didn't he cough up? Is that what happened Kai. Did he stiff you on the money, so you decided to make him pay in a different way?"

Kai put down the boulder he was lifting and stood upright, he was clearly upset at the accusation.

Rachael scanned the floor for her taser, but she knew that it wouldn't stop the giant man so soon after its recent discharge.

"Now you listen to me Pākehā," spat Kai. "I never touched that bloke ok… and I never took no stinkin' money either… got it?"

He'd stopped calling her 'copper' and instead, he'd reverted to the word 'Pākehā'. It was a deliberate switch, clearly intended to emphasise his belief that he was being victimised—so Rachael decided to use that chip on his shoulder, for extra leverage.

"Listen, Kai," she said. "I'm trying to believe you, I really am, but you need to give me something more. The killer obviously hates you and your Māori brothers, just as much as he hated Jonno Hart. The killer is the real villain here, not me. Help me to catch him before anyone else gets hurt."

Kai laughed.

"Before anyone else gets hurt? Well, you're too late for that love. That pathologist bloke died yesterday so I heard, and you know what, it's good riddance. Whoever this killer is, they're doing the world a favour if you ask me."

"The pathologist?" said Rachael. "Are you saying that Bob James was murdered too? By the same person that killed Jonno Hart?"

Kai didn't answer, but even in the fading light, Rachael could see him rolling his eyes at her stupidity; she shrunk back from the dominant stance that she'd assumed. Clearly, she had missed some important clues about the relationship between Jonno Hart and the town's pathologist.

Pippa Barrett must have been instructed by her boss to find a fishing guide, and she'd known to ask Kai simply because of their association at the Rugby club. The poor girl was a victim of circumstance and had no doubt felt scared to reveal her part in the story, for fear of incriminating herself in Jonno Hart's murder.

'That's probably why she called me about the necklace…' thought Rachael. *'The poor girl must have realised that Kai was being stitched up and she wanted to make sure that any evidence against him would be put in doubt.'*

But if Bob James really had been murdered, then he couldn't be Jonno's killer either, and that had to point the finger squarely at his son, Scotty. The bungy jump owner was a frequent and unchallenged visitor to the hospital, a place where he could easily have stolen drugs, and then used them to dose his father before he set off in his car.

'Scotty must have wanted the mining company all to himself?'

It was the logical assumption, reasoned the policewoman, and the easiest way to do it was to get rid of his fellow share-holders—the fishing celebrity, and his overbearing father.

'But why frame Kai for the murder?' she thought.

As far as she knew, the man's saboteur antics had never affected the bungy bridge, but on the other hand, he *had* rejected Scotty's proposal for a joint tourism venture and Scotty's plans to rip up the valley would no doubt have met similar resistance from the Māori. If he'd invested as much in his mining business as Rachael suspected, Scotty couldn't let Kaihautu put a stop to his digging before he'd even got started.

Rachael scanned the gold-lined walls of the cave once more. If Scotty was prepared to murder his own father for the few scraps of gold still left in the valley, what would he do for the mother-load that was hidden inside the mountain? Rachael was starting to see things more clearly now and she needed to get the word out to her colleagues. She was starting to suspect that the explosions had been no accident, and if Scotty James wasn't stopped soon, then who knows what would happen to the waka and the three of them trapped inside the cave.

Chapter 34

"If you're looking for another way out, you're out of luck," shouted Kai from the darkness.

They had hit a rock that even the giant Māori could not move and while Rachael climbed up to investigate a chink of light, Kaihautu had crept back to his hiding spot behind the waka.

"The hole in the roof is now the only way out of here," Kai continued. "And unless you've got a Batarang in that utility belt of yours, we're gonna need wings to get up there."

"That's it!" said Jenny. "But not wings... we need rotors! Detective, try and see if you can get a phone signal, we'll call the air rescue team and they can lift us out through the roof!"

'Oh, so she's back in the room, then is she?' thought Rachael, climbing down from the rocks.

"Miss Sunley... Oh, I'm sorry, Mrs. Sunley... Listen... you know I was probably wrong about what I saw in the tunnel. I'm sure Owen's just fine and he'll be waiting for us when we finally manage to get out of here."

Rachael didn't believe a word of what she'd just said, but the bimbo had snapped out of her daze and she needed her to stay calm.

"Yes, I think you're right," Jenny replied. "Owen's probably out there right now, organising a team to dig us out through the tunnel… he's good at organising things you see."

The stupid blonde was clearly in a state of denial about the severity of their situation, but Rachael decided that it was best not to challenge her optimism.

She pulled out her phone and waved it around, praying that the gold-lined walls of the cave might somehow boost the signal. But the phone wouldn't connect and the policewoman smacked it with the heel of her hand, like a doctor trying to resuscitate a patient.

"Try from the middle of the lake," offered Jenny, "If you can climb up on the canoe you might be able to get a signal through the hole in the roof."

"Don't even think about it!" shouted Kai from his hiding spot. "Nobody's stood inside that waka for nearly two thousand years and I'll be dammed if I'm gonna let a Pākehā be the first one to do it! Throw me the phone and I'll do it for you."

"No way," said Rachael. "How do I know you won't throw it straight into the water? You might know of another way out and then just leave us here to rot."

She might have convinced herself of Kai's innocence with regards to Jonno's murder, but his sabotage could still be the cause of the cave-in and he might do something stupid to cover up his actions.

"I told ya," shouted Kai. "There's no other way out—I promise. And even though I mucked up those explosives, I'd rather go to jail for that, than die in here with the ōrea."

Rachael didn't fancy being eaten by the eels either, so she told Kai to come out of his hiding place and threw him the phone.

"Just dial 111 and then press the green button," she instructed.

"Thanks for the tip," he replied. "All this technology mumbo jumbo is a bit much for us simple Māori folk ya know."

His temper was clearly starting to fray and Rachael worried that his sarcasm although justified, might be a sign that he was about to lose his rag.

'Perhaps the situation was starting to scare him too?' she thought, as Kai's enormous hands fumbled with the phone's tiny buttons.

Perhaps there really was no other way out and he was just as nervous as she was about spending the night with the eels?

Or perhaps there was something else in the cave that worried the big man, something even more dangerous than the snake-like predators?

She realised that her mind was starting to run away with her now, but she couldn't help feeling that the cave still had more secrets to reveal. The weathergirl must have been thinking the same thing, as she piped up again with her annoyingly breathy voice.

"You know, if Kai's story about the Waka really is true, then perhaps there's also some truth to the other Māori legends as well?"

"What do you mean?" asked Rachael.

"Well we both heard him dismiss Kupe's story of the giant

octopus that destroyed his boat, and like-wise with the story of the Takitimu, he was quick to claim that no monster ever existed to wreck the great vessel."

Rachael realised what the weathergirl was getting at, and her already low opinion of the woman now sunk to new depths.

"I hope you're not suggesting what I think you are. That there really was some great sea monster, and it really did wreck this canoe? Next, you'll be saying that it's still out there now, hiding in this cave, waiting for its moment to strike."

Jenny laughed off the policewoman's rebuke, but Rachael could tell it was exactly what she'd been thinking.

But the eel attack to her leg had also affected her more than she'd realised, and she couldn't help but glance across the water to satisfy her curiosity. The cave was starting to play tricks with her mind and a movement at the centre of the lake sent a shiver down her spine.

"Kai, have you got a signal yet?" she shouted. "I really need to get Mrs. Sunley out of here."

"Yep," said Kai, "It's dialling now—but your battery's running low—they'll have to answer it pretty quick."

The phone connected and Rachael listened as Kai blurted out the story of their predicament, relaying instructions for how the rescue helicopter could find them.

On hearing it all explained, it was obvious really and Rachael wondered why nobody had ever discovered the cave before.

"Perhaps it's because of the lake?" whispered Jenny. "Perhaps it just looks like any other pool of water when viewed from above. Perhaps nobody ever thought that it could be sitting 30ft below a hole in the ground."

The weathergirl had beaten her to it and she couldn't think of a single reason why her supposition wouldn't be correct.

'...*Bitch.*'

"They're on their way," said Kai, as he tossed Rachael's phone back across the water. But before she could respond, he had already disappeared into the darkness, leaving her thanks hanging on her lips. He was like a wraith from the underworld and it was unnerving that he could see them, but she had no idea of where he was hiding.

Rachael looked at the phone's screen and noticed that the battery had just two percent of its charge remaining. If they needed to make a second call, they'd be lucky if it even managed to connect. Rachael turned off the phone, just to be safe.

"I suppose all we can do now is just sit and wait," said Jenny, as she sidled up next to the policewoman.

"Well, maybe not sit," Rachael replied. "There's still eels out there remember, even if there are no monsters… and there definitely are NO monsters."

Rachael studied the weathergirl again as she looked up at the ceiling. Moonlight was shining through the roof and its icy blue light sparkled on the woman's flawless skin.

She was beautiful, that was a given, but Rachael recognised

something else in the weathergirl now, something that was more than just her good looks. Several times now, she had taken control of the situation, when it should have been the policewoman leading the way. And although it pained her to admit it, Rachael now realised that she'd severely underestimated the woman. Jenny may not have been the sharpest tool in the box, but she was clearly resilient and didn't give up easily. It wasn't usually in Rachael's nature to apologise, but she coughed gently to get Jenny's attention, before offering a handshake as a sign of friendship.

"You know, we've never actually been introduced. I'm Detective Sargent Rachael Blunt… but please, call me Rachael."

"Yes, I know who you are," said Jenny. "We met at the bungy bridge, didn't we? Owen mentioned that you're investigating Jonno Hart's murder."

'So, he talked about me?' thought Rachael, *'I wonder what else he said?'*

"I suppose it must be weird for you…" she said. "You know… working with your father-in-law—and weird for Owen too I suppose?"

"Oh no," said Jenny. "Markus isn't Owen's father. I know they look very similar, but Owen hasn't seen his dad since he was a kid."

'Markus?' thought Rachael, before guessing that she meant the TV executive—the owner of the Volvo in the car park.

"No, not your boss," she continued. "I'm talking about your cameraman, Dave Norman—Owen's father."

Even in the poor light of the cave, Rachael could see the confusion on the weathergirl's face, but instead of doing the polite thing and enlightening her, she left the woman hanging, fishing for clarity. She had begrudgingly accepted a modicum of respect for the blonde, but she didn't have to like her, and it felt good to have ownership of something that should have been common knowledge for the woman.

"Oh no, you're wrong," stammered Jenny, incredulous at Rachael's suggestion. "Davey Boy isn't Owen's father… he couldn't possibly be… they're nothing alike."

But her look of quizzical confusion belied her confident rebuttal, and Rachael waited for the inevitable…

"…But they do have a similar nose, don't they?"

The policewoman couldn't help but smirk and the darkness of the cave did nothing to hide her giggle.

"Ah, it's a joke," said Jenny. "You're winding me up to lighten the mood, aren't you?"

'Incredible,' thought Rachael. The stupid cow really didn't get it, did she?

But Rachael's pleasure at getting one up on the blonde was quickly replaced by guilt for her bad behaviour and she suddenly felt the need to explain.

"I'm not joking," she said. "Your cameraman—Dave Norman—he really is Owen's father. I only learned it myself when I spoke to Scotty James."

"Scotty James? So that's why Owen wanted to get out of there so fast."

Rachael watched as the pieces started to fall into place and she wondered what other connections were finally being made behind those mascara caked eyelashes and precision plucked brows.

"Your cameraman…" Rachael blurted. "Did he ever mention anything about his work here in Queenstown?"

The weathergirl still seemed lost in thought about Rachael's revelation and she replied with a simple, "No, not really."

But Rachael knew from experience that 'Not really' often meant, 'Probably… but I wasn't paying attention.'

So, she pressed her again, hoping to tap into the blonde's beautiful, but mostly vacant head.

"So, Dave never talked about his relationship with Jonno Hart? He never mentioned whether he actually liked the man or not?"

"Oh yes," Jenny replied. "He did mention that Jonno was a bit of a diva… 'a demanding dick head', I think he called him. But in answer to your original question… no, he never talked about their work here in Queenstown, or anywhere else."

Jenny could feel the policewoman's hawk-like stare inspecting her for weaknesses. She'd been prepared to give the woman a chance, but she was proving herself to be just the sort of snotty-nosed bitch that she thought she'd left behind in England.

"Where the hell is that helicopter?" she mumbled, as Rachael paced impatiently beside her. If they were going to be stuck together in that cave all night, she was going to have to do something to make the policewoman relax, or at least shut up with her stupid jokes about Dave being Owen's father.

'Honestly,' she thought, she'd never heard of anything so ridiculous. She may have grown fond of the cameraman thanks to his appreciation for nice shoes and reggae music, but to suggest that he and Owen shared the same genes, well it was just ridiculous.

'...But they do have similar eyes?'

She stopped herself there—it was just too ludicrous to consider. The possibility that the drag queen cameraman, with his hideous Hawaiian shirts and decades-old cargo pants, could really be her father-in-law, it made her burst out laughing and her giggles echoed around the cave.

'Oh, now that's just great,' thought Rachael, as the weathergirl's laughter bounced off the walls. It was like the hideous cry of some Harpy queen and she winced at every note. The woman was clearly starting to lose it, and they had no idea how long it would be before the helicopter would arrive.

But before Rachael could do anything to silence the hysterical bimbo, something else caught her attention, a large splash of water at the other side of the lake. It was too far into the darkness to see, but its sound was quickly followed by a wave that travelled towards her at great speed, like a mini tsunami.

The ledge where Rachael and Jenny were standing was about a foot above the surface of the lake, but the wave was sizeable enough to breach its defences and the water came flooding over Rachael's feet.

Liquid fingers clung to Rachael's skin as the water first splashed up her legs and then receded down again. For a second it almost felt as if the lake was trying to draw her back in and the policewoman rubbed her legs frantically to shake off the feeling.

The weathergirl must have been equally surprised by the icy deluge as her laughing stopped suddenly and she began running up and down the ledge, trying to keep her feet dry.

Rachael half expected to hear the laughter switch once more to Kaihautu, still hiding somewhere in the darkness. But instead, he shouted from his hiding spot, with a panic in his voice that stopped the women in their tracks.

"Hey, where's that fucking helicopter? We need to get out of here now!"

Chapter 35

Kaihautu could feel his heart pounding in his chest, he knew that he had to calm its beat—before the beast could sense it. The two women had probably attributed the splash to a falling rock or rumblings caused by the earlier explosions. But Kai knew that it could be down to something else and he didn't want to find out if his suspicions were correct.

The water inside the cave may have seemed cold when splashed unexpectedly on the skin, but it was still a good two degrees warmer than the rivers outside and Kai knew that it was the perfect environment for creatures to grow big and strong. The eel that had attached itself to the policewoman's leg may have had some fight in it, but it was just a tiddler compared to the monsters that could still lie hidden in the darkness of the cave.

"Get away from the water!" Kai shouted. "We're getting out of here right now—even without that helicopter."

"I knew it!" shouted Rachael. "You've known another way to get out of here all along, haven't you?"

Kai was clearly a skilled manipulator and Rachael now realised that her initial suspicions of the man were probably correct. He was Jonno Hart's killer after all and Pippa was just mistaken about the fishing hook found on the celebrity's body.

Rachael realised that if the helicopter didn't arrive soon, Kai could easily plunge both her and the weathergirl to their deaths, and after the eels had had their fill, there would be no way to question his side of the story. She was normally unfazed by even the most challenging of situations, but with the upper hand so clearly in the Māori's favour, she had never been so scared in all her life.

But just as quickly as her fear had surfaced, it was suddenly replaced by relief, as a light from above pierced the darkness of the cavern. The rescue helicopter had arrived, and it was searching for its passengers. Reflecting first, off the surface of the lake and then dancing across the cave's gold streaked walls, the searchlight was like a light from heaven and Rachael was overwhelmed by its purity. Tears welled within her eyes and she struggled to hold them back as their rescuer dropped slowly through the hole in the roof.

"Thank fuck for that!" shouted Jenny, against the noise of the helicopter's rotors. Her candour was a vulgar counterpoint to the almost spiritual emotions that Rachael was feeling, but it seemed to strike a chord with the policewoman and she too let out a string of obscenities as her relief spilled over.

The two women embraced in a fit of giggles as the helicopter's winchman landed on the canoe and then signalled to his colleagues to indicate that he was safe. Standing on the prow of the great waka his face was illuminated by the helicopter's light and it was impossible to miss the look of disbelief as his eyes took in the spectacle beneath his feet.

He unclipped himself from the line and the helicopter lifted away, taking its roar with it.

"Ok ladies," he shouted. "Your carriage awaits."

Then he waved with a flourish, like a coachman welcoming royal guests.

The two women looked at each other with enormous grins, before realising that they had no idea of how to get across the lake.

"Kaihautu," shouted Rachael. "How do we get across? I know you didn't swim, and I doubt that you can walk on water."

"Over there," shouted Kai, pointing to a spot a few feet from where the women were standing. "There's a series of posts that lead straight towards the waka."

Rachael and Jenny headed to where Kai had pointed, but neither of them could see the posts that he had described. The policewoman pulled out her phone and switched it into torch mode, before shining its light at the water in front of them.

Revealed just below the surface of the lake, she could now make out a series of narrow wooden posts, all about five to six inches wide, and spaced roughly two feet apart.

"You should go first," said Rachael, handing her phone to the weathergirl. "You're a civilian and it's my duty to get you out of here safely."

"Are you sure?" Jenny replied, her foot already positioned above the water.

"Yes, you go first and then throw me the phone once you're over to the other side."

Jenny didn't need to be told twice and she quickly stepped onto the first post.

As she stepped down through the inch or so of water, circles radiated outwards across the lake, and from where he now stood at the side of the great waka, Kai held his breath as he watched the ripples like vibrations on a spider's web.

"Get a move on!" he shouted, as the weathergirl scanned the water for the next post. She'd made a confident start, but she already seemed to have lost her sense of direction.

"Not that way!" yelled the Māori in frustration. "Look straight towards me, the posts are positioned one and a half tuke apart."

Jenny looked up at Kai blankly.

"What the fuck's a tuke?" she shouted. "Can't you just tell me how far it is in metres, or better still in feet and inches?"

She was balancing on one foot and the light from the phone torch moved wildly across the lake.

"It's the distance from your elbow to your fingertip," yelled Kai. "But you've got little arms haven't ya, so it's gonna be more like two or three lengths instead.

Jenny steadied herself on the post and inspected the length of her forearm before guesstimating how long two lengths would be.

Then she pointed the torchlight out towards Kai and sure enough, just where he said it would be, she found the next post and the one after it too.

She wasn't keen to hang around any longer and she hopped to the next post, sending more ripples spreading outwards as she moved.

She quickly spotted the next posts in the chain and stepped deftly from one to the next, thankful that her early years as a gymnast were still paying dividends.

She was only six feet now from the island at the centre of the lake and she could feel the helicopter's downdraft as it hovered above.

"Only one more to go," shouted Kai, now standing at the water's edge.

'That can't be right?' thought the weathergirl as she searched out the next post in the causeway. "What do you mean?" she shouted. "I'm still at least six tuke lengths from the edge."

"Oh yeah, I forgot to mention, didn't I? Some of the posts rotted away, so you'll have to jump the next one."

"Well, that's just fucking brilliant!" Jenny screamed as she wiped the matted hair from her face.

She waved the torched wildly, searching desperately for the final stepping post. But she was now experiencing the full force of the helicopter's downdraft and the surface of the water was like frosted glass under its blast.

"It's just there," Kai yelled, pointing to a spot somewhere between Jenny's right foot and the safety of the island.

But she still couldn't see the post and she began to teeter on the six inches of wood that currently supported her weight.

"I can't see it!" she screamed, as hair whipped once more across her face.

She was wobbling wildly now on her tiny wooden island and she struggled to steady herself under the barrage of dust and water being blown down from above.

Behind her, still waiting for her turn to cross, Rachael could see that the weathergirl was in trouble and she shouted out encouragement to will her safely across.

"You know somebody once told me that the obstacles of the weak are the stepping-stones of the brave. You can do this Jenny, it's just one more post and it's exactly where Kai says it is. Just follow the line of his finger and then jump. You can do it Jenny—you know you can."

It was the most supportive thing that Rachael had ever said to anyone and more than ever before, she prayed that she was right.

"The obstacles of the weak"—whispered Jenny—"are the stepping-stones of the brave." She'd also heard that saying before and she knew that a certain dam engineer was the source of the policewoman's words of encouragement.

She repeated the saying once more in her head and she pictured Owen waiting for her at the edge of the lake. She'd already come further than she'd ever thought possible, but seeing him standing there, was the boost that she needed to take the final leap.

She looked down once more at the spot that Kai had pointed to and she still couldn't see the post. But with Owen's saying still ringing in her ears, she stepped forward into the unknown.

Plunging her foot through the froth, the weathergirl held her breath as her toes dropped out of sight. For a split second, she was convinced that she'd placed her aim incorrectly, but it was too late to pull back now and with her balance firmly committed to moving forward, she pushed with her back foot to seal the deal.

It was the extra momentum that she had needed and to her enormous relief the rubber beneath her toes suddenly gained purchase on something solid—she had found the final post.

Using her forward momentum, she made the final leap into Owen's waiting arms and she grasped him tightly to stop herself from falling backwards.

"Thank fuck for that!" she said as she looked up into her husband's eyes, but it wasn't Owen of course and the weathergirl's smile quickly turned to embarrassment as her hands smoothed their way down Kaihautu's enormous biceps.

Too embarrassed to say anything, Jenny quickly averted her eyes and she looked to the helicopter winchman, who was waiting to lift her out of there.

She walked to the front end of the waka and looked up at its intricately carved prow. Rising some six or seven feet into the air, the carved wooden figurehead was covered with dozens of spiral shapes, each of varying size, and all linked to a central stem that arched upwards towards its tip.

Sparkling green with an infusion of minerals, the beautiful carved lines reminded Jenny of New Zealand's famous 'silver fern', the emblem of the 'All Blacks' rugby team. But as her fingers stroked the surface of the waka, she quickly realised that this design was not intended to be beautiful. Instead, it was designed to incite fear in all those who saw it, for the spirals were not the fronds of a delicate fern, they were tiny eels, all connected to a giant mother beast, with dagger-sharp teeth, that curved inwards like a raptor's claws.

Jenny withdrew her hand, flinching away from the beast and its minions.

"It's alright," shouted Kai, over the roar of the helicopter. "I'll lift you up, so you don't damage anything beautiful."

"Ah, thank you," Jenny replied, feeling her face flush red at the Māori's compliment.

"I meant the waka," said Kai, bending down to lift her.

"Er yes, yes I know," Jenny stammered, as the man-mountain hoisted her onto his shoulder.

Still blushing with embarrassment, Jenny stepped onto the waka and immediately slipped on its shiny surface. Reaching out for the first thing that came to hand, she grabbed it hard and used it to pull herself back up. But hearing a loud gasp above the noise of the helicopter, she looked up to see the helicopter winchman, his face grimacing in pain. She'd gripped the strap that ran across the man's chest and with it a handful of his chest hair.

The weathergirl hastily withdrew her hand and then gently patted an apology on the man's chest. It was the same winchman that had rescued her only 24 hours earlier at the Homer Tunnel and Jenny's face flushed redder than ever as he strapped her into a harness.

When he'd fastened the last clip, he signalled up to the helicopter and feeling the waka disappear from beneath her feet, Jenny leaned in to kiss the man on the cheek.

"Thank you," she mouthed, as he stared at her like a rabbit caught in headlights. But Jenny didn't need him to respond, she was just grateful to be alive, and now all that she wanted was to see her husband.

Chapter 36

Rachael looked on as the weathergirl and the winchman lifted off from the giant canoe; she was relieved that she hadn't failed in her duty to protect the civilian.

As they lifted into the air, Rachael watched as a beam of light shone out from between them. Suspended in the darkness of the cave and with the helicopter's light shining from above, it looked like a spirit rising-up towards heaven and the atheist detective suddenly felt a rush of emotion that was overwhelming.

She had never believed in any sort of higher power or otherworldly beings, but in that moment, she found herself questioning whether they were being saved by rescuers in a helicopter, or by guardian angels who had more than just luck on their side…

…but then reality kicked in.

"The torch!" Rachael screamed. The light between the two people was the torchlight from her phone—and she needed it back.

"The torch Jenny, throw me the torch!"

But it was too late, they were already through the hole in the roof and on their way to safety.

The stupid cow had forgotten to do the one thing that the policewoman had asked of her, and now she had no way to find the wooden posts that lay hidden just inches below the surface of the lake.

"Fuuuuccckk!" Rachael screamed, as the severity of her situation hit home. She was going to have to make her way blind, or worse still, jump into the water and hope that she could out-swim the eels.

She stood at the edge of the lake and peered down into the water, desperately trying to make out the causeway that had carried the weathergirl across. She could see the first and second posts as they were only a few feet away, but after that there was nothing and she couldn't even distinguish the line at which air stopped and the water started.

She was going to have to swim for it and she took a few steps backwards, so she could build up momentum for a longer jump.

Pressing her back into the sharp rocks behind her, Rachael looked around the cave once more. The golden veins that lined its walls seemed to have come alive under the helicopter's light, but they also seemed to be closing in now, like the stomach of a beast keen to finish its prey.

Remembering the eel that had latched onto her leg only hours earlier, the policewoman couldn't bring herself to move and she stood like a statue, frozen to the spot. But unlike the giant waka in front of her, she was encased in fear, not minerals, and even the sharp rocks at her back did not make her flinch.

Sensing that something was wrong, Kai hopped swiftly across the lake. He'd walked across the causeway almost every day for the past 30 years and his practiced steps made easy work of the gaps.

"Come on copper, you can do this," he said, as he grabbed the policewoman by the arm.

But she didn't respond and instead she backed even harder into the rocks.

Kaihautu was getting desperate now and he shook the woman in frustration. She had locked herself away in a prison of fear and he needed to snap her out of it. Meanwhile, the winchman had returned, and Kai realised that he now had no choice but to carry the policewoman across.

Scooping her up, he slung the woman over his shoulder and then made his way back over the water. His journey was more difficult this time thanks to the extra weight, but once safely across he dumped the policewoman on the floor.

"Get up copper," he said, kicking the woman with his sodden boots. "Your rescuer's waiting for you, and if you don't move fast, I might just take your place."

"Rescuer?" she replied in a daze.

The woman was clearly not with it, so Kai lifted her once more on to his shoulder.

"So much for civilians first," he mumbled, as he handed her to the winchman. But in truth, he was glad that the woman was safe, and she'd made it across the water unharmed.

Kaihautu watched as the two passengers lifted into the air and he knew that his moment to escape was now or never. The policewoman would soon regain her senses and she'd probably radio ahead to make sure that officers were waiting to arrest him.

His sabotage of the explosive devices had to be the cause of the tunnel collapse and if the dam engineer had indeed been crushed as the policewoman suspected, he'd no doubt be tried and found guilty of manslaughter. It was a justice that he knew he deserved, but at the same time the thought of losing his son Nīoreore was just too much to bear.

Kaihautu looked around the cavern. For nearly 30 years he'd protected the cave from the outside world and now he needed its help. He needed an escape route from the mess that he'd created, and a way to evade the fate that awaited him if he lingered too long.

He knew that there must be another way out—one that didn't require a helicopter's winch— but in 30 years he'd never found it. The eels had to find their way in somehow, but they could never have made it through the thick scrubland that fronted the cave's tunnel entrance. There had to be another way in, but one that also allowed water to flow back out into the valley below.

Kai cursed himself for his lack of knowledge and for not fully exploring the cave when time had been a luxury. But he also considered how much time he'd have on his hands once he was locked up in prison for a murder that he did not commit. He knew every twist and turn of the rivers and valleys for nearly 50 miles in all directions and if he could only find his way out of the cave, he was sure that he could stay one step ahead of the police.

He'd been paid to kill the fishing celebrity—and his cameraman too if required. And in truth, he probably would have done it for a lot less money, if he'd had to sit and listen to them for much longer. Jonno Hart had been a pig of a man and although he clearly loved to fish, his skills were mediocre at best. The useless prick was so full of self-importance and bile towards others, that every day, Kai had wondered if he might wake up to find that somebody else had killed him first.

But for all the man's failings, he was still a man and Kai's heart pounded in his chest as he remembered the moment that he'd pulled his hand away, instead of pushing forward to send the man to his death.

His plan had been to drown the celebrity in one of the holding ponds that fronted the dam, and with its vertical walls rising nearly 12 feet above the surface of the water, the fishing celebrity would have had no means of escape. His colleague would have tried to save him of course, but even with Jonno's fishing rod to aid him, the ageing cameraman would have struggled to reach the vile bastard.

Kai laughed at the memory of Jonno's ridiculous selection of kit. He had fished for ōrea like he was hunting great white sharks and although it was clearly to make the eels seem more dangerous for the camera, his heavy rod & reel had made it impossible to react quickly if he ever got a bite.

If only he'd taken the Māori's advice to fish in the old way, with wool to hook the eels' serrated teeth, he would have at least caught something in his final few hours. But instead, he died, in the fog of ego and the whiskey that he'd used to drown his sorrows.

Kaihautu had seen it all from the shadows, high up on the walls that rose above the iron bridge. But instead of acting to stop the murder, he'd stayed silent, watching as Jonno's killer finished the job that he'd been paid to do.

Kai looked down at the swirling black water just inches from his feet. If he jumped in now, the eels would take him and serve the punishment that he sorely deserved. He should have stopped Jonno's murder, or at least have had the decency to kill himself for letting it happen.

His foot hovered above the surface of the lake, held fast like a needle caught in the pull of a magnet. But instead of pointing true and in the direction of freedom, it was pointing downwards to the underworld and the goddess Hine-nui-te-pō, who was waiting to eat his soul.

But before Kai could enact his suicide, an angel from above came to his reprieve. The winchman had returned and was beckoning him to climb the waka's great prow. Kai looked down again at the water, he wasn't ready to go just yet—at least not to the underworld. His boy needed him and though he had to face justice for sabotaging the explosives, he knew that he had to clear his name over the death of Jonno Hart.

He quickly made his way up the side of the waka, reaching behind one of the planks as he did so, to retrieve the real treasure of the cave. And when he was standing on top of the canoe, he stretched out his arms and waited patiently as the winchman strapped him into a harness. The man loosened the bottom webbing as far as it would go, but it still only just made it over the Māori's enormous thighs. The chest strap, however, was stuck fast and wouldn't loosen up, and the winchman tugged at it in frustration. "It's alright," shouted Kai. "I'll be alright—I'll just hold tight to the cable."

The winchman nodded in agreement before signalling up to the helicopter and then for the first time in Kai's life, his feet left New Zealand soil as he lifted skywards towards redemption.

'Thank goodness for that,' thought Rachael, as the two men appeared from the darkness. Almost as soon as her feet had left the ground she'd come to her senses and realised her mistake. She'd left her prime suspect behind, with the perfect opportunity to escape. She was convinced that Kai had known of another way out all along, but she had no idea where his secret escape route would have taken him.

She looked out through the window and watched as the cable lifted the two men up from the cave below. They were being buffeted by the downforce of the helicopter's blades and a spiral of red dust whipped around them, surrounding them like a blood-shot eye. Rachael found herself willing them on to safety and she flinched as a large boulder tumbled down the mountainside towards them.

Suddenly the helicopter lurched sideways, and the policewoman's head was thrown against the glass of the window.

"What the hell?" she said, before looking to the cockpit to see what was going on.

All manner of lights and switches were flashing on the console and the helicopter pilot appeared to be struggling to maintain his position.

"What's going on?" screamed the weathergirl's voice over the intercom.

"It's the mountain," replied the captain. "I think there's an earthquake—we've got to get out of here fast."

Rachael looked out of the window. The two men were still hanging below but they were swinging wildly on the helicopter's cable. The winchman appeared to be ok, but Kaihautu was dangling upside down from his harness. The policewoman's heart leapt into her mouth as she saw the Māori starting to slip.

"You need to speed up the winch," she shouted into her microphone. "He's going to fall!"

"It's going as fast it can," responded the captain. "But I might have to lift out of here if any more rocks fall from above."

Suddenly a vibration shook the air around the helicopter and even above the noise of the rotors, Rachael could hear its dark, ominous bellow. The mountain was angry, and it didn't like the mosquito that was buzzing it flanks. Rachael watched helplessly as boulders tumbled down towards the men, before plummeting into the darkness of the cave.

Out of the corner of her eye, she spotted a boulder, sliding towards the two men. The rock was about the size of a car and it was starting to gather speed on a sled of gravel.

"Fly higher!" she screamed. "Another boulder's coming down—it's going to hit them."

But before the helicopter pilot could react, a human-shaped blur dropped from the cable and into the cave below.

She didn't see a splash, but Rachael was convinced that the Māori had dropped on purpose. She peered down into the darkness, hoping to see him surface. But her attempts to spot him were quickly thwarted, as the car-sized boulder tumbled down the slope and plugged the hole that Kaihautu had just fallen through.

"Shit!" Rachael screamed as she pulled off her headset in frustration. The Māori was gone, and if by some miracle he had survived the fall, he would soon find his escape route and disappear into the mountains.

The helicopter lifted sharply away from the falling debris and once safely above the mountain, the winchman finally made it back inside the cabin.

"I couldn't save him," he said; clearly distraught.

"It's ok," said Jenny, leaning forward to comfort the man. "There was nothing you could do."

But Rachael stayed silent. She knew that Kaihautu had fallen on purpose and she would chase the length of the Southern Alps to find him and bring him to justice.

Chapter 37

Kaihautu saw the darkness approaching and drawing on his years of rugby training he pulled himself into a ball, to minimise the pain that would surely be coming is way.

Cradling the object against his chest, he held tight as the first blow hit his side, followed quickly after by the stinging slap of water as he hit the surface of the lake. He'd never been a strong swimmer and he panicked as the water enveloped him in its icy cloak.

He'd hit the prow of the great waka and the pain that exploded in his side told him that he'd broken more than just a couple of ribs. Gasping for air and with only one arm free to paddle, he struggled to stay at the surface of the water. Looking up at the roof he could see the light of the helicopter, but it was blocked by the boulder that had lodged above him and it looked like an eclipse of the sun,

Kai looked around in desperation, he could just about make out the shape of the waka, but it seemed to be drifting away—like a dream that was no longer his.

"You've failed Kaihautu," sang a chorus of voices from the darkness. "You couldn't keep the secret and now even your son will forget you. The lies of the Pākehā will bleach his mind and they'll wipe out any memory of you and your kind."

Kai knew exactly what the voices were talking about and it hurt even more than the pain in his side. The Eel That Slept, was no longer his to protect and if the policewoman got her way, his son Nīoreore, would soon be lost to him too. The boy's identity would be white-washed, far away inside the walls of some Auckland youth prison, far from the river valleys that were the lifeblood of his hapū, his family.

"Leave me alone!" Kai shouted into the darkness, but his words simply bounced back at him in an ever-decreasing echo.

Then the voices came again and this time their song enveloped Kai like a net, pulling him below the surface of the water in a web of dissonant chords.

"Let go, Kai," sang the voices. "Give us your soul and we'll make it strong again, we forgive you, Kai, what's done is done."

Kaihautu looked around—he was surrounded by eels. Their bodies were black and insidious, and their eyes glowed green like Pounamu jade.

The eels' offer was as tempting as it was terrifying, but before Kaihautu could respond they scattered in all directions, leaving him alone in the darkness.

Suddenly in the distance, a giant swam out of the murk and its enormous tail swept from side to side as it approached the Māori. It was like a tiger of the deep, pacing in circles as it evaluated its prey and Kai closed his as he waited for his doom.

"You know me don't you Kaihautu?" said the great eel "I am the first, I am the last, and I am all."

Kai knew exactly who the eel was—and he was afraid. For it was Te Tunaroa, the one who had dared to defy Maui, the demi-god who had finally stuck him down with Ma-Tori-Tori, his great axe. It was said, that Maui had severed the eel god's body into pieces, which had then become all the eels of the world, but here he was, rejuvenated and whole—the most terrifying thing that Kai had ever seen.

"You know, I took your wife Kai... before she died," said Tuna. "She loved it, Kai, she wanted more—almost more than I could give."

The great eel's head moved slowly from side to side as it spoke and its eyes sparkled hypnotically.

"She drained me Kai. She was like an animal, basic and feral, and I gave her what she wanted Kai—I gave her everything that you could not."

Kaihautu knew of course that the eel was toying with him, but he was still enraged at its insinuation. He had been injured during a rugby match when he was a teenager and the doctors had said that he would probably never father children. So, it had been a joyous day when his wife had woken him with kisses and news that she was pregnant. But she had died during childbirth, never seeing the miracle son, the one who would be the last of the Waitaha bloodline.

Kaihautu was afraid, he realised that he was no match for Tuna, and if the eel god wanted to kill him, he could do it in a heartbeat. But at the same time, he knew that he deserved everything that he got. And even death at the hands of the eel was still better than the alternative that awaited him.

"Take me," he said to the eel. "Take my soul, before it sinks to the underworld".

"I don't want your soul," spat Tuna. "It's dirty and not worthy of my lips. I'll not sully my taste buds with the blood of a coward. The man who could not protect his son, the man who could not protect the secret of his ancestors."

Tuna flicked his great tail once more and it struck Kai in the ribs, sending shockwaves throughout his body.

"Go away Kaihautu Waitaha, I will see you again when you are worthy to challenge me. Only then will I take your soul, before feasting on your baby eel."

It was a clear threat to the boy Nīoreore and Kai realised that if he was gone, the threat to his son was now far worse than some state-run children's home.

He was about to respond and beg for the boy's safety, but Tuna was already gone and only the shadow of his evil remained. Kaihautu looked about to see if the eel god had tricked him somehow and was about to strike from behind. But there was only blackness and cold that was spreading from the shattered bones in his chest. Kai closed his eyes to fight against the pain, and he clung to the object that he'd rescued from the waka. He could hear the sound of his heartbeat, slowing to a stop. It was like a clock winding down and the world around him seemed to be spinning in reverse.

Then suddenly, just as the clock was about to strike its final chime, the Māori felt himself being lifted upwards and he realised that he was being dragged by the back of his shirt.

For a brief moment, he felt air on his lips and wind on his cheeks, but then he was dropped, and a foot pressed down on the back of his head.

"Bet ya didn't think you'd see me again," said a voice, as the foot ground Kai's face into the rocks.

Kaihautu recognised that voice and his heart sank at the sound of Jonno Hart's killer.

The foot lifted from Kai's head and he lifted his face out of the gravel, keeping his eyes shut to stop any sand getting in. There were small stones stuck to the inside of his lips and he turned to spit them out. After blowing the stones from his mouth, he opened his eyes to the orange glow that he could see through his eyelids. It was daybreak and the morning sun was rising over the hills. He was outside of the mountain—his life had been spared.

'The other way out?' thought Kai, he must have been sucked down through the eels' secret tunnel—although it felt more like he'd been spat out in disgust.

The sunrise in front of him was beautiful, but Kai's attention was drawn to something white, laying just a few yards away—it was a body.

'Fuck', he thought. *'Not you. You didn't deserve this.'*

Kai slumped back down onto the gravel, he felt sick.

Lying face down in front of him was the dam engineer, the weathergirl's husband. His clothes were wet, and his body lay motionless between two large boulders. He must have made it out of the tunnel before it had collapsed, and then fallen into the lake.

Kaihautu rolled over onto his back and looked up at Jonno's killer. He had escaped Te Tunaroa and his minions, but now the goddess Hine-nui-te-pō had sent her black devil instead to collect his soul.

"You fucked up good and proper this time didn't ya Kai. You couldn't kill the fisherman, but you managed to kill this fella instead—and all with just the snip of a few wires."

Kaihautu closed his eyes, he could feel the light of the morning sun warming his body.

'Oh, great Tama-nui-te-rā, take me away from all this' he prayed, but the sun god did not answer him and a kick to his ribs brought his eyes open again as he gasped in pain.

"I'm gonna give you one last chance Kai—and I think you should take it."

Kaihautu looked up at the figure looming over him. Any other day, he could have taken the bastard without even breaking a sweat, but today he was not the man he used to be—he was broken.

"What do you want from me?" he said, through gritted teeth.

"I want you to run," said the killer. "I want you to run and never look back."

The pain in Kaihautu's side was unbearable and he wasn't sure that he could even stand, let alone run.

"You're a good man Kai and it's obvious that you love your boy, so I'm gonna give you the chance to be with him before the cops take him away for good."

The thought of losing Nīoreore was like a dagger to Kaihautu's heart and even with the object still clutched against his chest to protect him, it pierced deep and raw.

"You killed a man," said the killer. "And although you didn't mean to do it, that makes you as guilty as me. You're a wanted man now Kai, but you've still got a chance—a chance to be with your son."

Kaihautu closed his eyes once more, hoping that when he opened them things would somehow be different.

Finally, the Māori breathed deep and opened his eyes. The killer was gone, and he was left with just the engineer's lifeless body for company.

Chapter 38

Jenny watched helplessly as the water level continued to rise behind the dam. The helicopter had been circling for nearly an hour and during that time they'd seen numerous landslides into the lake. The explosions triggered by Kaihautu's meddling were continuing to wreak havoc throughout the valley, and now the water inside the mountain was flowing out much faster than usual.

Thanks to Owen's team, the rise in the water level wouldn't normally have been a problem, but she'd heard over the radio that the dam's overflow systems were malfunctioning, and the emergency gates were stuck.

"I'm sorry ladies, but I'm gonna have to call things off soon," said the captain. "We've still gotta make it back to town and we're nearly out of fuel."

Rachael nodded in agreement, but Jenny could tell that she was pissed off. The policewoman seemed convinced that Kaihautu was Jonno Hart's killer and every now and then she could hear the woman cursing herself for letting the man escape.

"Captain, is there any word yet on my husband?" Jenny asked. "Have they sent a rescue team to find him?"

Although Rachael had assured her that Owen was ok, the weathergirl was still desperate to know that he'd made it safely out of the tunnel.

"No word yet, I'm afraid," said the captain. "They're doing their best though Miss Sunley, I promise."

Jenny peered down at the world below. The long shadows of the morning sunrise were beginning to shorten, and features of the rocky landscape were beginning to emerge from the darkness.

"Over there," she screamed suddenly. "It's him, it's Owen!"

Close to the northern edge of the lake and bobbing up and down on the surface of water, a white blob was dangerously close to being washed over the dam. Jenny had instantly recognised it as Owen in his white shirt and she grabbed the pilot's shoulder in panic.

"You've got to save him," she screamed. "He's gonna wash over the dam!"

The helicopter swerved in response as the pilot corrected his flight path and he urged the weathergirl to sit back down in her seat.

"Don't worry Miss Sunley, I'm on it. Just sit back down and we'll have him safe in no time."

In seconds they were directly over Owen's white shirt and the winchman launched himself through the door to retrieve him.

Jenny watched as Owen's rescuer landed with a splash and then proceeded to strap the dam engineer into a harness.

"He's alive," said the winchman over the radio. "But he's not looking good, he must have been in the water for some time."

"He's alive," Jenny repeated, as a wave of emotion flooded through her body. She'd only been married to Owen for a few months, yet the love she felt for him was like nothing she'd ever felt before.

Finally, the winchman appeared at the open door and he heaved the stricken dam engineer on board.

Jenny rushed to his side and as the medics swung into action with oxygen and thermal blankets, she cradled Owen's head in her lap.

"Don't you die on me Owen Penny," she whispered as she wiped the hair from his face. "Don't you die on me, you hear."

For a split second, she saw a movement on Owen's lips, but then a long beeping noise sounded, and the medics pushed her out of the way.

The rest of the night was a blur as the helicopter flew them back to Queenstown and at the hospital, Owen was whisked away by a team of doctors.

Jenny tried to keep up with them as they sped down the maze of corridors, but suddenly everything went black and when she awoke, she was lying on a hospital bed with a familiar aftershave wafting from the chair beside her.

"Gidday gorgeous," said a man's voice. "How ya feelin' love?"

It was her cameraman Dave, and he offered her a cherry from the bowl that he cradled in his lap.

"What's the matter?" he said. "Don't ya wanna pop my cherry?"

Jenny had barely opened her eyes and he was already being his usual inappropriate self.

24 hours earlier the weathergirl had started to find him quite endearing, but with Owen's health already on her mind, she simply got down from the bed and walked out of the room. The cameraman was left staring after her, and he quickly put down the bowl before running to catch up. His arm was in a sling, and he yelped in pain when the weathergirl stopped abruptly in front of him.

"I need to find Owen," she said. "I need to find out where they've taken him."

"Owen?"—the cameraman looked confused.

"Yes, Owen... my Owen... I mean your Owen... our Owen—we need to find him."

"Let me get this straight," said Dave. "Your husband, his name's Owen—and he's my son—my boy?"

"That's right," Jenny replied. "He was in the water and the helicopter rescued him—I need to know if he's ok."

The cameraman looked stunned, as if his brain couldn't process the information that it was being fed.

"My Owen," he said. "My Owen, he's here? He's here in this hospital?"

"YES!" shouted Jenny. "Now, are you gonna help me find him, or what?"

The cameraman beamed and grabbed the weathergirl by the shoulders.

"Just try and stop me," he said.

Chapter 39

Rachael and Liam quietly entered the room and the policewoman could tell that her boyfriend was shaken. One of his best friends was lying in a coma and there was nothing he could do about it. She'd seen Liam upset before, but it still seemed strange to see him looking so vulnerable.

"He's gonna be ok," she assured him. "It's a medically induced coma, they can pull him out of it anytime."

The dam engineer had been in the water for several hours and Rachael knew that he wouldn't be well again for some time, but she kept quiet about the other information that the doctor had given her before Liam arrived. Owen had suffered a severe blow to the head and only time would tell if he would make a full recovery. Rachael knew that it was the doctor's code for 'possible brain damage', and it was devastating to think that such an intelligent man could be left without the full use of his thought processes.

"I'm just gonna go get some air," she said, as the emotions of the past 24 hours caught up with her. Seeing Liam cry may have been a rare occurrence, but she'd never let herself slip in front of him and she made for the door before he could see her tears.

Outside in the corridor, the policewoman slumped down against the wall, she was struggling to catch her breath. Rachael hadn't cried since she was a young girl and even now she could hear her father's words, telling her to pull herself together. But everything seemed different now, changed somehow, and the world no longer made sense. The walls that she had built up and maintained for so many years seemed pointless now and they suddenly come crashing down as she began to cry.

Unfettered and unleashed, Rachael's tears flowed uncontrollably. It was no surprise that she failed to see Jenny as she sprinted along the corridor towards her.

"What's wrong?" screamed the weathergirl. "It's Owen isn't it—something's happened?"

The policewoman looked up and was about to respond but the blonde was already halfway through the door.

Rachael looked back down at the floor, waiting for the weathergirl's inevitable wailing as she was confronted by the sight of her stricken husband. But instead, the door opened again, and she looked up to see a man entering the room. His arm was in a sling and he groaned as he pushed against the door.

"Excuse me," said Rachael. "It's just friends and family for now."

The man stopped and looked back through the doorway.

"It's alright love—you don't need to worry—I'm his dad."

'His dad?'

Rachael jumped up from the floor. It was Dave Norman—Jonno Hart's cameraman.

She rushed back into the room.

Owen's father was already at the engineer's bedside and it was obvious that he was in bits.

Rachael was desperate to question the cameraman, but she realised now was not the right time and she was grateful when Liam spoke instead.

"Shit mate, what happened to you huh? First, you whine over a little sprained ankle and now you decide to go swimming in a freezing cold lake, you must have a death wish or something."

The dam engineer did not respond, but the weathergirl flashed a smile instead, showing gratitude for Liam being there.

"Don't worry," said Rachael. "He's in safe hands now—he's gonna be ok."

Jenny looked exhausted and even though it was out of character for the policewoman to show compassion, she was beginning to reassess her first impressions of the woman.

"Jenny, you look tired, why don't you sit down, and I'll go get us all some coffee."

The weathergirl nodded and Rachael did a quick check of what everybody wanted before leaving the room. As the door closed behind her, she looked up and down the corridor for a vending machine, but there was none to be seen. She suddenly remembered the unusual coffee making facilities that Bob James had constructed in his lab and she turned towards the lift.

She hadn't spoken to Bob's assistant since hearing of the

pathologist's death, so it seemed like a good excuse to go and see Pippa, to express her condolences.

When the lift doors opened at the basement level, Rachael stepped out into the corridor and quietly entered through the pathology lab's yellow doors. She was hoping not to find a body lying on the slab, but she was out of luck and as her eyes focused on the bloated corpse laid in front of her, she suddenly realised that it was Bob James, the deceased pathologist.

Lit up by the table's harsh inspection lamps the doctor's flesh glowed white and Rachael felt sick at the sight of his bloated stomach. It had been less than 48 hours since the doctor's death, so the breakdown of his internal organs couldn't possibly have been the cause of the swelling; Rachael was confused.

Bob James had been overweight but not obese, so ether his white lab coat had done a very good job of hiding his weight, or something else had created the swelling.

The policewoman approached the table and she gagged at what she saw.

The doctor's torso had been opened up and then professionally stitched closed again. There were strange bulges under his skin, and it looked like something had been placed inside his stomach.

She leaned in close to study the odd-looking shapes, all the while, fighting down her urge to vomit.

"What are you?" she whispered, as she inspected the doctor's torso.

"I'm sorry?" came a reply, from the adjoining room.

It was Pippa, the junior pathologist, and she walked into the lab carrying a beaker of hot coffee. She was wearing a black rugby tracksuit instead of her usual lab coat and she looked like she'd been awake for most of the night.

"Oh, you're here," said Rachael. "I was just wondering what the swelling was inside the doctor's stomach, that's all. Oh—and I'm sorry by the way—it must have been a hell of a shock."

"Not really," said Pippa. "He was overweight, and he drank too much, it was just a matter of time really—he was well overdue a heart attack or a stroke."

"And what was it in the end?"

"Oh, erm, a heart attack I think."

The girl seemed nervous, unsure of her assessment, but that was understandable considering the pressure she must have been under.

"So, what's with the bulges?" Rachael asked, pointing towards the doctor's swollen midriff.

"Oh erm, that's just my poor packing I'm afraid. There's nearly a mile of intestines in there and I struggled to get them back in."

The girl looked embarrassed and Rachael gave a reassuring shrug to show that she understood.

Pippa was clearly struggling to cope with the doctor's death and the policewoman reached out a hand to console her. But as she did so a movement on the slab caught her eye and she looked down at the doctor's corpse. The bulges in his stomach were moving and Pippa's neat stitches suddenly burst open.

Back upstairs, Owen's three remaining guests sat in awkward silence, each not knowing what to say.

"Maybe I should go give her a hand?" said Liam, poking his head through the door.

He popped his head back inside and flashed a smile, before heading off to find his girlfriend. He was a nice bloke, thought Jenny, but they seemed like an odd match. The policewoman was cold and aloof, but in the brief time she'd spent with Liam both at the cafe in Te Anau and now there at the hospital, he seemed warm and eager to please. He was clearly one of Owen's closest friends and she trusted her husband's judgement of the man.

It was odd though that Owen had never mentioned him, but then again, Owen never really talked about anything to do with his old life—before his move to England with his mother.

Jenny, looked over at Dave, cradling his son's hand in his own. They looked nothing alike, but she could see where Owen got his caring nature. Why had he never talked about the cameraman before? The man was no ogre, and with his secret revealed during their trip down south, he was clearly no womaniser either—but perhaps that was the problem?

On the night of their engagement, Owen had mentioned that he wouldn't be inviting his dad to the wedding. Apparently, he'd left his mum for another woman and she'd never forgiven him— perhaps that woman was Lady Gloria, the cameraman's stage persona?

Jenny watched as the disowned father gently stroked the hair of the boy that he'd never stopped loving, and she suddenly broke down in tears at the beauty of it all.

Down in the basement lab, Rachael jumped back in fear as a wide and slimy head burst out from the pathologist's abdomen. The creature's soulless black eyes seemed to lock onto her own as if sizing her up for its next meal.

"What the fuck?" screamed the policewoman, as she looked to Pippa for answers.

But the girl had disappeared, and Rachael scanned the room to find her. What the hell was going on, she thought. But before she had her answer, a hand grasped her from behind and something pricked the side of her neck.

The policewoman fought desperately to free herself as a second hand reached around her body, but just like a snake that constricts its prey, her attacker's grip tightened with every breath she took, and she quickly felt the world turning black. She was scared and confused, and she screamed inside her head, hoping that somebody would come to save her—but nobody came. And the last thing that she heard was the voice of Jonno Hart's killer…

"I'm sorry, but you've seen too much."

Chapter 40

Jenny blew her nose and silently thanked Dave for the tissue. She'd barely stopped crying since Liam had gone to help with the drinks and she was gagging for the promised cup of tea.

They sat in silence for a while, each holding one of Owen's hands, before the cameraman finally broke the silence.

"Where the hell's she gone for that tea?" he said, apparently just as parched as the weathergirl.

"It's alright," said Jenny. "She's had a rough night as well you know, give her some slack."

She hadn't intended for it to sound like a telling off, but it seemed to have that effect and the cameraman retreated into silence once more.

Jenny desperately wanted to ask him about his relationship with her husband, but somehow the words just wouldn't come out.

Instead, it felt easier to mention Jonno Hart, and she expressed her condolences for the cameraman's loss.

"You know, I was really sorry to hear about Jonno Hart—it must have come as a shock when you woke up huh?"

"Jonno?" said Dave. "What's wrong with Jonno?"

Suddenly a beeping sound interrupted their conversation and the weathergirl jumped up from her seat.

"What's that?" she screamed, "Is it Owen, is he ok?"

The cameraman inspected the machines that were keeping his son alive and he shook his head.

"It's definitely not Owen, everything seems to be working just fine."

"Then what is it?" Jenny asked. "What's making that noise?"

And then she saw it.

The policewoman had left her radio behind and somebody was trying to call her. Jenny picked it up and pressed the button.

"Hello," she said. "This is Jenny Sunley speaking. If you're looking for DS Blunt, she'll be back in a minute I think—she's gone to find coffee and some tea."

"Yeah, via India," chirped Dave sarcastically.

The weathergirl scowled at the cameraman.

"Is that you Davey Boy?" said a voice on the radio. "Long time no see mate, it's me, Tony."

"Ah Tony, nice to hear from ya mate, how's Shirley?"

"Yeah, she's good mate. Still nagging at me to go see one of your shows, but what I can say, she always did have bad taste."

"Cheeky bastard!"

"Listen, Dave. I really need to speak to Rachael—I mean DS Blunt—it seems the dam could collapse at any minute."

"Shit, that sounds serious."

"It is mate. Scotty James has already evacuated the bungy bridge and we're starting to evacuate the eastern side of the town."

"Don't worry," said Dave. "We'll find your colleague and we'll tell her to get in touch."

"Thanks mate," said Tony "Oh, and one more thing—if you don't mind—can you tell Rachael that I got a hit on the license plate she asked about—the one at the Homer Tunnel. The car belonged to Bob James, but I don't think it was him driving it."

"Ok," said Dave. "Will do."

"Ten-four… oh and erm, I'm sorry about Jonno, you two had a long run together didn't ya."

The radio beeped and Dave put it back down on the chair.

"The Homer Tunnel?" he said. "Do you think he was talking about the crash—was there another car involved? And what the hell did he mean by, 'You and Jonno had a good run?' What's that bastard gone and done now? He'd better not have taken another job without me. He won't find another cameraman that puts up with his shit like I do."

"I think you'd better sit down," said Jenny, placing a hand on the cameraman's shoulder. "I've got some bad news I'm afraid."

For the next few minutes she relayed the news of Jonno Hart's death and she recalled her interview with the pathologist whilst the cameraman had lain unconscious.

Dave seemed to take the news well and Jenny couldn't help feeling that he almost seemed pleased to hear of Jonno's death.

"So, somebody finally topped that old bastard eh. What else did Bob say?"

"Not a lot really, but that's the other thing I'm afraid-he's dead too—apparently he collapsed behind the wheel of his car."

"Huh… well, wouldn't ya know."

The cameraman looked surprised, but not upset.

"Are you ok?" Jenny asked. "It's a lot to take in isn't it?"

"Yeah, I suppose."

It was a bit of a strange reaction, but not unexpected considering some of the things that Dave had said about the fishing celebrity and his friend Bob James.

"I should go find Rachael," said the weathergirl. "You've got a lot to think about and you deserve some time with Owen."

She exited the room and scanned the corridor, perhaps some time with Owen was exactly what Davey Boy needed. Perhaps his lack of emotion was just another example of his warped sense of bravado, a macho persona that he'd been forced to inhabit, but even now with Jonno Hart gone, he still couldn't let it go, not even to grieve for his old colleague.

The policewoman was nowhere to be seen and Jenny wondered where she might have gone to.

Remembering her interview with the pathologist in his basement laboratory, she headed downstairs to see if Rachael had sought out one of Bob's 'beaker brews'. His young assistant may have had an unusual technique, but it certainly smelled like good coffee.

The lift arrived at the basement level and pushing cautiously on the lab's yellow swing doors, Jenny prepared herself for the smell of death.

She stepped into the room beyond and immediately froze in shock. Spread out on the mortuary slab before her, lay the pale, lifeless corpse of Bob James. It was a sight that was dreadful enough in itself, but wriggling beneath him on the floor, was the grotesque, serpent-like form of an enormous black eel, revelling in a pool of blood and guts.

It was a sight that made the weathergirl gag and she held a hand to her mouth as she struggled to contain her vomit.

"Rachael!" she cried. "Are you in here? You had a call from the station."

But there was no response, only the crackling of a radio, tuned to the local police frequency.

Jenny scanned the room for any sign of the policewoman having been there, but apart from a syringe lying on a chair, there was nothing, just the pathologist's intestines smeared all over the floor.

She looked down once more at the pool of blood and guts—the eel had certainly been enjoying itself. The blood had been smeared in a wild and random pattern by the creature's feeding frenzy, but for some reason, one particular mark stood out and Jenny bent down for a closer look.

There was a definite smudge in the fringes of congealed blood, and it was clearly leading towards the door. Something or someone had been dragged from the laboratory and out into the basement corridor.

'Rachael!'

The policewoman must have come down to the basement for coffee, but she'd stumbled upon something that she wasn't supposed to see.

Suddenly everything started to click into place and Jenny realised why she'd never warmed to Bob's pretty lab assistant.

Turning on her heels, she dashed back to the lift and impatiently pressed and repressed the button.

"It's Rachael!" she screamed, as she finally stumbled into Owen's recovery room. "She's gone—and I think Jonno's killer took her."

Davey Boy looked up from the bed, he was still holding Owen's hand, but the strength of his grip was now being reciprocated… Owen was awake.

"Hey gorgeous," he mumbled, as his wife rushed to his side. "What were you saying about Rachael?"

"She's gone Owen, she went to get some drinks and I think she's been kidnapped."

"What do you mean?" said Dave. "What makes you think she's been taken?"

"An eel," Jenny replied. "A big, fat, ugly eel, just like the ones that were inside the cave."

"The cave?" said the cameraman. "You were inside the cave?"

"Yes—it's incredible isn't it—and I think it's the reason why Jonno was killed."

"Jonno was killed because of the eels?" said Owen.

"No, not the eels—the gold. Jonno would have wanted to protect the eels, but his killer would have wanted the gold, and they would have done anything to get their hands on it."

Both men nodded in unison, seeming to agree with Jenny's summation.

"So, you know where I'm going with this?" she said.

"Yeah, I think so," said Owen. "Scotty James—I never liked that bloke, and it's no secret that he wants to mine the valley."

"No, not him," said Dave. "She's talking about Markus. He's wanted rid of Jonno for years, and a show about gold mining would certainly bring in the viewing numbers these days."

"You two really are alike aren't you," said Jenny as she grasped her companions by the hand.

The two men looked confused.

"Surely you can't mean it's both of them?" said Owen. "But you said Rachael had been kidnapped by Jonno Hart's killer, not killers."

"And what about Bob James?" said Dave. "Scotty's a little shit, but he always looked up to his dad—there's no way he would have killed him—not even for a ton of gold."

Jenny grinned, it wasn't often that she held all the cards, but she knew that it was time to reveal her hand.

"It's neither of them," she said. "Not even close in fact… and if the bitch was here now, I'd punch her in the face."

"I hope that's not my girlfriend you're talking about?" said a voice as the door swung open.

"What? Oh no, I didn't mean Rachael," the weathergirl replied, as Liam plonked himself on a chair.

"Hey, you're awake!" he exclaimed suddenly, as he spotted his friend sitting up in bed. "It's good to see you mate—for a moment there I thought we'd lost you. You know I…"

"She's missing," Jenny blurted, interrupting the friends' buddy moment. "Rachael's missing and we think she's in danger."

Liam stopped in his tracks.

"I think you'd better explain Jen," said Owen, as the truck driver looked on dumbfounded.

Chapter 41

Ten minutes later Jenny sat down on the wet vinyl seats of the Queenstown jet boat ride and strapped herself in as Liam searched for the spare key.

They'd sprinted from the hospital to the lake, where one of Liam's friends kept the boat as a spare.

"Better to ask forgiveness than permission," said the truck driver, as the boat's engine roared into life. He quickly steered them towards the Shotover River and pushed the throttle forward, pinning Jenny to her seat. They were about 10 kilometres south of the bungy bridge, but at this speed, Jenny realised they'd soon be there in no time at all.

"What makes you think the killer will take her there?" shouted Liam, looking back over his shoulder.

"The radio in the pathology lab…" Jenny replied. "It was tuned to the police frequency. She would have heard that the bridge had been evacuated."

"And this girl—Jonno's killer—she's the junior pathologist, you say?"

"That's right," Jenny replied. "I think she must have heard Jonno and Bob talking about the gold, and she wanted a piece of it for herself."

"And what about Owen's dad…" shouted Liam. "You think she tried to kill him too?"

"That's right…. at the Homer tunnel. I think she drugged you and set you on a course to collide with us."

"But how did she get there? You said she doesn't have a car."

"While you went looking for Rachael at the hospital, one of her police colleagues called on the radio. He said that Bob's car was spotted at the Homer tunnel. I think his assistant took it while Bob was performing Jonno's autopsy, and then she returned it again before he had a chance to notice."

Liam scratched the back of his neck, seeming to contemplate the plausibility of Jenny's suggestion. But he quickly returned his hand to the wheel, when the boat jumped suddenly on the water.

The rocks on either side of the river were closing in sharply and Liam slowed the boat as they approached a bend in the river.

"I've been up here a few times," he shouted. "But I'm not as confident as those blokes that do the tourist runs. I'll slow down until we're safely through the other side."

"How much further to the bungy bridge?" Jenny asked. "We need to hurry, not just for Rachael's sake, but for our own as well. The dam could collapse at any minute and we don't wanna be stuck in one of these channels if it does happen."

"Ok," said Liam. "But hold tight eh, things are about to get pretty hairy."

Back at the hospital, the cameraman cradled his son's hand in his own.

"So, you've been here all these months, but you never came to say hello?"

"I'm sorry," Owen replied. "You know I wanted to don't you, but I just couldn't, I wouldn't know how to tell mum that we'd been in touch."

"It doesn't matter mate, we're together now eh and that's all that matters, isn't it?"

The two men hugged and as they pulled themselves apart the cameraman smiled at his son.

"So, you're married huh, and she's a nice girl—I'm proud of you son."

"Thanks, dad."

"But we need to keep her safe, don't we—if only we had a way to see what was happening?"

"Like an eye in the sky, you mean?"

"Exactly," said Dave, "If I had my drone, we could see where she was going, and we could let the cops know how to find her."

"This drone…" said Owen. "Is it about this big? Looks a bit like a flying saucer?"

Owen gestured with his hands, describing the size and shape of an object that he'd seen before.

"That's it—have you seen it?"

"It's at the dam—Jenny left it on top of my car—it'll still be there now unless one of the construction guys picked it up."

"Perfect!" exclaimed the cameraman. "Now, where did I put that police radio?"

Rachael opened her eyes and quickly shut them again. She was lying face down on what felt like wooden planks and her arms were tied behind her back.

She opened her eyes again and forced herself to keep them open this time, even though she was terrified at what she saw.

She was some one hundred feet above a river, with steep, rocky walls rising up on either side. She was at the bungy bridge and Pippa was going to throw her off!

"Let me go!" she tried to shout, but the words would not come out, and instead her tongue lolled around inside her mouth.

Whatever the girl had used to drug her, it was still having an effect and she suddenly realised the feeling of helplessness that

Jonno must have felt before he was thrown to his death.

"I'm sorry it had to end this way," said Pippa leaning in close behind her ear. "But you've seen too much. You don't deserve to die, but those old bastards did, and I'm not gonna go to prison for what happened."

Rachael turned her head to look at the girl, she could almost feel the anger in her breath.

"You must know they deserved it?" said Pippa. "They were dirty old pervs—and you cops did nothing."

'So that's it?', thought Rachael. *'That's why she killed them. It had nothing to do with the gold at all, it was all just about revenge—but revenge for what?'*

The girl seemed to read her thoughts and Rachael felt herself being rolled onto her back.

"The bastards did this to me," said the girl, pointing to her chest.

She'd unzipped her top to reveal a circular burn mark, about three inches in diameter.

"They never remembered me of course—but I remembered them—and when I saw the job at the hospital, I knew what I had to do. But it wasn't just for me ya know, it was for all those other little girls, the ones that couldn't fight back."

Pippa was clearly implying that she been abused by the two men when she was a young girl and it was obvious that the anger had never gone away.

"But what do you care eh? You just want to close your case—

you don't care about justice."

The lab assistant placed her foot on Rachael's chest and pushed hard. The policewoman was already struggling to breath and the extra weight made her eyes water as the oxygen to her lungs diminished further still.

"How does it feel?" said Pippa. "Not being able to breathe, not being able to resist?"

The girl was wearing tough walking boots and the heavily grooved sole dug deep into Rachael's chest as she twisted her foot left and right.

"It burns, doesn't it? Now imagine you're 12 years old and it's a hot cup of coffee resting on your skin, as a sweaty old man forces himself on you, while his mate holds you down."

Rachael looked up at the girl standing over her. She desperately wanted to tell her that she knew exactly how it felt—but even her own anger that she'd buried deep inside, couldn't fight against the drugs that held her tongue.

"Ya know, even the Māori didn't care enough to help," said Pippa. "And I thought he was different. But in the end, he just gave back my ten grand and I had to make other arrangements."

Rachael felt sick, she'd accused an innocent man of murder and now justice was coming for her instead. Pippa had clearly lost the plot and even with a good reason to feel sorry for her, Rachael sensed that nothing she could say would pull the girl back from the madness that now gripped her.

The lab assistant was starting to ramble now and as she paced backwards and forwards on the bridge Rachael tried to loosen the bonds that tied her hands and feet. She would only have once chance to escape and if she could only find a way to stand up, then maybe she could make a run for it.

Pippa leaned in close once more, seeming to sense the policewoman's desperation.

"I didn't want you to die, you know that don't you? I didn't want any of this to happen, but how could I just do nothing, when instead of being punished, they were gonna be rich instead?"

Rachael stared at the girl, she knew about the gold after all and its lure had been enough to help tip her over the edge. Revenge on its own was rarely powerful enough to incite murder, but when combined with greed, its skewed form of justice could become further twisted still.

Back at the hospital, Dave fiddled with the buttons on the policewoman's radio. It was a combined CB radio and satellite phone model and he grinned as he moved his finger along the device's colour touch screen.

"I've definitely gotta get myself one of these," he said, as Owen leaned in beside him for a closer look.

The cameraman had phoned one of his colleagues back at the TV station and they'd managed to patch him through to the drone that

Jenny had left on the bonnet of Owen's car. And now using the phone as a controller, Dave was steering the drone from nearly 10 kilometres away, while watching its footage on the TV in Owen's recovery room.

"Over there!" said Owen, pointing to a tiny spec on the screen. "It's Jen, I'd know those eyes anywhere."

Dave turned the drone 10 degrees left and spread his finger and thumb to zoom in with the camera.

The weathergirl and Liam were moving fast, heading upstream towards the bungy bridge.

"Move forward," said Owen. "You need to get closer."

Dave swiped forward on the screen and the drone followed suit. Flying high above the river valley it passed over churned-up ground and abandoned diggers that had been left by Scotty's gold mining team.

Outside in the corridor, a group of nurses had gathered at the window to watch the action unfold.

"Fucking nosey parkers," muttered Dave as he steered the drone closer to the bridge. "Haven't they got better things to do?"

"No point worrying about them," said Owen. "This is being broadcast across the whole country isn't it?"

"Well I've gotta say one thing for your missus buddy, she sure knows how to get the ratings doesn't she."

Back in the jet boat, Jenny clung desperately to her seat, they were storming up the river now and the ride was getting bumpier by the second. Liam's maneuvers had become more erratic with every rock they passed, and Jenny got the feeling that he was starting to panic.

"Perhaps we should slow down a bit?" she said. "We don't want to spook the girl. We might force her into harming Rachael."

"You're right," said Liam. "We should probably sneak up on them, shouldn't we?"

With that, he pulled back on the throttle and the jet boat slowed to a stop, its engine idling just enough to keep them in position against the current.

They were about 80 metres from the bridge now and Jenny could see a figure standing at one end.

"I think that's her—I think it's the girl—but where's Rachael?"

"Over there!" said Liam, pointing to the centre of the bridge.

Jenny held a hand above her eyes as she tried to make out the shape of the policewoman. The criss-cross ironwork of the bridge structure made it difficult to tell what was going on, but finally, she spotted her, lying on her side, with her head hanging limp over the edge

"The bitch tied her up—she can't break free—what are we gonna do?"

"I don't know," said Liam with a gulp. "I wasn't expecting any of this."

"What do you mean?" Jenny asked, confused by his response.

"I don't know… none of this was supposed to happen."

'What the fuck is he talking about? Of course, this wasn't supposed to happen.'

Suddenly a shout from above drew Jenny's attention skyward, and she looked up to see the lab assistant staring down at them.

"What are you doing here?" shouted the girl. "I thought I told you to leave this to me?"

"What is she talking about?" said Jenny—and then suddenly the penny dropped.

She looked at Liam and he stared back at her; panic written across his face.

"You? You're involved—you killed Jonno Hart?"

The truck driver looked up to the sky, his secret had been discovered and he held a hand to his mouth as he considered what to say.

"I didn't want to do it," he said finally. "You've got to believe me Jenny—I only did it because I had to."

He reached out to touch the weathergirl's arm as he spoke, but she pulled away, desperate to create some distance between them.

"You killed a man…" she replied. "Two men in fact."

The realisation that she was so close to a murderer had made her legs buckle and she grabbed the railing as she clambered to get away from him.

"You've got to believe me," pleaded Liam. "There had to be justice."

"What are you talking about?" Jenny screamed as she climbed over seats towards the back of the boat. "Justice? What justice? You murdered two people and now you're gonna kill me too."

"I didn't, I swear I didn't," Liam begged. "I just helped that's all. She needed me to lift Jonno's body—I didn't kill him I swear."

"But why?" said Jenny. "Why would you help her—what is she to you?"

"She's nothing, just a friend that's all. But she needed my help and Jonno needed to be punished."

Liam was moving towards her now and Jenny climbed up on to the back of the boat, desperate to get away from him.

"He hurt her…" continued Liam. "They both did, and I couldn't let them hurt anybody else."

But Jenny wasn't listening anymore, she'd made it to the back of the boat, and she was deciding the best way to jump off.

Chapter 42

"What the hell is she doing?" said Owen, almost falling from his bed. "She looks like she's gonna jump."

The dam engineer and his father had been watching the action unfold, along with a growing audience of doctors and nurses, all gathered at the window.

"I'm not sure," Dave replied. "I'll try and get a better look."

He zoomed in closer with the drone's camera and even at a distance it was clear to see the fear in Jenny's eyes. She was standing on the back of the boat, with Owen's friend apparently trying to coax her down.

"She's scared," said Owen. "But scared of what?"

"Liam!" exclaimed the two men in unison, as things suddenly became clear.

Rachael's boyfriend had gone to help after she'd left to make coffee and he only returned after Jenny's discovery of the policewoman's disappearance.

"Liam's working with her," said Dave. "He's working with the girl—the one who took Rachael—the one who killed Jonno."

With that, Dave swiped up on the touch screen and the drone-powered forward.

Speeding directly over the bridge they caught a brief glimpse of the lab assistant standing at its centre and she quickly ducked out of sight behind the maze of ironwork. Now that the drone had been seen, they'd have to act fast, Pippa would know that she was being watched and she might do something desperate to secure her escape.

Once they were clear of the bridge, Dave tapped twice on the device's volume control. It caused the drone to drop like a stone, but at the very last moment, he tapped again to stop it from splashing into the river. It was the first time that he'd ever used a police radio to control a drone, but his skills as a pilot had been honed over hundreds of filming shoots, in every corner of the globe.

"Get him dad!" shouted Owen as the lorry driver came into view once more. His back was turned to the drone and he hadn't noticed the buzz of its rotors.

Jenny, on the other hand, had spotted the flying camera and she was staring straight at it, praying that its operators would notice her engagement.

"She's seen us," said Owen, slapping his father on the back.

"Aaarrgh! Go easy will ya," replied the cameraman as he winced in pain.

The drone seemed to sense the cameraman's discomfort and it lurched sideways as Dave's finger slid across the touch screen controls.

"Fuck," said the cameraman, as he fought to stabilise the device, but it was too late and it crashed into the river in a spray of water.

It may not have been what the cameraman had been hoping for but it was enough to catch Liam's attention and he turned at the disturbance behind his back.

The drone's crash was also disappointing for the weathergirl, as she'd been hoping to see it attack her assailant instead, but she took her chance anyway and jumped from the back of the boat.

If it had been the old Jenny Sunley, the girl who constantly doubted her abilities, she probably would have jumped straight for the water. But this was a new Jenny Sunley, the weathergirl that had faced blood rain and tunnel crashes, and she'd had enough of being afraid.

So instead of diving into the water, she chose a different direction and dived straight towards Liam instead, kicking the truck driver squarely in the back with both feet.

The man was tall and heavy, but he was unprepared for the weathergirl's attack and the force of her kick sent him tumbling into the river.

Jenny, meanwhile, landed on the deck with a thud and for the fourth time in less than three days, she banged her head on something hard.

"Fuck!" she screamed as pain shot from behind her ear and down the side of her neck. Then pulling herself to her feet, she looked over the railing and studied the water below. The truck driver was nowhere to be seen—he'd been washed away with the current.

Jenny looked up at the bridge, the lab assistant was staring down at her, with a look of disgust on her face. The policewoman's body was sitting at her feet, bound and motionless, and Jenny gasped as the girl's face changed to an evil-looking grin. She was going to push Rachael off the bridge and there was nothing that she could do to stop it.

Rachael looked out across the valley through tear blurred eyes and she waited for the inevitable to happen. She'd seen Liam falling into the river and now she was about to join him.

The lab assistant may have been involved in Jonno Hart's killing, she might even have been the one to toss him from the bridge, but she'd done it out of revenge, out of a need for justice, and it was a need that Rachael could understand.

But Liam on the other hand, he'd been in it for the money. The girl had paid for his brawn when the Māori had refused to do her dirty work and for every tear that she was now shedding through fear, Rachael had two more for the betrayal that she was feeling inside.

Liam had accepted the money without question, without morality. He was just as evil as the man that he'd helped to kill, and Rachael felt dirty at the memory of allowing him to touch her.

"Stupid prick," said the girl as she kicked an iron post in frustration. "I told him not to come and now he's fucked everything up—why do men have to be so fucking stupid?"

Rachael felt herself being rolled onto her back once more and she looked up at Pippa standing over her. The sensation was starting to return in her tongue, and she tried to talk to the girl, to try and form a connection.

"Yoooo dnt haf to do this," she stammered. Her words were slow and disjointed, but the girl seemed to understand.

"No!" Pippa yelled in response. "You've seen too much."

It almost sounded like she was trying to convince herself with her own words and that glimmer of hope made Rachael press her again.

"Isssss not yurrr ffffault," she continued. "Heee mmmade yooou do it…. he deserrrrvved tooo die."

Pippa looked down at her, studying her like an insect under a microscope. She appeared to be considering her words and Rachael deliberately locked eyes with her, hoping that her own pain, kept hidden deep inside, might somehow afford her some notion of kinship or sisterhood.

"You're just playing with me, aren't you?" said the girl finally, before kicking Rachael in the ribs. "You're just buying time, so somebody can come save you."

The policewoman might have hated wearing her cumbersome and outdated stab jacket, but at that moment she would have given anything for the protection of its heavy steel plates.

"Well guess what, Detective… Sergeant… Blunt…, nobody's

coming to save you this time, just like nobody saved me. And that dumb bitch down there in the boat, she's gonna watch you fall, while I disappear with my money."

'Wait a second', thought Rachael. *'She kept the money? She didn't pay Liam after all?'*

Her head was spinning, she couldn't make sense of what was going on.

"Can you believe it though," said Pippa. "Two blokes, and neither of them wanted the money—how fucked up is that? One of them just didn't have the balls to go through with it, and the other just wanted to help a poor damsel in distress."

The lab assistant struck a seductive pose as she talked, to illustrate how she had won over the truck driver.

"The stupid prick thought he was gonna get me into the sack, but did you see the state of him? What kind of woman would lower themselves to a bloke like that?"

Rachael's tears were unstoppable now as she felt the guilt welling up inside her.

Liam was a good man after all. He hadn't taken the girl's money, instead, he'd taken her word that Jonno had assaulted her and he'd wanted to help her find justice. That's was the Liam she'd fallen in love with, not a paid assassin, or a mindless thug.

The policewoman rolled onto her stomach, struggling to free the ropes that bound her. The lab assistant's drug was beginning to wear off, but her bonds had been pulled tight and Pippa laughed at her futile efforts to escape.

Rachael knew that she had to do something, the girl was seriously unhinged and even Jonno Hart's murder might not be enough to satisfy her lust for revenge. It would have been lazy to blame the girl's mental state on her abuse as a child, but Rachael wondered how many other men might now face her wrath as her sanity continued to unravel.

'That's it!' thought Rachael, she just needed to unravel things.

She'd suddenly remembered the fishing hook that Bob had found embedded in Jonno Hart's scrotum, and the badly formed knot that had been used to secure it.

"A highwayman's hitch," was the name Bob James had given it, but from the photos it had looked more like a friction hitch, often used by climbers to secure an anchor point. It was a type of knot that offered great strength when pulled downwards, but it could be easily unravelled if the rope was pulled in the opposite direction.

Pippa was leaning over the side of the bridge now, looking down at the jet boat that was weaving from side to side.

"Stupid bitch. She still thinks she can save you, but she doesn't even know how to control a boat."

The girl started pacing up and down, appearing to consider what she should do next. Her back was turned to the policewoman, and Rachael took the opportunity to put her plan into action. She was praying that the girl had tied her ropes from a standing position above her, and if that were true, a forceful tug downwards on the rope would loosen its spirals enough for her to slide out her wrists.

Arching her feet up behind her back, she managed to position the frayed rope end between them. Then, gripping as tightly as her ankle bindings would allow, she kicked down hard and prayed that her guess was correct.

If Pippa had tied her knot in the opposite direction, she would at best lose her grip on the rope and drive her feet into the ground. But at worst, her kick would pull the rope tighter and maybe even pull a shoulder from its socket.

Fortunately for Rachael, her guess was correct and as her feet kicked downwards, she felt the rope unravel from her wrists.

The lab assistant was still turned away from her and she quickly reached down to untie the bindings at her ankles. Her fingers were numb from a lack of circulation and she struggled to grip the shiny blue rope. It was the type used to tow vehicles and the policewoman cursed that it could be so useless at the job it was intended for, but so efficient at stopping an escape.

"Hey... you... stop right there!" came a voice suddenly and Rachael looked up to see the girl staring angrily in her direction. But instead of rushing towards her she turned as if to run away and Rachael suddenly understood why.

It wasn't the girl that had spoken, it was Tony, and he was standing at the end of the bridge. Rachael's colleague had come to her rescue and he was walking towards her with his police taser outstretched in front of him.

"Get on the floor!" he shouted at the girl, but she dashed towards Rachael instead, grabbing her as a human shield.

"I said get on the floor!" shouted Tony once more as the girl dragged Rachael away from him in a chokehold.

Locking eyes with her elder colleague, Rachael seemed to connect with the man, and she knew exactly what he was going to do. She could see his finger moving on the side of the taser, turning a dial to ramp up the volts. He was planning to electrocute them both, just as the weathergirl had done in the cave when she'd tasered the eel that had attached itself to Rachael's leg.

But when that had happened, Rachael had been soaking wet from her fall into the lake and the eel's body had created an arc as it connected with a puddle of water on the floor.

Rachael knew that Tony's plan wouldn't work and instead of sharing the jolt with her attacker, she would instead take the full force of the shock. She had to do something, she had to stop him before it was too late.

Unable to shout out a warning, Rachael attempted to gouge her attacker's eyes instead, but her fingers will still numb from her bindings and the girl simply rolled them away with a turn of her head.

"Stay back!" she shouted to the approaching police officer. "Stay back, or I'll throw her off the bridge."

Tony stopped advancing, but Rachael could see that he was simply sharpening his aim.

She would have one chance to save herself, but she would have to move at exactly the same moment as her colleague. She looked straight at Tony, hoping that he might give her some clue when he was about to fire.

And then it came—the smallest of winks—and Rachael twisted her body hard in response.

Using her full weight to pull her attacker forwards, she rolled her body at the same time so as to turn the girl behind her. She had reversed their roles of target and human shield and she heard Pippa groan loudly as the taser's prongs delivered their charge.

Falling forward as the girl collapsed on top of her, she reached out to stop her fall and grasped one of the iron bars that formed the structure of the bridge. She looked down at where her hand had settled and staring back at her she saw the head of an eel, one of the guardians that ran horizontally along the railing. For a brief moment, Rachael saw the beast's gold-leafed eyes crackling wild with energy and then suddenly she felt its anger burning through her body.

"Oooooooohhh," came the sound from the corridor as the taser delivered its charge.

Davey Boy and Owen had managed to resurrect the drone from its ditching in the river and had flown it upwards to see if they could help the policewoman on the bridge.

"Ouch!" said the cameraman as they saw Rachael drop to her knees. The lab assistant had collapsed on top of her and they were both spasming from the charge that was coursing through them.

"They must have both touched the railing," replied Owen. "It won't be an efficient conductor, but it'll be enough to hurt."

Dave zoomed out on the camera and they watched as the policewoman's colleague rushed in to help. He was quickly followed by several other officers who appeared from opposite ends of the bridge and the two voyeurs sighed in relief as the lab assistant was dragged away.

"Better late than never, I suppose," said Dave, as the police officers bundled the girl into a van.

He turned the camera around and tilted downwards towards the jet boat which Jenny had finally wrestled under control.

"You've got a real keeper there, son. But make sure you look after her eh, otherwise she'll drop-kick you into next week!"

Owen laughed at his father's joke and the two men embraced in a congratulatory hug. "Don't worry about that—I know my place, and if Ms Jenny Sunshine wants to be the boss, I'm certainly not gonna argue with that."

Chapter 43

Four days later, it was finally time for Owen to leave the hospital, and Jenny couldn't wait to see him. The doctors had kept Owen in for a bit longer than normal, but they'd now given him the all-clear and the weathergirl had plans lined up for their reunion. She'd secured a few more days off work due to the stress of recent events and with Markus' body now uncovered from the rubble at the cave site, she needed time to process everything and come to terms with all that had happened.

Rachael had been convinced that she'd seen somebody inside the tunnel before it had collapsed and although Jenny was relieved that it hadn't turned out to be her husband, she was still upset at the loss of her employer. Markus had rebooted Jenny's career, giving her new faith in her abilities, and it was devastating that his own life had been cut short so abruptly.

"Ladies first," said Davey Boy as he held the door from the reception area.

"That reminds me…" said Jenny, squeezing past with a coffee in hand. "Haven't you got something to tell me? About a certain lady friend of your own… one that wears a bright pink wig?"

The cameraman stopped in his tracks and Jenny turned to face him. She thought that he might have been embarrassed by the revelation, but instead, he simply put his hands-on-hips and flicked an imaginary lock of hair.

"What's wrong with pink? Don't you think it suits me? I think it goes with my shirts."

"No Davey Boy, NOTHING goes with your shirts."

The weathergirl shook her head to emphasise her distaste.

"You know I think Lady Gloria and I need to go on a bit of shopping spree when we get back to Christchurch. I've got a reputation to keep don't you know, and I can't be seen with a girl who doesn't even know how to match the essentials."

"Like collar and cuffs, you mean?" chuckled Dave. "I can assure you now, all that stuff matches perfectly my dear, and even if they didn't, it's nothing a bit glitter couldn't fix."

"Eeew!" said Jenny, choking on her coffee. "I think that's enough of that, don't you? After all, we're family now aren't we, and I really don't want to be thinking about my father in-law's...

...pejazzle."

"What's a pejazzle?" asked a voice behind them and Jenny turned to see Rachael strolling through the reception doors. The policewoman appeared to be on duty with her uniform freshly pressed and her boots polished to a mirror shine.

"Oh, it's just a decorated male, erm... never mind... how are you anyway—don't you ever have a day off?"

"Oh, I'm fine thanks," Rachael replied. "And a day off? What's one of those?"

"Well you should look into it," insisted Jenny. "You had quite a shock didn't you."

"A shock? Oh no, I'm fine. I had a human shield to take the brunt of it, so it really didn't hurt too much."

"Oh, I erm, I meant Liam. It must have been a shock, finding out that he was involved in Jonno's murder—I know Owen was gutted about it too. They were good friends at school, he can't figure out how Liam got involved with it all."

The policewoman took a deep breath, she was clearly just as upset as the dam engineer, but she didn't look angry and she merely shrugged as the words to respond failed her.

"I take it you've arrested him?" said Dave. "I saw on the news that your guys found him hiding out, somewhere up north."

"That's right," said Rachael. "He took my car and appeared to be heading towards Picton. I don't know what he thought was gonna do when he got there, all the ports had been given his description and the car's registration details. He wasn't thinking… he never does."

Jenny placed a sympathetic hand on the policewoman's arm, she knew what it was like to be let down by somebody that you loved.

"But at least he didn't do it," she said. "At least he didn't kill Jonno—that's something isn't it?"

The policewoman shrugged. She appeared to agree with Jenny's sentiment, but the weathergirl could sense that Liam's betrayal was hurting more than she was letting on.

"Why don't you join us for lunch?" she said, trying to lighten the mood. Davey Boy here, has offered to take us out for pizza, haven't you David?"

"Have I? Oh yeah, yes, of course, you will join us, won't you?"

The policewoman smiled, but a beep on her radio, signalled that she was still on duty and she mouthed the word "Sorry," as she responded to the call.

"DS Blunt receiving, go ahead Tony."

"Hi Rachael, it looks like we might have found him, well a whiff of his trail anyway. What do you want us to do, should we send in the dog handlers?"

"No, let him go," she replied. "We've got no reason to charge him now, but just seeing you guys on his tail will keep him out of our hair for a while. If you bring him back to town now, he'll only cause more trouble for the team up at the dam."

"Ok, 10-4, I'll see ya later yeah."

Rachael let go of her radio and turned to the weathergirl once more.

"Kaihautu?" said Jenny, sensing the policewoman's unease.

"Yes," she replied. "I feel guilty about letting him run, but he's a pain in the neck and I'd rather he stayed away until the dam team has made the area safe."

"So, you're not gonna charge him?" asked Dave. "He tampered with those explosives didn't he and he got somebody killed—that's manslaughter isn't it?"

"Not this time. We took some fingerprints from the control board. Somebody set them off on purpose and I think we all know who."

Jenny and Dave nodded in response, but neither of them mentioned the word, Pippa. It was as if the lab assistant's name had become toxic to them both and they each took a breath to wash away the bad taste that it left.

"Come on," said Dave. "Let's leave this little lady to do her job, she's got better things to do than stand here talking to us all day."

"But that's actually why I'm here," said Rachael. "I need your help one more time I'm afraid—It's a matter of public safety."

"Sounds interesting, what do you need?"

"It's the dam. The engineers think they've finally made it safe, but they need a drone to scan the entire structure for any cracks that they might have missed."

"Now you're talking," said Dave. "When do I start?"

"Well now, if you don't mind?"

"Just try and stop me," replied the cameraman, as he flashed Jenny a grin. "You don't mind, do you?" he asked.

It was the first time that she'd really seen him smiling face on, and Jenny suddenly saw Owen's features reflected in the older man's face.

"Er, no. You go ahead, that's fine with me," she stammered.

But her words barely mattered anyway, as the cameraman was

already leading Rachael away, asking her questions about the type of shot that was needed for the safety team.

Jenny turned back towards Owen's recovery room—he really was the cameraman's son after all, wasn't he—she really did have a drag queen for a father-in-law.

She smiled at the thought of Davey Boy in his bright pink wig and she remembered how he'd studied her bright yellow stilettos so enviously—her beautiful, expensive, Jimmy Choos.

"Oh yes Lady Gloria, we'll definitely be going shopping you and I… and if you mention just once about that trip to Milford Sound, I promise you this, you'll be the one footing the bill."

Kaihautu turned on the tiny hand-held TV and plunged a spoon into the cold tin of beans that balanced awkwardly on his knees. He'd waited for nightfall before returning to the cabin and he shivered in the cold, damp air. The police might have called time on their search for now, but they'd be back on his trail in the morning and he needed to maintain his strength if he was going to stay ahead of their dogs.

As he chewed silently on the flavourless beans, he flicked over to the news and waited impatiently for an update on the police team's search.

But instead of hearing about an ongoing mission to apprehend a cold and calculating Māori killer, he instead saw pictures of a boat anchored at Milford Sound, a hundred miles away.

The ship's captain was being interviewed by a male reporter and the man looked as dishevelled as the journalist's badly press suit.

"And it was bigger than the boat?" said the journalist, shoving a microphone in the man's face.

"That's right," replied the captain, lighting up a cigarette.

The picture zoomed in on the man as he dragged medicinal nicotine into his lungs. He looked badly shaken and his hand trembled as he pulled the cigarette from his mouth.

"It was at least 30 feet long, and it's eyes… it's eye's… well, they kind of… glowed".

The camera panned back to the reporter, who seemed amused at the man's description. He clearly thought that the captain was drunk, and he smirked as he passed back to the studio with his closing comment.

"Well there you go folks, it looks like Nessy is alive and well, but she's taken a bit of a holiday from the cold waters of Scotland this year and decided to take a trip down under to visit us here in New Zealand instead.

- Now back to you guys in the studio."

Kaihautu put down his spoon and stared at the object on the table beside him. He may have escaped the cops and Jonno Hart's killer, but he was yet to escape his fate.

Te Tunaroa, the great eel god, was on the move and he would

need to act fast if he was ever going to escape the beast and its plans for his soul.

The End

Printed in Great Britain
by Amazon